THE OFFSPRING

In a huge house in a suburb of a midwestern city lived a little girl named Peg, her older brother Eric, their beautiful mother, distinguished grandfather—and one other. Like Eric and Peg, the fifth member of the family is Elizabeth Porter's child, but there the resemblance ends.

For this child was conceived thousands of years ago. It is a child of infinite cunning, infinite evil—an evil as old as time. Its powers are beyond the capacity of men's minds to comprehend or control.

They thought it had died in the blazing inferno, but nothing can destroy the . . . EVIL OFFSPRING.

Also by J.N. Williamson:

PROFITS
THE TULPA
THE LONGEST NIGHT
PREMONTION
PLAYMATES
WARDS OF ARMAGEDDON
BROTHERKIND

J. N. WILLIAMSON

LEISURE BOOKS NEW YORK CITY

A LEISURE BOOK

Published by

Dorchester Publishing Co., Inc.
6 East 39th Street
New York, NY 10016

Printed in the United States of America

For Mary, always; in memory of my mother; for Jane Thornton, who's always been in my corner; and for Ray Peuchner, James Kisner, Bob Weinberg, Stan Wiater, F. Paul Ganley, Don Gazzaniga, Alan Rodgers, Milburn Smith, Tom Millstead — among the good people in this bizarre business of dredging up one's nightmares and reporting them on paper.

EVIL
OFFSPRING

"What if this night prefigured the night after death . . . ?"

—F. Scott Fitzgerald, "Sleep and Waking"
The Crack-Up

PROLOGUE

RED—the world had gone *rouge, merah, akai, rosso, kirmizi, rot, ahmar, piros, rood, RED*!

Generously lashed cow eyes nearly popped from the enormous head. While the shock remained, was sustained, it was momentarily brushed aside by an upwelling of the bleak and consuming fury that always lurked in the shadows of the great, all-knowing brain.

It had not yet become terror.

The relatives, being dragged by the hand away from the bolted-down bed, being saved from wrath by that old woman! Boy and girl getting tugged through fast, shimmering, many fast-moving walls of—

RED!—*ruga, krasni, vermelho, czerwony, crven, punainen RED*!

Frantic to understand, sensing others' desperation to flee, to escape—reading their minds but finding none of the infinite number of words known to it, finding only images of terror and all-consuming desire to be outside—the Offspring's incomparable mind strove to understand the meaning of the moving color in French, Indonesian, Hebrew, Japanese, Portuguese, Polish:

What—mean—RED? And, *What—mean—outside*?

One instant when boy Eric looked back at the monster lying beneath the window and helpless on the bed against the wall—one second to learn why terror, WHY they all run toward outside, by scanning boy Eric's bright, developing brain . . . one second to see whole world of outside as boy Eric see it, not as the Offspring saw it—always—in books and on television and in endless miles of recording tape. *Quick*! Read boy Eric's *fright—*

FIRE! The monster struggling to sit up saw the image, made the connection, instantly translated it to absorb every conceivable connotation given to it by the people of the world: *Vuur, moto, tuz, api, Feuer, fogo, tuli, agon, nar*—memories of Grandfather saying, "A nation is learned through its citizens but the history of the citizens can be learned through its language, its words;" synaptic lockings and a network of speedy connections summoned the meaning needed by the monster in image after memorized image of human beings' agony and loss—FIRE! *FLAME*!

Others, gone. Smoke, known from Grandfather's cigars, suffusing the average American upper-middleclass bedroom—sweeping above the Offspring where it lay, helpless and abandoned. *Help me,* it thought, the prayer intended for boy Eric's bruised and bewildered brain, a brain battered by the Thing itself. *Aid! Assistance*!

Turgidly, unprettily, with far greater effort than it had ever before expended physically, the Offspring sought to suck air into its scorched young lungs and then *rolled* ponderously on its bed, struggled with what might have been notable valor in a less monstrous Thing—labored mightily to sit *up*, to *get* up for what would be the first time. This was also the moment when it realized for the first time that Mama's great Hammond organ—doubtless blazing with red and warped both by fire and a bizarre electrical short—was moaning its anguish like a beast that had dropped into a stake-lined pit. Sonorous, senseless chords and a span of high-to-low piercing notes that would have been beyond the reach of human hands trumpeted, roared, and bayed. When the *real* burning began—when its hairless, fleshy arms were singed and the Offspring flung them beseechingly into the ruined air—it knew finally what its victims had experienced. It shared the agony belatedly of the damned and recalled plainly that it *was* the *Damner*—

And longed, its generously lashed eyes lolling back in the head, to torture and slaughter, slowly, just for one more second.

And what *did* penetrate, inform, and motivate the monstrosity was the fresh realization that then enflamed its great mind. In another place, in quite differing circumstances, the Offspring would have insisted upon pondering and exploring every strange aspect of the phenomenon which shocked its brain with the amazing news:

This *vermelho/rosso/ahmar/crven/RED fuego/ ogien/foc/agon/fotia* FIRE was—was—was going to...bring...*DEATH*!

The whole concept, the remotest possibility, that *it* could *die* could not have astonished the Offspring more if wings had shot from its meaty shoulders and it had flown through the bedroom window to safety. Never capable of anything more than rolling over on its side, the Offspring seized control of itself, spoke to the pain centers of its body, and silenced them for a carefully calculated four-point-eight seconds. Deep buckets of perspiration, bathtubs full of dime-sized globular stinking sweat, boiled up from the pores of the Offspring's simmering form and, sliding off the edge of the now-ignited bed, brought steam like geysers where it splashed onto the blazing floor. There was so little *time*. This FIRE must surely—

Yes! That was it, *precisely*! What it was in the process of doing was *losing time*. As it began to die, the problem could be logically seen as time, expiring—running out! The red fire was using up its appointed quantity of *time* . . . but time was not an absolute. Time was *relative*. All its studies had informed the Offspring of that! Now the scorched thing on the bed knew it had made a major connection with the means to liberty, to NOT dying, and literally experienced the passing joy of excitement—because it had also experienced fear and learned *much* since it slew Grandfather and inadvertently began the burning process. It raised its head, reflectively; it thought. *No—room, no space—left in time. Need OTHER—time, to—enjoy—NEW space*!

But its control of the pain centers snapped like a twig—another first; no one and nothing had ever interrupted its machinelike control in the past—and hideous pain came swirling, snarling, rushing in upon it, and inside of it.

Feeling . . . *frantic* . . . it peered down its rolling mass and saw that each leg and the lower portion of one all-but-useless arm were blackening; one leg was now entirely sheathed in crackling flame, as if it might be steadily cooked for the culinary delight of somebody or something even more monstrous than it. Evaluations of the dying process which the Offspring had studied in order to bring cessation of life to many others in varied and inventive ways informed it with computerlike quickness that it could now . . . *die* in any of several painful ways.

Death is COMING! it thought, its fact-stored, finely tuned, always half-insane mind rising above the acute agony of its burning prison of flesh, soaring out of the charring nightmare to record and perceive the facts, and to quest—with *seconds* to go—for the way out.

. . . and remembered, as if the data were buried deep in the innate cells which had needed to be raw and exposed before it could reach them, the long-forgotten beliefs of the people in its own distant origin—its own world of true family:

Leave—body! Yes! To . . . live . . . must leave—*body*!

Seeking a method, it turned its head, saw the ripped and flaming sections of its life-supporting oxygen tent spread and beat and flap as if a Phoenix were trying to rise. It encouraged, emboldened, the bedded monster—but then the legs of the bed gave way unexpectedly and spilled it rudely upon the burning floor. For the first time, it made audible sounds. It *howled,* a high-pitched, horrible squealing sound midway between that of a pain-wracked human and a ravening mad boar. Then it had tugged its way to a kneeling position and, clinging by fingertips that had begun to resemble remnants of a Christmas tree in February, the Offspring peered through the jagged emptiness of where its window had been. Only infrequently had it ever seen Outside; never before had it looked out at night for any period of time. Down below it recognized *the family*—that term came perversely to mind, unbidden; it'd had no time to track the emotional interpretation and never had done so before, never had considered loyalty and certainly not love—which was quite safe on the sidewalk. Yet it had also turned back to gape with pale, upturned faces and, for a fleeting moment, the Offspring believed *the family* would try to save it. *Help—me,* it cried telepathically, forcing the words into conveyed thought, hopeful of reaching any of them. *SEE—me*! it commanded the trio, *I am here—I . . . need . . . HELP . . .*

But the maid was making the children drop to their knees, leading them in prayer. *It* did not understand, that instant, their actions; it had to dredge from clouded memory the concept of someone superior to the Offspring, and the concept maddened, infuriated, it. *How—dare—they? Will . . . get . . . them, will . . . exact . . . REVENGE!*

But its coughing started then, rackingly, overpoweringly. *Moarte*, the monstrosity whispered deep within its mouldering bulk; *koulema, tha'natos—I must first . . . leave body. Depart—body—at precise* point—*of death . . .* And its mortal torment wafted out the windowframe like billowing spitballs, like the product of cruel emphesyma magnified a thousandfold. For a moment, it was almost overcome. Behind where *it* knelt, browning, its bedroom had become a forest of fire. Spirals of blackness columned upward like shadow trees. Thickets of smoke lay beneath the ceiling like gray, dessicated foliage. The downstairs organ's dying wail slithered among the shadow trunks like things of covert serpent mein, stalking the one who still lived in the dying house. Flames furnished the ambience of daylight in the ghastly forest, innovating the fast-passing present and erasing the past.

And still on its wobbly knees in sinister mimicry of the God-fearing prayer being conducted beneath it, the Offspring commanded its pain to retreat, become bearable. *Must focus! Concentrate* . . . But absence of air was smothering it like something feral and furry that had emerged from the forest. And as its long-delayed demise began, its inner eyes glittered in amazement and, for a matter of moments, the only instance of peace it had ever known . . .

It stood—shocking enough surprise—in a bleak, black tunnel of slightly shifting darkness—and far in the incalculable distance from where it stared upon its untested spiritual legs, that stygian tunnel *forked*—headed in two distinctly different directions. From one, a warming light—the most brilliant it had witnessed, yet the luminosity did not hurt the gaping eyes—at once beckoned and intermittently *faded*, as if uncertain about the Offspring's admittance.

But that which the Thing saw down the other fork in the tunnel road was unstinting, unremitting, dolefully welcoming—hypnotic, even—and the Offspring knew simultaneously that it must float eerily, psychically, toward the second division in the universal tunnel and punishment much worse than even it had visited upon its victims. Now the flames in the room in which it had spent almost all its life were consuming, *eating* it—smoke was imbedded in and crisping as well as remorselessly collapsing its lungs—and it knew that death was certain. Unwillingly, without volition, it had floated straight toward the branching blackness which, it perceived, was shimmeringly framed in the same red that lurked behind it—except that *this fire* surely burned for all times, forever and ever . . .

It remembered astral travel; it remembered the concept of purgatory, and *earthboundedness*—

It remembered and sought that survival which was not life nor was it quite death—the survival of its brain through an exact merging of its perpetually sacrificed mortal soul with the very time and space surrounding it—oneness with the molecules of the scorched night air, melding with the unsatisfying but viable Hereness of the only home it had ever been permitted to know. It turned inward, upon itself; it focussed its total intellectual power upon the spark of mind and personality that was all it had ever cared about; it *willed* that spark to *abandon* the fusing cremation of the helpless hulk that had housed it—

And the Offspring burst *from what had been its body and hovered above it in twisting, cavorting, miniature spirit as the corpse fell thumpingly upon its side and caved into itself with a sound like that of a mammoth belch. Then the bodily corpulence, hollowed, the face like a gross and grinning mask, went on smouldering and smoking and stinking while the surviving monster giggled and frolicked, overhead—safe. In its own peculiar and malevolent manner . . . alive.*

Vengeful.

Filled with fresh plans.

Able to do what it wished, to whom it wished to do it.

Fifteen years old, a genius, a lunatic—forever.

PART ONE
WELCOMING

"The earth is cool across their eyes;
They lie there quietly.
But I am neither old nor wise;
They do not welcome me."
—Dorothy Parker, *The White Lady*

1

June, this year

Of all the possible ages he could have been, of all the places where he might have found himself, and of all the people he could have been, Eric Porter thought that God had made the arrangements absolutely ideal for him. Which was the way it was supposed to be, after all, since God *was* perfect and young Eric Porter was doing his level best to achieve the same heady plateau.

At not quite twenty-three, there were times when it troubled the bespectacled and bookish graduate student that life wasn't always ideal, because that appeared to cast a measure of doubt upon the Creator's current track record, if not His very existence. Yet those were the only moments he was disposed to question the viability of his Maker—unlike most of Eric's less confident cronies over the past four and a half years at Dayton U.—and there'd even been times lately when it occurred to Eric that maybe his own behavior in life comprised a few minor and distinctly dubious flaws. Frequently philosophical of bent, Eric had perceived how that could explain God's disinclination to allow him an unbroken string of accomplishments and joy.

But it also made the mutually advantageous partnership he'd sometimes imagined he enjoyed with God rather less equal than he had conceived it.

Happily, such ruminative second thoughts were in the past these last few weeks due to a newer relationship Eric had formed, one with a person of quite accessible flesh and blood: Jennie Dorff. Asprawl on the rumpled bed in their off-campus apartment, Eric stretched and sighed with the joy known only to young men who have learned, conclusively, that their favorite bodily parts function at peak efficiency. Beautiful, sensual, playful, brilliant Jennie. He wasn't exactly certain of her age, but Jennie had admitted once that she was "about three and a half years your senior, junior," and that put Jennie in her late twenties. Marginally, perhaps, but nonetheless factually. And Eric's added gratification stemmed from the realization that he hadn't conquered a girl, a mere child, but a fully flowered, mature, experienced adult.

And for all these reasons Eric was, for the first time, pleased that he'd saved himself—virginity wise—until Jennie's transfer to Dayton where she meant to earn her master's. True, with respect to those facts, "saving it" had actually been more a case of finding no coeds with a sufficiently mature approach to the sex question. Often enough, he thought ruefully, he'd been quite willing. *No*, Eric rethought and rephrased it, *much more than often enough and much more than merely willing*!

And while he was being honest with himself, waiting for Jennie to get home, maybe he shouldn't confuse the facts in other areas. For example, Jennifer Dorff was not beautiful, *per se*; she was pretty and she suited his tastes. *Meaning your horniness*, he amended the thought, abruptly skinning out of the tank top he'd worn while they played tennis that afternoon. And she wasn't so much sensual as willing—from time to time—and disinclined to make a big deal of sex. In addition, she wasn't so much playful or brilliant as witty, well-read, and interested in the same things he was. *At least, she* is *a woman*, Eric concluded with a private grin.

His first, as he thought of it. The one who'd shrugged and then nodded when he'd worked up his nerve to ask her to move in with him. "Why not?" were her precise words, as Eric recalled.

All of which—including his graduate status and diminished class schedule, the new season of spring bursting upon them, his youth, and his location—enabled Eric to reestablish the Creator at His former plateau, not to mention permitting Eric to restore their former, cozy partnership.

"Location" was definitely a major factor in the mosaic of Eric's fulfillment, less because he and Jennie were together in Dayton, Ohio, than because he was no longer a boy living with his sister Peg in Indianapolis—with Peg, and with . . . others.

But those memories had always been best left alone, left in the past, he reminded himself, removing his bottlebottom glasses, blowing carefully upon them and then wiping the lenses with a relatively dry spot on his discarded tank top. Mildly disturbed even by thinking briefly of his boyhood, Eric sighed and flopped over on his side, wishing Jennie would get her butt in gear and bring it home. But just at that moment, he needed to feel her arms around him even more than he wanted Jennie Dorff for sex. *I worked out all that jazz about my relatives a thousand years ago, even before I started college,* Eric thought broodingly. *If I hadn't, I'd be just like Peg is now.*

Funny, the way Peggy Porter had been the brain when they were kids and he'd been Big Bro, protecting her all the time—or trying to—and thinking of himself as an All-American in the making. Maybe it was the way he'd been batted around, almost killed, before Mildred, the housekeeper, dragged them out of the house and saved their lives; maybe he had decided, down deep inside, that a guy had to be sharp, mentally, and know what was happening, just to survive the crazy things that went on in the world.

And maybe the reverse of that, in a way, was what had gone wrong with Peg. He shook his head in old awe, recalling how very bright his little sister had been, how independent and brave in the face of a terrible danger neither of them had understood. Yet when it was finally over and the two of them were safe with Mildred raising them in Dayton, poor Peg had sort of caved-in for a while—and she had never again been the promising student she had been as a child. Worse, Eric admitted to himself, Peg had seemed . . . well, unstable to him, ever since. Still a sweet kid, a nice girl, but something of a flake.

Simultaneously feeling guilty that he rarely saw his sister any longer and that they never even corresponded, and also relieved—because, when he was with Peg, Eric sometimes imagined he could see the frightening image of the Offspring lurking deep in her haunted eyes—he forced his thoughts back to Jennie Dorff, the healthy, "now" woman in his life. Earlier today, they had played tennis on the

Dayton intramural courts and he'd had his hands full with her, as always. That was a part of what he enjoyed about being with Jennie, and it made Eric feel good about himself. Although she was able to do nearly everything he could do, which he liked—thereby avoiding the onerous label of male chauvinist pig—she also *lost.* Almost all the key games and matches, and always when he really felt that he *had* to win.

From the standpoint of a competitive and aggressive person like Eric Porter, that made Jennifer Dorff damned near perfect, too.

She came flashing into the tiny apartment minutes later, shoulder length brown hair rising behind her as if she'd run to get there, and it was almost as if they'd never been parted. Eric looked from her wide, smiling eyes to legs that were not so much naturally athletic as driven by sheer Jennie Dorff will power, and back up to her wide, expressive mouth. It fascinated and confused him, that mouth. When it turned up in merriment, it was always a count late, as if her mind controlled it and she denied anything automatic, reflexive. Yet it also kissed more openly, sometimes ravenously, than any mouth he'd known.

"Did you leave any hot water?" This question was her sole remark since she had arrived. Hand on her hip, gripping her racquet, Jennie stared with a frown at Eric where he lay on their bed, smiling his appreciation of her beauty and playfulness. Almost his height—

something, possibly a boyhood terror, had halted Eric's early promise of being quite tall at rather less than six feet—Jennis reminded him of an imperious, myopic and therefore awkward princess. If she'd give in and buy glasses, she'd stop lunging at the ball and kill his ass at tennis. Squinting, she seemed to notice for the first time that he still wore his tennis whites. "Oh, *Lord*, boy—you haven't even showered!"

"This is my gallant stage, lady," he told her airily, bowing the best he could while lying on his back. "I have sacrificed my own comfort for yours."

"You've sacrificed your cleanliness," Jennie snapped, making a face. Tugging at her sleeveless blouse, she raised it over her head and, braless, headed toward their miniature bathroom. "Unclean, unclean!" she called over a bare shoulder.

I wonder how Peg'd like her, Eric thought, sitting up in more ways than one. What Mildred, who had raised them, would think of him living—unmarried—with a woman like Jennie, Eric knew without a doubt. He'd told neither Peg nor Mildred about persuading Jennie to move in because he felt funny about mentioning it to his sister and unwilling to hear another lecture from the old woman. He was pretty sure Mildred was getting senile by now. Besides, she'd never adjusted to the fact that he had become the scholar and Peggy the drop-out.

He left his shorts and jock strap in the short hallway, next to Jennie's tennis top.

"Why, hullo there," he said in a debonair, throaty voice as he slipped into the tub and wrapped his arms around Jennie Dorff.

"Get away from me, you dirty pig!" she cried, twisting to look at him in mock surprise and disgust. But she glanced down the length of him as he did her, her needless question unspokenly but definitely answered. "I don't share my shower with jocks who like to humiliate helpless young things like me on the field of honor."

Eric grinned. "The jock has disappeared," he said, taking the soap from her hand and working up a generous lather on her breasts. "Can't you tell?"

"I've already washed there," Jennie snapped, groping for a second bar of soap.

"How about here?" Eric asked, obligingly opting for another potentially unwashed area.

"How about that?" Jennie whispered, gasping. She began searching for a portion of Eric that might prove to be in dire need of hygienic assistance. Then she noticed he was still wearing his glasses! "You idiot!" she cried. "You have your glasses on!"

"Certainly," he said with a grin. "I'm a genius, remember? And geniuses don't like to miss a thing!"

When both of them were scrubbed clean and they'd made love, Eric and Jennie stretched out on the bed with the apartment window held open by a stick, thoroughly relaxed, feeling affectionate and soothed by a gentle spring breeze. "Do I seem a little overconfident sometimes?" he asked, face snuggled between her breasts. "I mean, do I get too big for my britches?" The term was one Eric had heard, many times, from the former housekeeper who'd raised him.

"Sure," Jennie said. "You're a man." Playfully, she rumpled his light brown mop of hair, left her hand there, amiably. "But whenever you do get too big for your britches, kid, I know a sure-fire, really *fast* way to reduce them!"

The one-liner completely escaped Eric. Unbidden, an image from the past had come to mind. A mental picture as clear and familiar as if it had been yesterday when he last saw his tall, domineering tyrant of a grandfather—the most brilliant man Eric had known and the one, despite his every effort, whom he most grudgingly admired.

"Now and then," Eric said softly, approving the way Jennie had begun to caress his head and the back of his neck, "I can't hide from the fact that I'm quite a bit like my grandfather. *Too* much like him. I think I know everything. I get bossy as hell. I've even started walking around with a cane—the kind he used to crip around on!"

Her hand, Eric realized, stopped moving. For

an instant, Jennie said nothing but simply lay motionless until he wondered if she were dozing. At length, he tilted his head and chin to nibble on the nearest breast. "Don't stew it, York"—she called him that on occasion; her own affectionate derivative of his first name—"because whatever *you* can do, buster, *I* can do. That is, if I really want to."

"Not quite," Eric corrected her, obliged to lift himself up on his elbows, "anything."

She stared up at him and smiled. "If you'll take off those dumb, soapy specs for a while," she retorted, squirming down in the bed, "I'll issue you a challenge: Two falls out of three, or ninety minutes—for the championship of mudless wrestling!"

Eric grinned. "Let's just make it ninety minutes, and a tie . . ."

Walls of flame formed like five fingers on four sides crawled up the edges of the world, and wriggled, semenlike globules of fire spitting out from the scarlet walling and hissing around her. Yet even with the intensity of the blaze, the peril it posed even while, strangely, she did not appear to be burning—merely miserably, uncomfortably hot—the little girl with the streaming yellow hair stared fixedly at something *else*—a mound, a fetal ball, of pink fatty tissue. The blob hung suspended mere yards away, but, as the child reached out with a shaking hand to touch it, to probe at it with her small fingers, it remained tantalizing inches away—and the walls of flame squeezed in, *closed* in on her, remorselessly, mercilessly. Now she was perspiring profusely, fluid gushing from the pores of her skin, and yet she remained determined to poke the pink substance. It was, she thought with a dreamer's disciplined and detached terror, as if all the surplus poundage lost at a weight reducing studio had attracted and blended itself and acquired independent sentience, volition—because it quavered, just faintly . . . it seemed to breathe, like a monstrous heart with each and every artery and capillary clogged and choked by the disgusting fat of some gross and unnameable beast.

The fatty glob rolled upon its back, exposing itself.

And rather than genitalia, what the little girl saw was a set of elephantine jaws lined by foot-long, ferocious teeth, fangs, even tusks.

It rolled again, toward her, the drooling, avaricious jaws concealed coyly with each complete turn before being exposed once more, closer, nearer . . .

Peggy Porter sat bolt upright in bed, a half-naked man with his powerful hands locked around each of her arms, *shaking* her!

"Peggy, dammit, wake up!" His earnest young face was thrust close to hers, real concern etched into his regular features. "Shit, Peg, it's *me*—Danny!"

"Do not ever call me by that name," she said instantly, automatically, closing her aqua eyes with dignity and then opening them to glare at the man. "If a monster is going to devour me, you and he can at *least* call me by my correct name."

Now Danny Stanwall was even more anxious. "Come outta it, babe," he pleaded with her, touching her cheek lightly with a trembling finger. "I won't let nothin' hurt you."

Peggy laughed, the nightmare receding once more. It always did, sooner or later; but it seemed to consume more time, require more effort if she were to forget about it, as the weeks passed. "I was teasing you," she said, patting his cheek with an instant impression of patting a dog or cat. *How much do I want him around just for security when I have my bad dreams—so* someone *is around in case I can't get back by myself? Lord knows, he's as dumb as a box of rocks*! "I'm sorry if I woke you up."

"Well, shit, that's all right." Relieved, he lay back against their headboard, simultaneously scratching his head and ribs and yawning. Raised up that way, he looked like an affable giant. "You just scared the piss outta me, babe, that's all."

Peggy, kneeling, shook her long, blond hair back from her head and gave Danny a genuinely affectionate smile. Maybe she did love him; how was she supposed to know? Only once before had she permitted anybody to sleep with her—that was just Cary, after the senior prom, when they'd both been frightened about going to college and terrified they'd flunk out—and Cary was a friend, so he didn't count.

With Danny Stanwall, Peggy understood fully, it had been a case of his needing her to tutor him if he was to remain eligible for school. At six-two, he was a basketball guard, and marginal; but in the classroom, Danny was obviously sinking without the help of a nineteen-year-old woman who'd never gotten her collegiate act together. Then, too, there were the several former sorority sisters Peggy knew who would have surrendered their left titties for one night with Danny. But he appeared to be genuinely fond of her.

Besides, with her brother Eric becoming the reigning family brain and always busy, and her job in the new downtown shopping mall boring Peggy Porter silly, Danny was all she had left to provide the faintest gleam of a bright and interesting future. Except for Mildred, of course—who'd have just *died* if she knew her "charge" was sharing bed, board, and body with a boob of a basketball player!

"Listen, do you ever have other sorts of nightmares?"

She turned her head curiously. "No. Not since I was little. Why?"

"Well, shit, it's obvious." His bland young face was screwed into a professorial image. "I mean, havin' the same goddam nightmare all the time—shit, it's got to *mean* something."

"But it doesn't." Peggy shook her head, warmed by his interest. "Don't think I haven't mulled it over a million times, Danny. Walls of fire . . . an ugly glob of fat . . . the way it *rolls* toward me, trying to eat me or something." Peggy shuddered. "How can crap like that mean anything?"

"Well, it does," he mumbled. Lapsing into momentary silence, he pawed around on the nightstand by his side of the old bed, found a beer can, tried to squeeze out a few more drops of Miller Lite. "You sorry you decided to lay out of college a year?"

Peggy leaned over him, impulsively, with a swift kiss. "*I* didn't exactly decide it. I'll have to petition to get back in. If I decide to do so." She settled down in the bed again, resting her head on the side of his rather broad chest. "Sometimes it seems so funny, Bro being the wizard now when he was sort of a nerd." Peggy giggled. "Well, he's *still* a nerd, sort-of; but he's taken to college like a duck to water." Her face was wistful as she half-raised it to Danny. "Once upon a time I was the whiz kid. Mildred said I was going to be a scientist, like Mama."

"Your mother was a scientist?" Danny said, impressed. "What kind?"

"She was—" A dark expression drifted over her pert face. "She was sick when I was little, Danny. She died before I was even ten years old."

"Hey, Peg, that's your answer!" Danny sat up in bed so quickly he nearly decapitated her. "*You're blocking it out*, your whole childhood—but your *nightmares*, shit, *they're* tryin' to make you remember!" He frowned, vastly. "Hold on! Maybe they're what are keeping you from remembering. Shit, I'll bet the goddam nightmare is preventing you from being the real *you*!"

"Come on," Peggy growled, batting at him. Danny, she knew, was something of an anomaly. He didn't read much—couldn't—but he'd always enjoyed analyzing what other people thought or believed. "This is a bed, not a shrink's couch!"

"Dammit, I'm serious, babe!" He snapped his fingers. "And I'll bet I'm right, too—'cause you didn't even get mad at me when I called you Peg! The nightmare is blocking the *old* part of you from the *now* part, so you're . . . divided! And you can't really grow up and . . . and fulfill your potential 'til you're *one*!"

"All you know about blocking is what you do with those big thyroid cases on the court!" Now Peggy, too, was sitting up again, annoyed because Danny's theory seemed to make sense and she hadn't been the one to come up with it.

Then there was the feeling, twisting deep inside some nearly forgotten corner of her brain, that however accurate Danny's theory might be, there was a great danger that awaited her if she chose to explore it. Abruptly, her expression changed, however, and she looked at her first lover with hope shining in her face. "Do you really believe there's . . . *more* of me . . . that I could use to make something of myself?"

"I'd bet a hundred bucks on it," he said promptly, and grinned. "Except Coach and the NCAA don't exactly appreciate athletes laying bets." Danny put out his hand, placed it firmly, gently, in her lap. "Honest t'God, babe, I really think they'd rather I laid something else!"

Peggy called him a name and smooshed him with his own pillow.

Even when she'd lived in the Baldwin mansion, taken care of the lot of them, the old woman had slept soundly every night. Scoffing at insomniacs, along with an uncounted and possibly uncountable array of opinions and prejudices, had been as much a part of Mildred Moag Mannin as her dyed jet-black hair, her covert practice of numerology, and her firmly principled adoration of children.

Now, however—only the past few weeks, the same period of time that she had been ill and done nothing about it—she tended to fall into a deep, troubled sleep the instant her head nestled into her pillow and to awaken, staring into the gloom of her solitary room, early-morning-alert, less than an hour later.

It was this night, nearing 2 AM, that she elected to call upon old Ouija again—her way of personifying the occult board, as if the strangely named game had been darkly christened on behalf of an actual, individual spirit—for the first time in years.

How long had it been? Mildred, alone at a dining room table that had once rung with the laughter of two children—recovering from a living hell, because a housekeeper in her late middle years had taken them to raise—put back her head to remember. Lighting from the chandelier above the table was trapped by her unnaturally black hair and gleamed in its tangle like desperate fireflies. Why, she hadn't called upon old Ouija since Peg, Eric, and she had dwelled in the Baldwin mansion! Small wonder, too, considering the evil that had transpired there and the torments which the little ones had narrowly survived with God's own sanity left in their heads! Of all the things in that fire-gutted house in Indianapolis, old Ouija was one of the few to emerge intact. The box containing the weird, predictive game had been crisped along the edges, smudged; the board and planchette, strangely, suffered no damage whatever. That in itself seemed an omen now to Mildred.

She missed those children something dreadful, that was the truth. But it wasn't why she had decided to consult the spirit world and there was never any point in hiding from the truth; it found you out. Eric was a man now, leastwise in the legal sense of the word, and being on his own was merely right and proper. Not that what he was up to, aside from his studying, wasn't a concern to Mildred; it was. *I'm no ignoramus and I've not lost my wits, not by the half of it,* she thought, frowning fiercely. She raised the lid off the old box, took out the board bearing the letters of the alphabet—plus the oft-terrifying, indicative words YES and NO—and set the wooden planchette on top. *Just like his grandfather, that young Eric does what he wishes to pleasure himself.* But like the late Senator, he would be all right until he did something against God's *special* ordinances—*until,* the old woman thought darkly, *he breaks the rules the Bible* didn't *put down in black and white. 'Cause simply* mentioning *'em could be the worst temptation of all*!

She knew she was stalling, might as well pose her questions to old Ouija, but hesitated all the same. Using the Board wasn't to be done lightly.

It was her Peg—Peggy Porter—who was on Mildred's mind tonight. That poor child and the way she'd abandoned her studies, her with that good head on her shoulders just like her mother's! But Elizabeth, bless her memory, had also been a haunted woman, had consumed years of Mildred's tender care and precious time—not that the old housekeeper begrudged a moment spent on any of them. Sighing, without asking a question, Mildred moved the planchette slowly around the board in sweeping aimless circles, warming herself up and seeking the initial contact with old Ouija. At least, she thought, sweet little Peg was a true good person and wasn't careless in her sleepin' habits like her big brother!

At last, after saying a brief prayer, Mildred rested both gnarled hands on the board and cleared her throat. It was a silent night outside, so still it was as if Ouija was waiting, already listening. With considerable clarity and more than a note of command in her accents, Mildred asked aloud: "Is somethin' bad happening to my kids?" Nothing. The planchette didn't budge. "Is there anything goin' on that Peg and Eric Porter should *fear*?"

Immediately, unwaveringly, the wooden planchette took off across the board, then stopped abruptly, pointing to the printed word YES.

Good Christ, Mildred prayed, blinking. She paused again, carefully removed one husky hand from the indicator, and took a sip of the coffee she'd brewed for herself in strict disobedience of her anxious doctor's orders.

After replacing the cup in its saucer, she replaced her fingertips and asked, in little more than a whisper, "*Who* is it? What should my Eric fear?"

No hesitation. The device scurried up and began pointing first at one letter and then another; Mildred found it hard to keep her fingers pressed against its hard surface.

Four letters were spelled out, and she didn't need to put them down on the pad of paper at her left arm for later research.

Old Ouija had spelled for her the name . . . LYNN.

But Lynn is dead, Mildred protested, by no means speaking the thought. The wise did not go out of their way to offend Ouija.

"Thank you," she murmured politely. Now her hands were discernibly shaking. She found it hard to keep from scooting the planchette all over the surface of the board. Exercising an iron effort of will, Mildred inhaled, closed her eyes for an instant, then opened them and asked: "And my Peg? What of *her* dangers, *her* fears?"

Whizzing up from the base of the game board, the indicator again began spelling out an answer. Mildred gaped at it in terror, incapable now of voluntarily withdrawing her trembling hands before old Ouija uttered the secret but now-unwanted truth.

L, the first letter was picked out, and something seemed to hover over the dining room table, breathing; then, *Y*—

The housekeeper's outflung hand struck her best china cup and sent it flying across the dining room floor. It disintegrated and black coffee stained the dining room wall, ran toward the baseboards like dripping blood.

She had not torn her hands away from the planchette *voluntarily*.

Staring down at her fingertips, going "Oooooo" softly in fright and in pain, the old woman perceived that several of her fingers had been badly burned.

2

The fact that she hadn't had a father around the house had bothered Eric's girl, Jennie, very little during her childhood. Later, she discovered the reason why: people who grew up under Communism without wanting to foment a revolution had no way of knowing that human beings in the Free World lived much more liberated, rewarding, and opportunity-studded lives. Whatever they experienced themselves, as individuals, seemed simply the way of it—everywhere.

Although Jennie hadn't grown up behind the Iron Curtain, the principle, she perceived eventually, was exactly the same. All the recollection of a father figure Jennie had possessed was a shadowy, deep-down little girl's memory of a man who seemed only to drop by and then head somewhere else, always on missions that he, and Mother, described as "important," or "significant." Consequently, she'd had nothing more than a periodic sense of loneliness or incompletion during her formative years, because she had no way of connecting her yearnings to a dead father who was, after he died—Mother never made any formal announcement of the fact; there were no tears, there was no funeral—never mentioned again.

Nor was there any reference, in Jennie's childhood, to the fact that her father had probably been summarily and brutally executed. Murdered.

She'd grown up with half her parentage forgotten, a cipher, occasionally bothered by the way Mother skipped carefully over details in her past, at those rare moments when they communicated their personal feelings, until, during her middle teens, Jennie'd become aware that her friends generally had *two* parents. Questions that she put to her mother were evasively answered, if at all; Mother was thinking about marrying the most recent in a series of men she had dated since Jennie was small. Once, after Mother came home from a party somewhat intoxicated, she'd told Jennie that "your father's life was taken, his greatest achievement in life stolen from him, thousands of miles away."

But she hadn't told Jennie who murdered him, why they hadn't been brought to justice, or one other matter Jennie was left to discover on her own, shortly before she began college.

The fact that she was the *illegitimate* daughter of a mysterious, murdered, and forever-disappeared father.

Some facts involving the parents can be safely kept from modern teenagers, perhaps *should* be kept from them. Most of the others may not even faze today's youth, who are inclined to consider anything occurring before their own births of little consequence.

In Jennie's case, however, her life at twenty-six—when she transferred to Dayton with the express purpose of getting to know another grad student named Eric Porter—had almost amounted to the prolonged piecing together of a jigsaw puzzle. Sometimes, it seemed to her that her life had been a lie, a contrivance, with the end result that she didn't really know exactly who she was. A few years before, after graduating from college, Jennie had spent considerable effort and time—not to mention imagination; many of the aging persons she wrote or telephoned attempted to lie in the face of the facts and deny that they'd ever heard of Senator Adam Baldwin—striving to learn what had happened to her father during his final journey to Iraq. What she had discovered was helpful; it filled in some of the missing pieces, but not all. Not in the least.

When she had found that Senator Baldwin was dead—had been since his grandson Eric, was only a boy—she'd almost become frustrated to the point of tears. But that would have finished her investigations; she'd have had no recourse except to explain why she wept over the demise of a man she had never met. Not Baldwin, of course, but her father. On the surface, Eric was a good kid with a lot of charm, a lot more male ego, and a first-rate if unsophisticated intellect. Despite herself—despite the way that Jennie wanted enormously to loathe every member of the Baldwin clan—she'd really liked young Eric. He seemed eons younger than Jennie was, but there'd been the fun of competing with him, establishing herself as an equal, or better.

But all that had been a far cry from saying "Yes" to Eric when he'd had the nerve to ask her to move in with him—the implication of their sharing a sexual relationship as unavoidable as a rhinocerous in a pup tent. Her feelings for him, other than passing friendship, were not only guarded but clouded by her solitary quest for the truth concerning her father's death. Worse, those emotions were tempered by the way the kid appeared to be following in his late grandfather's footsteps. When he had begun effecting a cane, which Senator Baldwin had also used, both to support an arthritic hip and, presumably, for the same reason Eric now lugged one dramatically around with him, Jennie had reluctantly agreed to live with Eric.

Perhaps, she had thought it through, he knew more about what happened in Iraq than anybody else; that monster of an old man could well have confided in Eric since his daughter, Elizabeth, reportedly had become an invalid. Even, Jennie had intently heard the hints, the innuendo, mentally ill.

Or maybe, she thought, two weeks since her last tennis match with the kid, *when I've learned all I can possibly find out about Daddy's death, there'll only be one person on whom I can avenge my father.* Eric *himself.*

He was preparing their dinner meal, showing off as usual, and Jennie had changed her clothes for the evening. She'd started to depart their bedroom.

But she stopped short, glancing back at a dresser drawer she hadn't closed firmly. Instantly, she seized the telltale, monogrammed blouse and quickly stuffed it all the way down in the drawer, beneath her lingerie.

Jennifer Dorff's monogram revealed the initials: "J.S."

The blob was rolling toward Peg-the-child, gathering momentum, raging toward her now and bigger—more bloated somehow, more hungry looking—than ever before. And now, it made a sound. A terrible sound born in its bottomless gut and yet gouged from the source of all violent storms at the same time, the long lamenting line of its screeching wail shrieking at little Peg from everywhere at once: *Linnnnnnnnnnnn*, it howled, coming closer now, the massive mouth wide and lusting for her whole frozen-in-place little dreaming body *—Liiiiiiiinnnnnnn . . . wwaaaants . . . YOOOOO-OOOOOOOOOOOU.*

GO AWAY, she screamed at it; but the vicious winds tore the words away as they left her terrified mouth, whipped them into sinister, laughing shards, like fragile glass breaking and sprinkling the cosmos with innumerable piercing bits of madness. GO AWAY AND LEAVE US ALONE!

Nooooooooo, yowled the cyclone of death, fangs flashing near Peg's horrified face; *nooooo, Lynnnnnnn WANTS you*!

"Why did I say 'us?' " wondered the logical side of Peggy Porter's brain. "Who? Eric and I?"

Then she was flung deeper into sleep, far deeper into the developing nightmare, and was dashing down a flight of steps, others with her—*two* others, shouting at her to hurry, to *escape*. Yet even while she forced her little legs to pump, to send her partly running, partly tumbling down the stairs, Peg sensed that she had not escaped the great, fat blob, would *never* escape it. She felt its telepathic tentacles reaching out for her, groping for her and the others as she reached the familiar front door. Now she felt invaded, virtually raped by the desperate, coiling probe of its psychic arms and cried out, strove to tear away and dash for freedom with . . . with Eric, and Mildred! *HELP MEEEEEE*, the awful, highpitched wind assailed her ears, her soul—*come back and HELP MEEEEEEE*!

But someone—Mildred—was fairly ripping the door open, admitting the night souls that seemed then to live vampirelike from the sap of the trees on the wooded lot, and upon the blood of her cousins who had died at the command of the disgusting, silly, all-powerful, vain creature even now expiring down the enigmatic second floor hallway. Clouds of severed, pointed teeth skittered in the doorway, blown cyclonically together in a chattering, rending ball of annihilation. And from the center of the nightmarish, nocturnal cloud, two beautifully lashed eyes peered seductively out at little Peg Porter and a cupid's-bow mouth made kissing sounds, visible drool trailing to the familiar front door welcome mat. Now the puckered lips strained, turned into the same immense mouth lined with teeth like daggers; and in the recess of the cavernous maw, wobbling like some thick and rooted thing at full erection, a great pink tongue flicked, in and out, in and out . . .

She began to scream, in two worlds; in neither, however, could Peggy Porter hear any sound except her own heartbeat and the slathering tongue and steady drool of the ravenous mouth that stood before her and freedom. She screamed again, louder. And recoiled from the smashing blow across her cheek from Danny Stanwall.

Sobbing, her face smarting, nineteen-year-old Peggy looked with a mixture of great relief and pained indignation at her athletic lover, still clad in basketball warmup pants and a shirt with a number twelve emblazoned on it. "Jesus, I'm sorry, babe," he was saying, the apologetic words falling out of his mouth, "I never hit no girl before but you were fucking *hysterical*!"

She tried to tell him it was all right, that she was glad he'd brought her out of the nightmare by *any* means. But now she was crying, hard, racked by sobs, temporarily beyond her own control and Danny's. Part of her—the vulnerable, hurting, terrified part—was still at the old mansion in Indianapolis in which she'd spent over a year of threat and outrage; and for one fleeting instant, Peggy knew what little Peg Porter had experienced, or *almost* knew . . .

"We're gonna wind up this bad shit for you, Peggy," Danny was saying. How long he'd been saying it, how long it had been since he rushed into the apartment and saved her from *Lynnnnnn* once more, she wasn't sure. The first half of forever had been her bad dream; the second half, the far more preferable half, Danny'd been talking her down and she'd been clinging to the athlete, thankful to God that he'd showed up when he had. *Maybe*, Peggy thought, being as honest with herself as she could be, *maybe he's what Mildred calls a 'golddigger' and found out about the property and money grandfather left us. But maybe, just maybe, he cares enough about me to stop this insanity before it kills me.*

"You're just blocked. That's the shrink's word for it," he was telling her, shouting and reminding her that she already had a blinding headache. "I looked it up. And the only way you're gonna be sprung from those goddam nightmares of yours is—t'confront your past."

"Confront it? I can't even *remember* much of it!" She allowed him to hold her comfortingly in his strong arms and rocked faintly against his chest. That moment, she wished they might be together forever. "Danny, if I *am* being . . . blocked . . . it started when I was a tiny girl. How am I going to confront a time that doesn't even exist any longer? Retrogressive hypnotism? Truth serum?"

"Uh-uh; Naaah. Too iffy and risky." He held her at arm's length as easily as if she were a child, to study her reaction to what he was about to say. "You are going back to that house you grew up in, babe. And make peace with it." He grinned and squeezed her biceps; it hurt. "I boned up on it at the school library and any shrink'll tell you that's gotta be where all your problems began, and that's where they're going to end. I'm goin' with you to Indy to protect you!"

It was preposterous to Peggy, but the plan, while it frightened her, immediately made sense to her. Apparently Danny really did care about her, wanted to care for her. But had she really told him about the Baldwin mansion—how she and her brother Eric had inherited the property after much of the place burned down? It was hard to remember; everything about that portion of Peggy's life was difficult to recall—without a grown-up little girl's imagination making the events an indecipherable chaos of reality and fantastic make-believe. But if he was only after the things she owned, maybe all Danny hoped for was to get her away from her job and the university to a place where she'd be dependent upon him. More inclined to agree should he elect to propose.

But where did you dare cut off the paranoia and allow trust to begin? *My Lord,* she thought, glancing away from Danny's imploring features, *how do I even have the* right *to assume that he's after my piddling little piece of property*?

It hadn't occurred to Peggy Porter that, after being a leggy, tomboy sort as a child, she had become a strikingly pretty woman, quite desirable on her own merits without a need to view herself as permanently desirable only because of her inheritance and Eric's. So much of what seemed sarcastic about her, the scarcely blunted jokes and easy criticisms, had been forged by her lifelong limited opinion of herself and a renowned grandfather who had treated her as if she were only an errand runner and a nuisance.

But whatever Danny's real motives or feelings, what he had proposed appealed to Peggy. It seemed to make sense; she was running around in circles here in Dayton, working hard but unenthusiastically at a shopping mall specialty store, not entirely out of university life but uncertain about returning to it.

"You'd go with me?" she asked him, and he nodded, eyes bright. She added, teasingly, "It might be haunted, you know."

"Ghosts are bullshit," Danny said instantly, and she remembered his Baptist upbringing. Danny Stanwall had been born dirt-poor; he'd only managed to get into college because of his basketball ability, on a scholarship. "But babe, *you're* haunted *right now*. By a lot of crap in your past that you can't straighten out." He pawed clumsily at her, tried to drag her back into the bed. "That's a lot scarier than anything we're going to find over in Indy!"

Peggy kissed him briefly and jumped up from the bed. "I hope you're right," she said casually, and quickly began pulling on her jeans and lightweight pullover. Then she looked at him frettingly through the lovely long fall of her blond hair and said, wondering why she felt a disturbing rise of doubt, "I really *do* hope you're right."

They'd eaten the meal Eric prepared for them and, to Jennie's combined delight and annoyance, it had been delicious. Surprise was not among her emotions. "Where in the world did you learn to cook like that?" she inquired, clearing the table and starting the dishes (*her* part of their live-in arrangement). "Didn't your mother die when you were just a little boy?"

"She did, but I don't remember when I told you so." Stuffed, he pushed his chair back from the table in their kitchenette and glanced at where Jennie had been in mild curiosity. "*Did* I tell you about Mama?"

"You must have." She'd rounded the corner and was hidden by the outcropping of space-saving cabinets. "How else would I know about it?"

Eric grinned. "Sooner or later, Kid Bigmouth will probably tell you everything that ever happened in his whole life.

"I certainly hope so," Jennie's voice reached him. Hastily, she added, "Are you going to answer my question or is your culinary expertise your one great secret?"

"Nope." He retrieved his cane from where

he'd leaned it against the table and worked it back and forth, fast, between his palms. "Our housekeeper, Mildred, who raised us after Mama died and all, must have been an early feminist. She taught me that when there was work to be done, that was all it was—that there was no such thing as man's work or woman's work."

"Mildred must have been a very wise lady," Jennie called above the scraping sound of an implement against tomorrow's garbage.

"I suppose she was," Eric said, amending it to *is. Was, is, always shall be, and I oughta be strung up by the gonads for never dropping by.* He brightened immediately. "Of course, it didn't hurt when I memorized the cookbook Mildred gave me!"

"All of it?" Jennie's face and neck materialized around the cabinets. She looked impressed. "What makes you work so hard at being a boy genius, kid? Do you think you inherited it from your mom?"

Eric slapped the cane back against the table, frowning and unconsciously wiping his hands on his cutoffs. "I don't know. She was one smart lady, but—I just don't know." He glanced up, hearing Jennie returning to the table and abruptly wanting to be entirely honest with her. "The primary influence in my life—where my craving for knowledge is concerned—is the Senator."

"Good old Grandpa Baldwin!" Jennie said,

keeping it light. She slid into a chair across from him. "You seem ambivalent about his influence in your life, York. But apparently he left you and your sister money."

"Let's not talk about him," Eric said shortly.

"Let's *do,*" Jennie persisted. She put out a hand, rested it upon Eric's. "If there's going to be any chance for a long-term thing between you and me, kid, I'd like to know everything there is to know about your background. Wasn't the Senator a candidate for the presidency at one time?"

A curt nod. "Adam Baldwin was a man who was"—he paused and turned his head to look out the second floor window and to his own past—"who was capable of doing anything." He squeezed her hand and pulled his loose. "But he was't a very nice man. He had no use for most people, unless they suited him statistically somehow, or as servants." He looked back at Jennie, realizing as he did that the sun had gone down already. Spring was bashful about coming, and staying; tonight would be another one when a light blanket was required. It seemed to Eric that second that his whole life had been spent waiting for the promise of spring to be fulfilled. "I told you he was capable of doing anything at all. I mean that. Scientist, inventor, superb politician, manipulator of people's lives—and of human life itself."

Jennie's eyes locked with Eric's. She looked slightly flushed. She'd never, he thought, looked more absorbed in what he was saying.

But before he could continue, there was a sound from the front room that made them both jump. The door was being pushed open slowly against the cheap, afterthought carpeting. They froze, listening.

"Don't you believe in burglars, Eric?" Peg, it was Peg, strolling nonchalantly into the kitchenette and smiling down at him. Then she saw Jennie Dorff seated there, too, and halted, her expression uncertain, expectant, and rather wary.

"I believe in music, love, and apartments—unlike this one—that allow puppies!" Eric bounced up to give his sister a bearhug. It was as if they had never been parted, as if his other half had arrived. Peg was even more casually clad than the last time he'd seen her, wearing an old blouse she'd had in high school and shorts that were tight in the seat now. But what really attracted his critical big-brother eye, and concerned Eric, was how weary she looked. "Sis, this is Jennie Dorff who—who's living with me now. Jen, my baby sister, Peg." He colored. "Did I get that introduction right or screw it up the way I usually make Miss Manners nauseous?"

Jennie'd started to stand, but Peggy was around to her side of the table quickly, reaching down to give the older woman an impetuous hug. Eric stared happily, lovingly, at the two of them, hoping Jennie could overlook his sister's impulsive, kittenish ways. Peg glanced up, hand left at the back of Jennie's chair. "You want to knock off that 'baby sister' label, Bro? It makes it very difficult, considering what I've come here to tell you. Danny?"

Feet scraped, and both Eric and Jennie turned their heads. Peggy had left the front door ajar. Ambling toward them was a tall guy somewhat younger than Eric, JOCK written all over him. He had donned a letter sweater that seemed hot for the season, and Eric, standing to shake hands loosely, disliked Danny heartily on sight.

Sister Peg performed the introductions breezily. That made her sound like his kid sister of old but Eric knew, by now, how unconsciously easy it was for her to imitate the person she used to be. Part of Peg, he sensed, remained the saucy pest he'd adored years ago in the Baldwin mansion. Grandly sweeping back her long, light-blond hair, Peggy told them they couldn't stay, adding, "Because there's a lot to do before we take off for the old homestead for a few weeks."

"Indianapolis?" Eric glanced sharply toward Jennie, who appeared fascinated by the conversation. "How can you stay there? Most of it burned up!"

"Just the second and third floors, mostly," Peg corrected him. "Besides, Eric, you yourself insisted that the place be partly renovated when you were sixteen or so. In case either one of us ever wanted to have a place to escape to."

"But there's very little furniture there," Eric argued. He turned to stare accusingly at Danny Stanwall, even while he continued addressing his sister. "And what's this jazz about *we* going home? You and this guy or what?"

Peg reached for his hand. "Your 'baby sister' grew up, Bro." Her light-blue eyes searched his face. He glanced at her, thought how everything about Peg was "light" or "almost," as if she were not quite finished yet and still needed his help to survive. "Danny and I are, well, sharing a place now."

Eric's hand began to tighten on hers until she had to pull it away but, for another moment, he said nothing. He looked the basketball player up and down, then snorted. "God, Mildred would just *love* what you're up to, wouldn't she, Peg?"

"*You're* doing what *you* wish," she argued.

He ignored her, smiled sardonically. "Of course, she might be glad to see you're engaged in some charitable work. Jocks don't make much money, do they, until they turn pro? Unless, of course, this dude is an exception to the rule *and* the rules."

Danny squared his shoulders, edged forward, on his toes. He was much taller than Eric and more muscular but probably did not outweigh him.

"Hey, kid," Jennie said quite directly to Eric, her voice low, controlled, "you're being a rude son of a bitch." She arose, headed around the table toward him. Needing glasses, she bumped against it as she reached Eric and peered up at him from her lowered lids. "Peggy has reached legal age. If she wants to take a lover and hang out for a few weeks at your old place, that's her business. So cool it, okay?"

Eric's cheeks worked and his fists doubled. He did not turn to look at Jennie.

Finally, he brushed past Danny Stanwall and headed, stifflegged, into the front room. "You have that all absolutely right, woman," he called his acknowledgement, and the apartment door creaked as he pulled it wide. "But the Baldwin house is *legally* half *mine*, too! And y'know, I think *we'll* find it just as interesting in Indianapolis as Peg and her gland case!"

He attempted to slam the door behind him but it caught on the old rug and his exit ended in a muttered, "oh, *crap*!"

3

"What a cocky little goddam fart!" Danny Stanwall exclaimed as he slammed his fist, hard, on the steering wheel of his Jeep. An '83 CJ7 painted a racy silver-and-black, it had a dynamite tilt wheel and all of the athlete's affection—or it had until Peggy Porter had agreed to tutor him. "Who the *fuck* does your brother think he is to talk about me that way?"

"My big brother," she answered promptly, and squinted through the narrow windshield to get her bearings. But it was dark now and, since Danny had a penchant for getting anywhere by barreling through side streets—he'd said the police pretty much stuck to the main streets and it was safer driving through neighborhoods—she had no idea where they were.

"Would you mind slowing down to a hundred and twenty? I heard a rumor that these things turn over easily."

"Just seems that fast, Peg," he replied, terrifying her by glancing in her direction at the same time he turned a corner. The fat right rear tire carommed off the curb and the whole vehicle zigzagged briefly before righting itself. "And don't believe everything you hear, okay? This sumbitch corners like Magic—Magic Johnson, that is!"

She nodded, remembering an earlier chat they'd had when Danny admitted he saw driving as a challenge and other cars as competitors, so he sometimes pretended he and the CJ7 were on a basketball court, sprinting for a layup on a fast break. "Eric still thinks of me as being nine years old."

"Yeah, well, I know about turkeys like that," Danny said, bobbing his head and narrowly missing a car at the curb with its door open. "And the sonofabitch can grow up like you did and quit being so fuckin' protective!"

"Our mother was not a bitch," Peggy murmured. She planted her feet on the floorboard of the Jeep, crossed her arms, and tried to appears fearless and haughty at the same time. "She was a brilliant scientist until—"

"Until what?"

"Until . . . Grandfather Baldwin overworked her."

"You're guessing," he snapped, glancing over

at her again. Relieved, Peggy detected their familiar old apartment building, near downtown Dayton, two blocks away. They might make it that far. Danny added, "You don't really know how your mom went of her kook, Peg, *do* you? That's one of the things we hafta discover in Indy."

"God, you're so *gross*," Peggy growled, sinking into her cockpit seat. "And you are *not* permitted to call me Peg, remember?"

"So you're gonna take your brother's side over me, right?" Danny looked darker, even saturnine, in the illumination cast by the few streetlights they were passing. "That it?"

"It was my *mother* you were insulting this time."

"Yeah, well, but my callin Mr. High and Mighty a goddam fart is what teed you off to start." He struck the steering wheel again, this time hitting the horn. It made the sound of a medium-sized animal struck a glancing blow and several black people on a nearby porch turned to stare after them. "I'm not gonna take shit like that from Eric in Indy, Peg. *Peggy*. You're the one who invited me there, not your stuckup little brother."

"He isn't my *little* brother," Peggy corrected him with a sigh. It was beginning to rain, the top was down, and her lover was getting tiresome. *Besides*, she thought, *you invited yourself. You're* making *me go there*.

Danny spun crookedly against the curb,

slammed the brake, and the Jeep squealed to a stop in front of their apartment building. It seemed gothic with rain lashing at the sides of the structure. "I meant it, girl," he threatened, throwing his door open and jumping out. Leaning down, he shook his finger in Peg's face. "Keep that smart-ass egghead off me if you don't want his brains scrambled!"

"Maybe he won't really come," she said, shoving the pointing index away and getting out. Without glancing back at Danny, she went straight toward the front door, yellow hair darkened by shadows from the night-etched branches of nearby trees. "In any case, I thought you were coming along to help me battle the ghosts of my childhood—not to play war games with my bro."

But Eric will be there, Peggy realized, smiling secretly, happily. *He's a pain in the butt but he's* always *there when I need him.*

She was ducking in out of the developing storm when she realized that she had dragged Danny to her brother's place to make *sure* that Eric would also be with her in the Baldwin mansion.

It was almost 2 AM when Eric unlocked the door to his apartment and, half-drowned from walking in the rain—sneezing loudly—found Jennie waiting up for him. She was wearing shortie p.j.'s and dozing in a chair, knees drawn up to her chin; but Eric ignored her long enough to make his point and announce obliquely that he wasn't through with his anger yet. He took off his shirt, wadded it into a ball and tossed it lumpily on their aged sofa, stomped around in a circle for two minutes, eventually slumped down to the floor beside her. "Parasite! That Cro-Magnon reject is just sponging off my sister!"

"Really?" Jennie yawned, head back and breasts raised. "Funny. I had the impression you liked her better than that."

He glanced up at her with his features squinched together. "I don't get you."

"I mean that your sister is quite pretty; vivacious. She seemed intelligent."

"So?"

"So I don't think she needs her paltry inheritance or yours to get herself a man." Suddenly Jennie lowered her head, tested him with her wide, taunting eyes. "I thought he was kind-of a hunk, too. Peg's a lucky girl."

"He's using her, dammit!" Eric howled. He started to push himself to a standing position but Jennie shoved his head and the rest of him back to the floor. Eric ignored it. "And *I'm* the only one who's allowed to call her *Peg*!"

Jennie shrugged broadly. "They've always told me that incest is best."

"Damn you!" Eric colored, started again to rise and wasn't hindered. But he'd realized how close he was to Jennie Droff's long, bare legs and that she wore nothing beneath her shorties.

"We went through a lot together, Jen!"

"You keep telling me that," she said smoothly, snuggling down until her nose—and mouth—were inches away from Eric's. "But I know next to nothing of the details. Was it all your grandfather's fault?"

"Yes," he said; and "No," he said, immediately correcting himself. *Lynn, lying in bed, watching them enter the room. The long lashes lifting, the hungry lips turning up at the corners. The knowing that anything Lynn really craved, Lynn was given. Or, anyone.* "It was just Grandfather who brought . . . someone . . . to live in the mansion. Right after he let us come to live with him for no other reason than to use Peg and me as—as *slaves* to Lynn."

"Slaves?" She pursed her lips, shook her head faintly in amusement. "You exaggerate more than anybody I ever knew before."

"Servants, then!" Eric agreed, frowning. "What else would you call a house where two kids couldn't play or make a noise and had to run errands all the time—for that 'relative' we were never permitted to see!" He was dimly aware that Jennie's interest had again mounted. "Every day, we had to take back huge sacks of library books and take out twenty or thirty more books. We were kids, Jen. They were heavy."

"For your grandfather, the Senator, to study?" she inquired softly. He shook his head. Jennie touched his temple. "For this . . . Lynn

. . . then? Who *is* Lynn?"

"*Was,*" Eric corrected her. "There was a fire." He shrugged. Unwilling to explain Lynn to her, he changed the subject slightly. "My sister was nine or ten years old so she forgot about most of the things that happened in that old house, *forced* herself to forget—which shows how basically bright Peg is! Mildred, who was our housekeeper and took care of us later, took both of us to a psychiatrist for a while and he said I'd snap out of it." Eric lay back on the floor, remembering more than even he enjoyed recalling. "In Peg's case, the shrink said, 'Let it come back to her normally, steadily, over a period of years. She'll piece it together and remember everything when her mind can handle it.' Except she never *has* brought it out, dealt with it, Jennie."

"Surely you or Mildred tried," she prodded him.

"*I* wanted to, but ol' Mildred took what the doctor said very literally and wouldn't ever let me broach the subject in Peg's presence."

"What about the rest of the family?"

"*What* 'rest' of it?" Eric demanded, crossing his wrists behind his neck and sighing. "Mama died in the house. Our father never did show up and Mildred eventually told us that she believed Grandfather had . . . well, had 'eliminated' him in some way. We had a couple of nice cousins, but they died in the mansion, too. If we hadn't been children and Mildred just the housekeeper, I think the police would have imagined *we* killed Grandfather and . . . the Offspring. I know they never believed the story I told them about what happened and what the great Senator Baldwin was working on in that hell house."

"The . . . Offspring?"

"Yeah; Lynn." He pretended to yawn. "Both Lynn and Grandfather burned alive there. Or Lynn did, at least." Eric felt foggy on the point. His memory told him that the Offspring had made Grandfather vanish, but he assumed that was only his child's interpretation of what had happened—or the pain Lynn had made him feel. "The rest of us barely escaped. It was an inferno, Jennie—yet the odd thing is, when I was in my teens and they sent us photographs and wanted to know what to do with the house, it didn't look nearly as ruined as it seemed during the fire."

Jennie looked down at him without speaking, thinking. Clearly, he didn't want to tell her—not yet—just what had caused the fire or, perhaps more significantly, who Lynn had been. A relative, apparently; perhaps aged, infirm. Yet something in Eric's tone of voice and in what he *hadn't* told her might have indicated his conviction that the Offspring was actually responsible for what had transpired.

She longed to press him for the rest of the story, considered trying to do so. Eric Porter had been reticent about nothing else since they'd met and what he knew would surely go a long way toward providing Jennie with the information she sought.

But if Eric *didn't* know what had taken place in Iraq when each of them had been a small child, and Jennie's scientist father had been murdered, the data she required might only be discovered in the house where Adam Baldwin had conducted his inquiries and experiments. Alarming Eric now, alerting him that she did not even faintly love him or intend to be involved in his plans for the future, could cancel the trip to Indianapolis and the place in which it had all occurred . . .

"Why were you mad at me when I came in just now?"

Jennie turned again to look down at him, startled. It was the kind of wistful, even sad, question that a small boy might have asked his mother.

"I wasn't mad."

He nodded. "Yes, you were. I can tell. But you also waited up for me." His eyes behind thick lenses were shiny, hurt and hopeful and curious and amazingly shrewd all at the same time. His arms reached up for her. "Was that because you were simply curious and eager to gossip, or because you were afraid I might have gotten pneumonia out there in the rain? Or rundown by a truck or something?"

She laughed fondly. "I suppose I was miffed at your assumption that I'd follow you to

Indianapolis. You might have *asked* me to go. But I *was* concerned about you, York, once it began to pour." *And that's the truth,* Jennie realized with surprise.

"You still haven't asked what I was doing out there all that time," he said insistently, but his arms remained upthrust to her. Invitingly. That moment, Eric Porter seemed twelve years old, to the woman seated in his chair—and a cunning, never-miss-a-trick corporate executive of forty-five. "Aren't you afraid I found a lady of the night to be unfaithful to you with?"

"Idiot!" She bounded up from the chair, spun, and suddenly lay atop him. Eric went "*Ooof*!" because of the unprepared-for weight but he didn't look as if he would object. "I'm not worried about you being unfaithful, kid," she told him, kissing him several times, briefly, on his unprotesting mouth. "You get all you can handle from your resident older woman. So tell me, York, what were you doing out there?"

She's wearing nothing under these shortie p.j.s, Eric thought a second time, immediately wondering how they were removed. "You're too late!" he said, laughing. "Baying at the moon!" He smoothed his palms against her buttocks, pressed. "Peddling stale candy to little kids! Mugging old ladies who wandered defenselessly onto the campus!"

Jennie brought her knees forward, sat up, Eric still pinned to the carpet. She did magical things and was naked to the waist, pale and statuesque. Light from beneath the almost-closed shades turned her breasts white as Jennie peered down at them. "Bay at these," she whispered.

He did, while he squirmed out of his clothes. Jennie helped. "Will you go with me to the old house in Indianapolis?" he asked as she raised her hips above him. "*Please*? That dumb jock might be right about going home helping Peg, and it'll probably take only a few weeks."

Jennie nodded, and neither of them uttered another intelligible word for some time.

But she wondered, then and later, if Eric's prediction would prove to be accurate. What had happened to Peggy Porter hadn't happened overnight and many years had passed since the deaths and the cleansing, consuming fire of her youth and her brother's. Apparently, Jennie pondered, her own long inquiry into her father's passing was obliged to end—not inappropriately—in the house of the terrible old man who'd murdered him. At last, she hoped, she might learn the nature of Daddy's greatest discovery and why he had been killed.

As well as what in the world Lynn and the Offspring had to do with it, and why Eric would willingly discuss most of his past with her but not them. In Indianapolis, with luck, she might be able to learn exactly who she was—and close her admittedly neurotic investigation. One way or the other.

Perhaps the reason why some very old people tended to think in black-and-white or right-and-wrong terms had to do with the way their own, aging bodies came to react to climactic change and the oft-hesitant turns of the season.

For Mildred Manning Moag, there'd been a moment or series of moments without the slightest warning when she had unwittingly passed forever from youth. Throughout her forties, fifties, and sixties, and well into her seventies, the retired housekeeper had awakened each morning and entered each new season feeling—in all the major respects—unhampered by the accumulation of time. Possibly, she'd reflected once or twice, had she been able to remember with all her limbs and innards precisely the way she'd felt at twenty-nine, forty-two, or fifty-three, her current condition mightn't have seemed so reassuring. Yet she had been able to continue doing whatever Mildred considered important; when pain presented itself, or sickness, there'd been bottles at the nearest drugstore which cured her—often by process of elimination.

Then, seemingly overnight, the bad moment or series of moments had come upon Mildred—or she had wandered into them—and she'd known almost instantly that she was, for a fact, old. For a while, resting in bed, Mildred had tried to sort it out, come to grips with it. It had occurred to her that, without meaning to, she had literally accumulated time; instead of merely getting older, she had somehow taken a year here, a decade there, collected an enormously weighty packet of the stuff during her years in the Baldwin house, acquired and stored-away—like bottled jams or jellies—several more heavier pounds of time while she finished rearing her Peg and Eric; and one day, there was more of the accursed stuff than she could handle! If a body looked at it in that light, she'd reasoned, perhaps it was possible to *lose* time—not all at once, by the drastic deed of dying, but slowly, gradually, the way a sensible woman lost weight. What was clearly needed was a diet book or newfangled video doodad with pictures of people reducing away their surplus time!

And then she'd gone and added another year or so when Peg and Eric moved away forever, and her body began notifying Mildred that it was past the time when the book or video would do her any good. Now, spring was not spring unless the temperature was in the seventies and there was no rain; "early spring" was the fancy of a young sprout, nothing for an old ash to take as a promissory note. The old, Mildred perceived, lived in an either/or world; summer was fine in the early eighties, but dog days were for canine companions, not old women whose ages matched the thermometer and fought desperately to avoid advancing in pace with the mercury. And winter was winter; zero degrees meant, at the very best, starting over, a fresh start.

Mildred went to catch a bus to the Dayton campus several days later, intending to warn "her kids" in person, not only about what old Ouija had told her, but of what she had felt—had *known*—in her mind, in the numerology charts she continued to create with awe glowing in her eyes like the rebirth of youthful vitality, and in her freshly aching bones. Mildred's feet wanted to move, to take her to Peg and Eric. Her back tugged at her, strove to pull her erect and send her on her way to them. They were in danger from Lynn, dead or not; there was nothing on the surface or deep inside the old woman that did not accept the warning signs for what they surely were.

But the illness had been upon her and rising to obey the commands of her bones, her belief, and her love had been impossible. Until today. Riding the bus to the campus, all the winter gathering within Mildred denied the silly notion of early spring and she felt quite sick, exhausted really. At this stage of her life, being able to stand, hobble to a bus stop, and prepare what she was going to say to the young people, however haltingly, amounted to the return of sparkling good health. She had thought of phoning them, then dismissed it promptly. People got exceedingly busy when they spoke into telephone receivers, and telephones could be hung up. What she had to tell her kids could only be accomplished face to face.

With the feeling that she was gliding upon ice and might fall through and drown at any step, hugging her coat and the shawl under it tightly around her shoulders, the housekeeper located Eric's off-campus apartment. As he'd told her, it was right across the street from the university itself, but what he hadn't understood—*couldn't* understand—was that crossing a wide, busy intersection and climbing a flight of steps to Eric's front door was equivalent to Eric running five miles.

She couldn't remember being as distressed as she was when she found a note stuck to the door. "Homeward bound. Leave mail and stuff at B-2." At first, Mildred believed he meant that he was driving out to her home, where she had raised the Porter children. Panicky, imagining him needing her and finding her away, she turned shakily and started back toward the stairs.

The door—not Eric's; a door with the legend B-2 painted on it—swung wide and startled her. A youth who was surely a giant, nearly seven feet tall, stood in the aperture staring at her. He was naked except for a pair of shorts and Mildred had never seen such feet in her life. "You Porter's old lady?"

For the first time in weeks, Mildred smiled. The term amused her. "I suppose I am, yes."

"Well, he booked for Indy, lady. His lady and him."

Mildred's mouth opened. Her heart skipped a

beat. "Do you mean his sister was going with Eric?"

"Beats me." The giant rubbed his navel. "Yeah, I think she *was* going with them, now that you mention it." The behemoth smiled, revealing great gaps where teeth were supposed to be. "And Stanwall from the basketball team." He appeared remarkably proud of his memory feat. From the depths of his apartment, Mildred noted, a smell issued that reminded her of the fragrance of a dead relative who hadn't wished to be embalmed.

Murmuring thanks, Mildred descended the stairs as swiftly as she dared, some of her sickness replaced by rising anger. What did those two children *mean*, dropping their studies and impetuously going back to *that place* without even telling her of their decision? She had to lean hard against the downstairs door to open it and, half-stumbling out into the uremic sunlight, she realized for the first time that old Ouija was right again.

Lynn—in some way Mildred could not conceive but she knew it, knew without a doubt that it was for evil—Lynn had wanted them back in the ruins of that house—and they were headed for it as if they'd been summoned!

Terror, in turn, replaced her anger, followed by two cumbrous thoughts which came in such quick succession that she was obliged to lean against the building and fight for another breath: *I must go to them at once*, and *I can't go.*

Bleak, barren of all save the ballooning press of her devouring yesterdays—feeling the winter that was hers alone creep through the aged body like icy water soon to freeze—Mildred forced herself to look across the street toward the campus, in search of a bus. Despite the fact that she hadn't doubted any of her thoughts and *knew* she could not reach Indianapolis, she was starting to work out the details of her departure from Dayton: writing and cashing a check, choosing between a bus and plane, although she had never used any of the Baldwin money for purchases of her own. Her eyes slowly focussed, took their time as they always had these closing days.

While she saw a bus across the way, half-filled with passengers and paused with the motor running, she also saw with her clearing vision what lay sprawled *atop* the vehicle. Fleshy, nude, mammoth, its eyes turned toward Mildred with the ridiculous lashes fluttering, the Offspring reclined as if enjoying the inceptional spring sun. And one plump finger was curled coyly to her, beckoning.

Mildred said, so loudly it was virtually a curse, "*Lynn*!"

Her own winter engulfed and pierced her caring and courageous heart. Before she had slid slowly to the pavement and closed her eyes, the dead thing on the bus had vanished.

4

The Baldwin family house, back when the distinguished professor brought his grandchildren to dwell in it with himself and his biologist daughter, had been the final, permanent holdout in the development of a *noveau* middle-class area called Central Eastwood. Ruggedly rooted in a past that Adam Baldwin pretended to be a part of, the huge, white brick two-story was rumored to interest the old man solely as a means of retaining his Indiana residency. For political reasons. And it was fact that, without living again in the state of his birth, Baldwin could not have become Indiana's senior senator.

Why else, asked the nearby farmers in suburban Lawrence and the truck-wheeling, beer-guzzling burghers of Central Eastwood, would a Pulitzer Prize winning scholar and bonafide member of the agnostic scientific fraternity *want* such an imposing—it was a mansion, compared to the prefab tri-levels of the fifteen-year-old community—yet unimportantly situated, old eyesore?

But Baldwin stayed, became a U.S. Senator and candidate for the Presidency of the United States, without doing anything more conspicuously bizarre than turning his attic into a partially-finished third floor with space for his own offices. In time, more rumors spread that Adam Baldwin was conducting some kind of weird experiments within the old mansion, and no neighbor was quite broken-hearted when the former professor perished in a fire that almost took the lives of his grandchildren and servant.

Other rumors, less prevalent, insisted as well that a person additional to Adam Baldwin had been roasted alive by the nocturnal flames.

More time passed, biographies of Baldwin were written, and his memory was eventually honored, if not revered or cherished. As houses in Central Eastwood exchanged owners and newer tenants replaced new tenants, realtors and a remnant of those who'd stayed enjoyed remarking upon the fact that the anomalous eyesore once had been owned by a versatile giant of intellect who, subsequent to his defeat in the campaign for high office, had spent his declining years inventing things meant to improve the lot of his fellow Hoosiers.

Nothing could have been, in general, farther from the truth.

Closer to verity was the further fancy that the now-unoccupied Baldwin property was haunted.

Eric Porter's initial surprise, when he and Jennie arrived in Indianapolis and drove out to his boyhood home, was that the house he'd considered enormous was merely a durable, commodious structure of the kind generally constructed between the turn of the century and the stock market crash of '29. During his teenage years and since, Eric realized, he had apparently exaggerated its size out of all proportions. His recollections of feeling isolated and almost imprisoned in his high-ceilinged bedroom on the second floor, of mounting stairs that went on ascending or descending endlessly, he saw, were nothing more than a mixture of imagination and the way that *everything* seemed giant-sized to a child.

His third surprise was how eerily restricting the place remained, once the two of them were inside the house. But surprise number two occurred while Jennie and he sat staring at it from his '84 fuel-injected Datsun 280Z (which had been Eric's gift to himself, courtesy of his half of the inheritance, when he'd graduated from Dayton): from the outside—from a street with the well-remembered succession of pickup trucks and rusty Fords and Chevies and the lookalike tract houses of aging Central Eastwood—it was very hard to believe that a terrible fire had seemed to burn the house down. Had, indeed, killed his grandfather and Lynn.

"I ordered the renovation when I was a kid mainly to prevent it from becoming a firetrap, an attractive nuisance," he said aloud. He went on looking at the old white brick structure but his hand reached for, and found, Jennie's. "I remember that when Mildred practically carried Peg and me out that door, I was sure the whole house was coming down. That it'd be reduced to ashes." He shuddered. "You could even hear the big Hammond organ that Mama once played screaming like an animal in pain as it burned."

She didn't know quite what to say, then saw Eric turn to her, looking frightened. "Honey—"

"Jen, the flames were *everywhere* when we were running down the steps from the second floor, trying to escape! You could hear things snapping—beams, I guess—and see the pictures on the walls melting, 'til the faces in portraits were part of the walls and—"

"York, you probably exaggerated it," she said. "Kids do that."

"Not *that* much." He shook his head wonderingly.

Jennie smiled and touched his nearly-beardless cheek. "Okay. Then you got a real break when you or Mildred hired the crew that did the renovation. Don't you see? They simply did a great piece of work!"

"I suppose it's possible . . ."

"There was probably a recession going on and the workmen had time on their hands. If they knew a teenage kid had the money to hire them, all the way from Ohio, they just decided to be thorough. To get asked back."

"You must be right." Looking dubious, he got out of the car and stopped in the street. "It's sure as hell as if somebody—or the house itself—*wanted* the place to look great whenever Peg or I returned." He headed up the walk and his words trailed off behind him: "So we'd *stay*. For whatever damned reason."

"What did you say?" Unaided, Jennie was struggling out of the Datsun and following him toward the front door of the house.

"Forget it." Yards from the door, he hesitated to withdraw a keyring from his side pocket. Frowning, he sorted through the keys until he located the right one. The sun over Indianapolis was bright but sullen, making Eric and the foot-high, yellowish grass faintly unreal in appearance. He took several steps forward. "No one's been here since I was sixteen so this may be kinda tricky; the lock's probably rusted."

He inserted the key and the door swung open almost before he'd touched it.

"There'll be a welcome wagon of ghouls and vampires by any time," Eric murmured, smiling humorlessly at the tall brunette.

"Oh, come *on,*" she snapped, preceding Eric into the house. "If you're gonna act spooky like that while we're here, a few werewolves can only brighten up things."

The foyer was devoid of furnishings and the floor thick with dust that swirled as they put the first footprints in it. But what troubled Eric was the simple act of closing the front door behind them. There was the sense of commitment to it, of reclaiming that which had only been partly his. When Jennie called, "What an unholy horror," he followed her into the great catheral-style living room with reluctant haste, unsure what he'd see. In that vast space, Grandfather Baldwin had once dared to play Mama's Hammond organ; she had come downstairs to join them for Christmas morning, quite against doctor's orders, and mentally collapsed when Peg showed her the ordinary pair of socks she'd knitted for the never-witnessed Offspring upstairs.

But Jennie stood alone in the center of room, gesturing. "York, did you hire somebody to replace some of the burned-up furniture?"

Eric nodded slowly. "My instructions were to buy some inexpensive chairs—plus a dining room table, maybe some old beds for upstairs—in case Peg or I wanted to visit the place."

"Now you understand the old saying, 'Never send a boy to do a man's work.' " Jennie's wide mouth grimaced in feminine disgust and disapproval. "And now I see why they worked so hard on the exterior. They can't have spent three-hundred dollars on everything *inside* the house and the foreman had an attack of conscience!"

Eric's audible groan acknowledged that she was right. It seemed that the people he and ol' Mildred hired by long distance had raided every fast food restaurant or diner for miles around. There were seven or eight small chairs and a single couch, bright red; the dining room table Eric saw when he'd rushed through the living room might have been used for picnics by Dillinger's family in the thirties! "It's Plastic World," he moaned.

"Well," Jennie sighed, "at least it looks too modern for a haunted house."

"It's as if Dr. Frankenstein died and was decked out in a tank top and jeans," Eric agreed, grinning as he walked toward her.

"Or the monster was being buried in bikini trunks!" Jennie added, hugging him.

She and Eric had intentionally arrived ahead of Peggy Porter and Danny Stanwall because Eric wanted to check out the house to make sure it was safe, "structurally, y'know; no roofs caving in on anybody." Jennie remembered that as he asked her to wait for him downstairs, and smiled affectionately. The kid had a kind heart; first he'd wanted to protect his younger sister and now he was doing the same for her, probably climbing the stairs with his heart in his mouth, waiting for old man Baldwin's spook to leap out and brain him with his cane. Eric had tossed his own cane in the back seat of the Datsun, and Jennie Dorff wondered about that as she gingerly perched in one of the red plastic chairs. Maybe Eric felt nervous about toting the stick around with him in the house where Senator Baldwin's *tap-tap-tap* must have scared him out of his wits.

Or maybe Eric and Peggy Porter both would be reduced to children again, in this silly old hulk of a house. She shook her head, wondering if she had made a mistake coming along, beginning to doubt that either Porter was capable of filling in the blanks about her own father's demise.

I won't lose my resolve or abandon the search, she told herself, crossing her legs and lighting a True Gold. *Daddy didn't deserve to be killed. But he* does *deserve for his daughter to know the facts, even if it's too late for Adam Baldwin or his child, Elizabeth, to pay.*

Because Verblin Spandorff—the latter was Jennie's real name—had also been a bright, promising young man once, then-Professor Baldwin's brightest student in ancient history, at Northgate University. Small and dark-skinned, homely and lively as a capuchin monkey, Jennifer's father had possessed qualities that even the great Adam Baldwin had lacked: an intense, wide-ranging imagination, a flair for believing in the damndest things until they'd been scientifically disproved, in time an archeologist with a quite unscientific but peerless intuition for locating the buried treasures of the past—and the unfortunate, untimely audacity to rub the noses of his peers and prestigious superiors in the ancient dirt.

By now, Jennie felt sure that her father, Verblin, had taunted the future Senator Baldwin—his ex-professor—into joining him at some digs in Iraq and, in the process, infuriated the haughty old bastard until he'd murdered Verblin Spandorff and taken the discovery as his own.

Yet there appeared to be no written record of it in newspaper files or those of professional journals, after a year of her devoted research—nothing that announced such a discovery on the part of either Baldwin or Spandorff. Jennie's courses and constant reading in psychology strongly suggested that a man such as Baldwin would've published a paper or book concerning such a thrilling find shortly after his return from Iraq, or, had the opportunity presented itself, employed such a major discovery to make another greedy fortune. Or to enhance his own renown. But Baldwin had bought *this* house, ultimately run for the Presidency and met defeat, then spent the rest of his long life in virtual seclusion here.

With no overt changes in his life, she suddenly saw the truth, *except for the presence—from nowhere—of a family member named "Lynn."* Excited, almost stunned, Jennie sat up straight and stared around the immense room as if its aged walls might yield the rest of the secret to her. *A relative he had to care for—Adam Baldwin as nursemaid?—and educate with library books brought home in droves by grandchildren he brought here for that purpose!*

For the first time, Jennifer was glad she had accompanied Eric. She realized that men like Adam Baldwin might be capable of patiently keeping astounding secrets and steer clear of the limelight if, at the end of a long road, they planned to achieve power again—power that might have been as great as, or greater than, that of the American presidency.

Who, then, *was* Lynn? And what did he—*or she*, the name was used by both sexes now that she thought about it—have to do with Verblin Spandorff's most important discovery . . . possibly the greatest archeological find of the century?

Three wheezing, powerful notes of off-key organ music from immediately behind Jennie sent her to her feet in shock and fear. But the Hammond no longer existed. It had burned in that awful fire more than a decade ago! Trembling, Jennie looked behind her and the absurd red plastic chair, put out a shaking hand, felt waves, *vibrations*, and an adhering warmth where nothing stood but the wall.

"Jennie!"

She whirled, heart almost stopping. But it was just Eric, striding into the room with an expression on his face that seemed mixed, ambivalent.

"There are places for you and I, Peg and the Neanderthal to sleep," he said, leaving a question in the air.

"Then we won't have to use the sleeping bags you threw into the trunk," she replied. *Power of suggestion,* she thought; *there is no organ so I imagined it.* "That's something."

"It's something odd as hell," he blurted, "like everything else that's happened since Peg and I lived here."

"Go on."

"In the bedroom where Mama used to sleep," he said, choosing his words carefully, "there's a nice double bed. Jen, it looks exactly like the one Mama had. But the worst part of the fire was concentrated on the second floor and the firemen would surely have hauled it away as a piece of junk." He held up a hand before she could comment. "There are cots in two other rooms, plain cots." He paused, blinking. "I didn't have the guts to go up to Grandfather's office becasue I was half-afraid I'd find the whole thing intact. But where Lynn slept" —Eric glanced away, as if he might have been followed—"there's a nice, brand-new bed. Jennie, it's a double-width *hospital* bed."

She shrugged, more determined after what she had imagined to downplay anything Eric considered peculiar about the house. "Everybody knows *somebody,* York," she argued.

"Without you or that woman who brought you up to keep an eye on things, someone you hired must have been able to get it for a really sharp deal. And *I* hereby select *that* room and bed as ours—or *mine,* if you don't have the balls to sleep there!"

Eric gaped at her, startled and concerned. So much so that he didn't bother to tell her the rest of the story.

That Lynn, the Offspring, had slept in a hospital bed exactly like the one he had found in Lynn's old room.

The rest of their first day in the Baldwin house, Eric and Jennie dusted, cleaned up, and washed down most of the first and second floors. There wasn't time for the basement before nightfall, and despite the fact that Eric remembered nothing terrifying that had happened there, both young people had seen enough low-budget horror films to be disinclined to venture into the basement at night.

But he had climbed the fire-scorched steps to the partially finished third story and, with Jennifer gripping his hand tightly, entered Senator Baldwin's office for the first time in his life.

Nothing much remained of the two wide rooms except several smashed test tubes on the floor of what had apparently been a laboratory and a blackened bookcase with a number of thoroughly charred leather-bound tomes and notebooks in the room Grandfather had kept as a combination of office and sleeping area. At a glance, without raising the warped and filthy leaf-front of the bookcase, nothing readable was left.

With Jennie retreated to the doorway, Eric stood in the center of the room, pivoting slowly with his face a cloud of forlorn memory. There, he assumed, was where Grandfather's bed had been—even if he rarely slept in it because of his insomnia and the fact that he was a workaholic. It was possible to peer through a window set into a gabled arch of what had been an attic storeroom, to stare haughtily from empyrean heights at the "ordinary" people of Central Eastwood as they sent their children off to P.S. 98 or John Marshall High School, then headed for their own day's chores as housewives who made do with the most inexpensive appliances or as employed people who worked long hours as maintenance men, clerks at nearby Fort Harrison, sales people at Victor's or People's pharmacies, checkout people at Kroger's, or line workers at McDonald's and Dairy Queen. Maybe, thought Eric, maybe they lacked the ambition or industry or imagination to dream of making more of themselves—Grandfather had genuinely believed that—and maybe they'd wanted less for themselves, *needed* less to feel content. Maybe Grandfather had hated them because, in the last analysis, he was afraid of them because they knew things he'd never grasped about love, and family life.

And children . . .

"We must do away with virtually every institution, every law—and start again. People will be grateful to the whole Baldwin family for generations yet unborn," Grandfather had told Eric and Peg. "There'll be no further toleration of ingrates and ignoramuses, people who cannot excel. For much too long a time, this country has abided people who contribute nothing but their bodily presence! Idlers, loafers without ideas, abilities, the necessary skills of the future—a future which will give humankind either all that it needs, or total chaos."

Peg had asked who'd decide what was needed. "Are *you* going to decide, Grandfather?" the twelve-year-old Eric had inquired. "Because all those ordinary folks wouldn't *let* you be President?"

And Grandfather had slapped Eric jarringly across the cheek.

For a moment, he'd feared that the giant of an old man might also strike him with his cane. But cousins Bernard and Sue, who'd come for Christmas, had interfered. And later, they had died. Hideously.

Grandfather was gone now, but the future—part of it—had come.

And what Eric Porter had seen of it on those rare occasions when he'd realized that his collegiate career was winding down, that he must make his way in the wider world, had deeply worried him. *Idlers without the necessary skills,* Eric recalled once more, turning to join Jennie at the door; *a future with all that it needs, or chaos.*

"You're limping," Jennie told him as they headed back downstairs.

"It's nothing."

But before they went to bed that night, Eric brought his cane in from the Datsun and he did not join Jennie in bed until the sun was starting to rise.

She'd watched him from partly-raised eyelids, dozed off once more without seeing him close his own eyes.

By the time his sister and her boyfriend arrived at the Baldwin house, it was nearing sundown the next day. Eric had gone with Jennie to the Lowell's market next to an Osco drug store and helped her stock up, clearly himself again to Jennie's relief. He'd ordered an inexpensive refrigerator to be delivered but, since it wouldn't be hooked up until the next day, they'd bought only enough perishable food to feed the four of them that night and the following morning. And with Peg's arrival, Eric seemed jubilant to see her, anxious to take her on what he called a "schnook's tour" of their childhood home. He'd even greeted Danny Stanwall, Peggy's lover, with an apologetic air.

Everything went well until the two young men began carrying Peg's trunk up to the second floor.

"What've you got in this thing?" Eric demanded, calling to his sister at the top of the stairs. "You manage to compress everything in your apartment into this trunk?"

"I can handle it, Eric," Danny said, meaning well. "You've got it this far and I can shove it the rest of the way."

Eric glared down at him. Now, the stairway looked as long and as deep as he'd imagined it when he was a boy. "There's no need for you to showoff, Stanwall," he snapped. "We all know what a big deal athlete you are. Listen, if you're named to the all-conference team this year, what'll that make you? All-Dipshit? It isn't exactly the Big Ten or the Big East!"

Angry, Danny shoved the trunk, forcing Eric to jump up a step to avoid the blow to his ankle. "Maybe so, Porter," Danny retorted, "but nobody on my team has to tag after his little sister so he has somebody to take care of him!"

"Take care of *me*?" Eric repeated, shouting and gripping the trunk by his fingertips, trying for better purchase. "I'm here to keep her from eloping with a pea-brained jock on the make! Without Peg or an NBA tryout, buddy, you'll be living at the local Y until you're sixty and working out with the other fat has-beens!"

"You snot-nosed little stuffshirt!" Danny shouted back, shoving again.

The trunk's edge went right out of Eric's grip, bounced against the step, rebounded—hard—against Stanwall's chest. Off balance, he caught it with one hand, threw up the other, and toppled away from the step on which he had paused so precariously.

Peggy at the top and Jennie at the bottom of the stairs screamed as Danny let go of the trunk, completely, and felt it crack against one leg, and—wigwagging with both arms—began falling backward.

But his body stopped as if encountering a bracing wall or a pair of powerful arms—and floated gently the rest of the way down.

5

Convinced that her eyes had played tricks on her and still unable to remember much of her life as a child, Peggy began unpacking her things and Danny's in the bedroom that once was her mother's. One wall was badly scorched from the fire and part of the flooring just inside the door had burned, but those things didn't matter. Simply being alone awhile and content to imagine that some last essence of her beloved Mama was watching over her helped Peg to reinforce that which she needed to believe.

Hanging dresses on hangers she had thought to bring, in Mama's enormous walk-in closet, Peggy again went over the incident of Danny's "fall" in her thoughts, quite calmly: while she mightn't be the brain everyone had believed she'd become and didn't know psychological behavior the way Eric's girl did, she *was* smart enough to understand the power of suggestion. They had all been half-way expecting some sort of peculiar occurrence, considering the unexplained fire and Grandfather's terrible death, years ago. Most of the kids Peggy knew tended to leap to conclusions; she had herself often enough.

Then too, she'd been at the top of the stairs, ready to help her brother haul the trunk to Mama's room, and standing at an impossible angle for perceiving *exactly* the way Danny fell—and Danny was easily the most athletic and agile of them. Hadn't she read somewhere, years back, that people in conditions of emotional stress were capable of doing things they were never able to do under normal circumstances? Her lover and her bro had been involved in another stupid quarrel; Danny, she believed, had simply been keyed-up enough to recover his sense of balance and sort-of walk backward down the steps.

Probably, if you paid him something, Peg thought, smiling to herself, he could teach himself to do that. And if you dared him, he'd learn how to do it in a minute!

She began to undress, not to bathe since the groaning old furnace in the basement had to pass another inspection before the gas company would hook it up again, but because her clothes were soiled from the trip and she wanted to change them. Peggy half-closed her eyes, dreamily, remembering what she could—all of it, on the conscious level, pleasant and soothing. Even after her mother had fallen ill—surely it had really been something *physical*, Mama was far too brilliant for anything to have hurt her *mentally*—Mama had managed to remember her "precious Margaret." Dimly, as she went to Mama's bed in only her bra and panties, to the heavier sweater and slacks she'd laid out for the chilly evening ahead of them, Peggy recalled Elizabeth Baldwin Porter's pale, drawn face, the widow's peak in her soft, chestnut hair, and how she had spoken to her children on her last Christmas morning: "My little birds," she'd murmured, fingertips caressing their faces with wonder, "how long I've neglected you in your nests!" But she hadn't *meant* to, Peggy thought as tears rushed to her eyes. It was all the fault of that—

Someone was watching her, but the cold shudder she felt along her bare spine told Peggy that it was not Mama's spirit.

Moving slowly, she turned, long blond hair stirring only faintly so that she was obliged to peer searchingly, apprehensively, through its strands. Peggy saw the fire-smudged vanity table that had been her mother's. Her eyes drifted to the side, saw the cracked and dusty mirror . . .

And a pair of eyes, nothing more, staring at her from the center of the glass, luxuriant feminine lashes batting above hard, mesmeric, and mocking pupils.

Instantly, Peggy dropped the sweater she'd been about to slip on, took an instinctive step of shock away from the mirror. At the back of her knees, the bed stopped her and she dropped onto the mattress with a gasp.

Quickly looking back at the mirror, too surprised to scream or call out, she saw the image of a frightened nine-year-old girl clutching a bright yellow kitten to her thin chest.

It dissolved at once and there was only her own contemporaneous face with the eyes wide and her mouth stretched open in a scream that never came.

It wouldn't be true to say that Jennifer Spandorff disbelieved in ghosts, especially since she was smart enough to understand that, in a way, she was herself haunted by her father.

Yet she was sufficiently educated and familiar enough with the scientific method to doubt whatever had not been established in a laboratory by means of repeated, verifiable, controlled experimentation. Alone in her own room while Eric and the athlete tried to build a fire in the ancient fireplace, to take the chill off the house and prepare for the kind of Indianapolis June night when the temperature tended to plummet, Jennie would have encouraged Peggy's less-rigid thinking, and echoed it, except that she was also an independent thinker in her own way. Failing to believe what she'd experienced with her own eyes or other senses was, to Jennie, as redolent of superstition as believing in things she'd *never* seen.

Worse, she thought, lying down on the double-sized hospital bed—Eric's surprise at finding it there was understandable, but there certainly seemed to be nothing supernatural or unreal about the bed—she had also heard organ music where no organ existed. The oldest and most mature member of their foursome had already experienced *two* inexplicable incidents!

And the only possible explanation for them, it occurred to Jennie Spandorff, if they had not actually occurred, was that she was beginning to come unglued.

Fully dressed, shivering despite the coverlet she'd drawn up over herself, Jennie wondered abruptly just *why* she had been chosen to be terrified twice—assuming the place was haunted and frightening people was the spirit's intent. Just as swiftly as she'd placed the question, the answer seemed whispered in her mind: *You're not really part of this. They're either toying with you—playing head games—or,* she realized, sitting up in bed and sensing her heart begin beating more insistently, *the ghost is trying to get rid of you. Make you leave.*

That was when the scratching sounds began in the walls, as if a small, unseen and possibly unseeable animal was trying to get out.

Jennie stared intently at the place in the wall from which the noises seemed to come, holding the coverlet to her. For a moment she thought it possible that the sounds—now the walls were being clawed viciously from inside—were merely seeping upstairs from down and linked to the work being done by the two young men. But that was wrong. Whatever it was was becoming frantic and violently digging from inside the wall just on the other side of the plaster and, if it kept at it long enough, would surely claw and chew its way through.

Rats, Jennie thought, the first entirely rational concept that occurred to her. But this house was unoccupied, had been for more than a decade. Didn't mice and rats make nests close to a food supply? Didn't most creatures?

Ghouls burrow up from graves deep in the earth, folklore reminded Jennifer, brought her quietly, cautiously, to her feet beside the bed. That was nonsense, of course, tommyrot and foolishness; but who could be certain that all of the people who died here were buried elsewhere? *If they're after new victims—if they want fresh flesh to replace the dead meat they dig out of caskets like an animal scooping the goody out of an egg, they must dig all the way up and out—seek the living.*

"I'm talking shit, here," she said aloud and

glared at the wall. "Go away!" The command had no effect. The scratching noises continued, unabated, louder if anything. *Paw, paw, scratch, scratch*. She tore a shoe from one foot, aimed it carefully toward where the sounds came from, and threw the shoe with all her might. "Leave me *alone*, damn you!"

The shoe bounced ineffectually away and stopped moving. Something quite distinctly *sniggered* at her, laughed at Jennie. It sounded—possibly it was only her imagination—half human.

And half thing.

The discarded shoe spun in a circle, stood up on its heel, and took a few experimental steps. It looked like someone trying on a shoe in a store, taking a tentative pace or two to be sure it fitted.

Almost hopping, Jennie rushed through the doorway—and realized that the sounds had stopped. Whatever had clawed and scratched and snickered and made the shoe come to life also wanted her to know that if she told anybody about it, she'd look ridiculous.

She wouldn't, in a fashion of speaking, have one foot to stand upon.

But she hobbled her way toward the stairs leading to young Eric Porter anyway.

Danny Stanwall was on his knees before the fireplace. The fireplace was crammed with old newspapers they'd found in the large kitchen where Mildred Manning Moag had worked so hard to continue feeding the avaricious Offspring on the second floor. Behind Danny, Eric stood with his hands behind his back.

"Fuck, man, when we light these papers, they'll just burn for a few minutes and turn to ashes," Danny offered without rising. "Maybe we ought to go out to the woods at the end of the driveway, see if we can find some branches down."

"I *found* something," Eric said expressionlessly. "On the third floor."

Danny looked around and up, saw the way Eric was standing. "What?" And then he watched as Eric deliberately began moving his hands into view.

Above his head, and well over Danny's, threateningly, Eric held a slab of wood, as if he meant to bring it crashing down upon Danny's unprotected head. To the athlete's horror, he saw how wild-eyed his host looked and heard a dreadful, *giggling* sound Eric made deep in his throat.

"Try this," said Eric, abruptly lowering the weapon and, with a grin, poking it into the fireplace with the old newspapers. "Part of my grandfather's shelving. It's dry, so it ought to burn awhile."

"Shit *fuck*, Porter, you almost scared the piss

outta me." Stanwall glared at him and accepted the cigarette lighter Eric was putting in his palm.

"Wait, let me write that epigram down," Eric murmured, pretending to search for paper and pencil. "By the time we go back to Dayton, my vocabulary will have been titanically improved simply because *you* were present."

"For a minute there, I thought you were gonna brain me," Danny complained.

" 'When you least expect it,' " Eric quoted the old movie ad, genuinely smiling now, " 'expect it!' " Besides, I couldn't possibly brain *you*. Certain essentials are missing!"

"You always got the needle out, or what?" Danny, quite gingerly, did what every man who ever built a fire feels obliged to do. He poked at it, with his naked finger, even though the scrap of wooden furniture had caught and heat was already issuing from the fireplace. "Your grampa's huh? You sure his ghost won't mind you bustin' his crap up?"

"*Another* jewel of lexicography!" Eric cried, applauding. Then he stood, retrieving his cane from a red plastic chair against which he had rested it. "The English department certainly lost a proud champion when you put on short pants again!"

Danny shot to his feet, fists balled. "I'm tryin' t'control my temper 'cause you're Peggy's brother."

"*And* your host," Eric added, turning to see Jennie entering the mammoth living room.

"Jen! We have a fire going! Did we remember to buy marshmallows at the grocery?"

"I'm not the dumbass you think I am, Porter," Danny said behind him.

Eric turned to face him. With a sigh, he extended his hand. "I apologize. Especially if I hurt your feelings." Danny clasped his hand, grudgingly at first. "And you're right, Stanwall—you're sharp as a tack. I got a friend of mine who works in the Dean's office to check you out and you get pretty damned good grades for a jock!"

"You did *what*?" Danny pulled his hand away.

"Peg's my sister and we survived hell together," Eric said simply. "Before I'm through, I'll know everything you ever did, and Peg will know it, too, bad or good."

For a long second, Danny gazed into Eric's unflinching eyes, then restored their handshake. "Okay, yeah, I can buy it. You've got no family and you're just lookin' out for Peggy. Well, I ain't done nothing I'm ashamed of, man. Check me out from stem to stern." He began squeezing Eric's hand very hard. "You wouldn't like for me to strip, would you, so you can make sure I'm man enough?"

"I even understand you, Stanwall," Eric answered, squeezing back, but he knew it was no contest. Danny was much stronger. "Like most people today, you try to reach down to the ignorant, instead of obliging them to reach *up* to us." The pain in his smaller hand was becoming excruciating. "But unless I work and live with a man, what else can I judge him by but the things he *says* to me? And please don't say, 'By what he wears.' Because the only thing trendier than slang is clothes, and each is changed completely every week or so!"

Jennie joined them. "Have you two become friends?" She reached for Eric's hand.

As inconspicuously as possible, Eric withdrew and gave the agonized thing to her. "Bosom," he intoned, "buddies."

"Pals to the end," Danny put in, smiling tightly. "You can take it pretty good, Porter."

"And the end is coming fast," Eric quipped and added in an aside, "Thank you."

Peggy soon joined them, suggested they have something to eat and, with no need to discuss it, the four of them found themselves dining in the front room, as close to the fire as possible. Eric had bought a small gas range but it hadn't been hooked up yet and they were obliged to make do with cold cut sandwiches and cole slaw washed down with Vernor's ginger ale or Diet Pepsi.

Neither woman volunteered to describe the strange things they'd seen in their respective rooms, and neither man noticed how forced their cheerful remarks were. On Jennie's part, it puzzled her how chilly it was for a June evening. She was unfamiliar with Indianapolis' sometimes-changeable weather but it seemed that the house itself was primarily responsible for her involuntary shivering. How much life did a house take for itself from those who dwelled in it over a period of many years? And if it were then closed up for well over a decade, was it possible that the unnurtured house grew lonely, withdrawn, eccentric, even iconoclastic?

"Sittin' in this plastic chair," Danny said, munching his way through a third bologna sandwich with catsup, mustard and relish, "I feel like this is the opening of a fancy new McDonald's." When Eric said softly, "Goody," the lanky athlete asked, "You ever eat in a McDonald's?"

"Once," Eric admitted. "But I recovered."

Jennie laughed. "York, here, is in the last stages—*I hope*—of what he takes for collegiate sophistication. But his real problem is that he's a living anachronism. He thinks nothing worthwhile has been developed or invented since he was born."

Eric's grin was distant. Peggy declared, "He hasn't changed, though. He was always an old grump."

They looked to Eric for another quip but he appeared not to have heard his sister's gibe. Peggy realized then that he wasn't actually a part of their good-humored banter and hadn't been for most of their makeshift supper.

Now, Eric was peering slowly around the high-ceilinged, cathedral-style room as if he needed somehow to acclimate himself, try to make peace with it and the memories it kept scantly out of reach. His young face was expressionless; his gray eyes, behind the thick-lensed spectacles, seemed owlish, hollowed. Peggy yearned to hug him, tell him she understood—except she remembered so little. Finished eating, her brother had grasped the cane so much like their grandfather's between his legs and was remotely tapping it on the carpeted floor from time to time. For the first time, Peggy was able to see Adam Baldwin in her brother. Not so much in his average-sized head or regular features, which were different from those of the tall, powerful old man, but in a tension Eric exuded and in the obvious difficulty he found in sustaining an easy, conversational affability. She suspected that it was not only around her lover Danny that Eric had become inclined toward times of pomposity and an inclination to lecture, to show off, to tell them what to do, each attribute having been basic to their grandfather's overpowering personality.

But it was this *place*, surely, that was at fault! Peggy didn't believe for a moment that the brilliant old man was attempting to possess Eric; if such worlds existed, Hell must have claimed Grandfather Baldwin the instant he died. Maybe, in a manner Peg could not conceive, Eric had witnessed her own failure to come to grips with life maturely and felt obligated, unconsciously, to fulfill the potential she had once displayed—just so one of them had a chance to scale the heights the way Mama and

Grandfather had. Without a doubt, in Peggy's mind, Eric was a decent guy and would always be her true Big Brother, Eric the Buffer, the Protector. That was one of the few really clear impressions she had taken from their childhood together. Her bro, she felt, would always remain a good person.

Although she yearned for him to tell her, to explain every awful detail to all of them, she decided then she wouldn't ask him, that she would wait until he was ready.

But something telltale in her pert, animated face communicated the hunger to Eric at that moment. His eyes, somber yet tender, fixed upon her. "You're going to need to try, yourself, to remember it, Peg, to piece it back together," he said. It was as if he had read her mind and the others, who had continued to joke and laugh, stopped when they recognized his tone of voice with the quality of a man abundantly older than he was. "Danny was right when he said you'd have the best chance of getting your act together right here, sis. And I—I can sense that you are . . . *wanted*. Welcomed." Then he shook off the mood, chuckled, and reached out to hug Jennie Spandorff. "Of course, I'm not sure the house will even *tolerate* the rest of us!"

Shortly after they'd all finished dining, Peggy gathered up the empty cans and bottles along with the toweling from which they'd eaten their sandwiches. Then she took out to the kitchen the four paper plates they'd used for their cole slaw, returning almost at once. "That's one good thing about meals like this," she said brightly. "There are no dishes to wash."

"And no way to shower," Danny said dourly.

"Or take a nice warm bath," added Jennie.

And at that point, a silence fell among them like deep shadow. Danny broke it. "I think maybe we oughta check out the woods tomorrow so we can keep the fire going in the fireplace till they get the furnace going."

"Maybe there are wild flowers we could pick," Peggy said agreeably, and looked at Eric.

"Sounds good to me," he shrugged, standing and stretching. He kissed his sister on the cheek and clapped Danny's shoulder good humoredly. "Want to turn in, Jen?"

"To *what*?" she asked, and the laughter that followed paved the way for the evening to end.

Holding Jennie's hand, Eric led the way from the great room and toward the foot of the stairs.

And there, they stopped, arms wrapped around one another, looking up. Because the steps were creaking as if someone were descending them.

The sole illumination came from the second story landing and it provided little light. But the young couple was able to sense that the unseen figure on the stairs was somewhat more than one third of the way down. And the closer the invisible entity came, the more the muffled footsteps increased in sound. Past the midway mark on the stairs, each step became ponderous and seemed to take forever. Then each step sounded like an explosion, a detonation, and it was difficult for Jennie and Eric not to imagine that a *shape* was forming—that of someone or something enormous and powerful, maliciously cruel in the way that its descent taunted them.

"Look!" Eric whispered, and Jennie looked where he pointed.

Four steps up from the foot of the stairs, there was a great depression, a creaking indentation, very deep and very wide, as if a creature of incalculable bulk were lowering itself, inexorably, toward them.

Eric gently disengaged Jennifer's arms and took a pace forward, his chin up, defiantly. "Hullo, Lynn," he said softly. "Finally get up off our dead posterior, did we?"

Smoke spewed up from the bottom step like a black cloud. It swept angrily from side to side, outward, until it filled the whole width of the stairwell. The strong smell of charred beef filled Eric's and Jennie's nostrils.

Then the smoke disappeared as if it had never appeared, and the bottom step was badly cracked.

6

"Then how can you explain those awful eyes I saw watching me from the mirror?"

Danny looked up from Mama's bed—at least, it *looked* like Mama's bed to Peggy. Her memory was none too sharp. Danny, naked except for his shorts, was clearly impatient for her to come to bed. "Imagination," he snapped. "Listen, that brother of yours has me thinkin', did you ever break that word down?" He enunciated more carefully than Peggy had ever heard him before. "Image-i-nation. You had a *image* in your mind, babe. And projected it to the mirror."

"But why would I imagine a woman's eyes?" she asked, pleading. Since they'd gone up to the room, buzzing about the bizarre incident seen by her brother and his girl, Peggy had been trying to tell Danny about her own instant of haunting. To counter his brash assertion that the bottom step had merely cracked. "At least, they seemed more a woman's eyes than a man's."

"Hell, yes!" Danny shot back. "They were the reflection of your *own* eyes!"

She'd slipped out of her bra and was sort-of holding it against her, unconsciously unwilling just then to appear quite naked before her stubborn lover. "What about the rest of me, then—the way I saw myself the way I looked as a little girl?" She raised a palm, waved it and headed back to the connecting bath. "Don't tell me," she sighed. "It was my image-i-nation."

"You've got it," Danny agreed, chuckling. "And I don't got it—yet. Are you ever comin' to bed?"

For a moment, Peggy didn't answer him. And for another moment, she wasn't even sure she knew him. Life was so odd. You spent your teenage years going to high school and the days crawled by and nothing much ever seemed to happen. Then, all at once, you were meeting somebody and deciding overnight to share your life with him—as if you just *had* to make up for lost time. Except that you never really lost it; if anything, you merely gave it away. Sighing, feeling very cold and suddenly quite lonely—or was the feeling actually one of aloneness? —Peggy gave her long, blond hair a quick brushing and slipped out of her panties.

"Turn off the light," she called.

"Aw, shit," Danny's voice complained from the bedroom. Mama's bedroom; for some reason, Peggy felt suddenly shy around the athlete, even unwilling to have sex with him. Especially in Mama's bed. On the far side of the bathroom door with darkness engulfing her, Peggy regretted having returned, certainly wished she hadn't come with this gross, obscene young man whom she scarcely knew. Now there was no other place to go unless it was to a cot in a solitary room, and almost any flesh-and-blood companionship was better than what could happen to her alone. At last, Danny agreed, then the bedroom lights went out and it was dark all over the world.

Scooting across the chilly floor, barefoot, Peggy slipped under the covers. Danny amiably raised for her and she felt his raw, muscular arms and implacable flesh waiting. It occurred to her for the first time that, so far as she knew, this stranger she had sexual intercourse with had experienced nothing . . . anomalous since their arrival.

Except for beginning to topple down the stairs backward and, according to Eric, being caught in midair. He was pulling her on top of him now. He was erect and his whole body seemed cold. Halfheartedly, she kissed him too, let his clammy hands roam. The house *was* haunted—she knew it then, believed it without doubt. But the really *odd* thing was, Danny Stanwall—a stranger to the house, to all the family living and dead—had not been scared or threatened. Why not? Did that deceased relative Eric called "Lynn" but would not discuss *like* Danny, for some reason? Or was it only that the spirit of the Offspring had other, *later* plans for him?

She found herself sitting up, Danny's rigid, icy member buried in her, her upper body exposed as the covers fell away. It was unbearably *cold* this way; Peggy felt she might well freeze if he did not finish soon and allow her to snuggle beneath the covers. Groaning, beginning to writhe beneath her, Danny automatically reached out to cup and fondle her breasts. He always did that and didn't know his own strength. Sometimes he pulled on or bit her nipples so hard in an effort to stretch them, that it brought real pain and the unstabilizing impression of nursing some cruel, wild thing. Moonlight from the partly drawn curtains across the way trickled across his face and made it older, both harder and simultaneously absurd as well as somewhat simpleminded. Having sex transformed people, Peggy thought; it knotted the muscles in the face and almost everywhere else and it bathed them with sweat and made them one with the animal kingdom. It changed them, so much, if only for a little while, and it was that—being transformed to a rutting, perspiring animal—which men seemed to like.

As if they resented having to go through each day like civilized people and *this* was the way they honestly preferred to be.

Danny began to buck, to cram himself up against and farther into her, his eyes rolling back in his head. Peggy leaned back, cooperated with him, breasts upthrust and sweat flowing freely between them. Her head went back, too, the ends of her hair brushing Danny's twitching legs; but her eyes were open, staring.

And it seemed to her that moment that someone was staring at her again, and not from the mirror.

Whoever or whatever it was, she thought with rising panic, it wasn't quite a passive observer and it wasn't just standing at the side of the bed, watching.

It was in the bed with them.

Sleep had been impossible for Eric. After he'd tried to drop off, spent more than an hour trying to clear his head of a swirl of fast-forming, frenetic thoughts and images, getting up had seemed the only fair thing to do. From experience, he knew that his arm and leg muscles would begin half-spasming with nervous energy before long and Jennie had a right to get some sleep.

He'd gone downstairs to the kitchen and

pinched two Lite beer cans off a six-pack, then walked back upstairs all the way to the third story, only realizing in a distant way where he was headed. He and Jen had bought enough beer for all of them but Peggy hadn't seen it in the kitchen and Eric hadn't wanted to offer it to Danny Stanwall. Not because he was being mean or cheap, but because he didn't think Danny could stop at one or two. Or that he himself could remain civil to a drunken Danny Stanwall.

He'd entered his late grandfather's bare offices and shut the door behind him before wondering why in the world he had come up here.

But since he had, and since he was young enough not to mind sitting on the floor, Eric slumped against the wall and slid down it until the floor stopped him. If anything remained according to Hoyle, two brews would make him so sleepy nothing could keep him awake; after the second, he planned to return to his room—*Lynn's room*, he thought, automatically; *no wonder I can't sleep there*—and Jennie for the rest of the night.

Grandfather's own office and laboratory . . .

Shaking his head and marveling, Eric opened a beer, took a healthy drag, and peered around him in remembered awe. It seemed almost that a favor had been granted him, since he had never been permitted here—or even on the partly-finished third floor—at any time. Grandfather had feared the clumsiness of a child, presumably, or had been unwilling to be interrupted in his labors. Seated just inside the combination study/bedroom and staring out at the ex-lab, Eric thought that the old walls held secrets which might, even today, change the very face of the world that he knew.

How could he help admiring a man like Adam Baldwin? What an astoundingly versatile mind he'd had! As sexless as a monk since his wife died, years before Eric Porter was even born, the old man had lived here when he wrote revelatory scientific tomes that spread his fame; here, he'd mounted a campaign for the Presidency; and here, in these rooms, he had commanded the development of the being called "Lynn" and planned nothing less than the complete renovation and transfiguration of the *world.* Nothing as paltry as overthrowing the government, experimenting with a slightly *different* government, had filled Adam Baldwin's mind when he'd encountered the resistance of his own party and the American electorate—here, in these rooms, Grandfather had planned to change everything about the world—and all the people who occupied it!

And Grandfather hadn't wanted to harm people, merely modify the way they thought and the things they did by means of Lynn's special, secret knowledge of "what must be done now to establish genuine order, logic, and peace," as the old man had once explained it to

Eric. Lynn, who'd been force-fed all the printed facts and wisdom of humankind while being kept from all living people except Grandfather, Mama, and Mildred, to "maintain the crystal-clear *purity*, the detached and uninfluenced viewpoint." Eric sipped his beer. Maybe Grandfather had made his mistake right there, in not allowing Lynn to *know* other people, ordinary persons, so that Lynn might have had the opportunity to *like* somebody, even love them; but Eric felt convinced that Grandfather had not *meant* for people to be hurt. It was just a natural, human error on Grandfather's part, not malice.

Even if it was rather hard to justify his concept, and Lynn's, of *replacement* people . . .

As for Lynn and *what* Lynn was, where Lynn had come *from*, even Mildred had been willing to help raise it, had felt pity for it. At first.

Suddenly, popping the tab on his second beer, Eric rather wished they had notified the old woman about going to Indianapolis, and why. Not telling her was what she would have called "the path of least resistance," after the fire and during the years that she raised his sister and himself. Still, without the housekeeper who'd also nursed Mama in her final illness and helped raise Lynn, the truth was that both young Porters would have died with Grandfather and the Offspring many years ago. *And we'd have been the ghosts haunting the place now*, Eric thought.

What did the fact that he hadn't seriously considered notifying Mildred about this crazy trip mean? That he really was getting more and more like Grandfather Baldwin, and not alone in the way he stretched himself intellectually or put his own ambitions and ideas ahead of other people's? If that were true, if he *was* becoming another Adam Baldwin, was it even possible just to be as brilliant as his grandfather had been?

Or was he going to go crazy the way both Grandfather and Mama had done?

Anguished, Eric pressed the cold can against his temple, trying to shock himself out of a grogginess that had begun to grow in him. Simultaneously, a panicky feeling had started to rush through his mind and his nerves; the phrase, *The seeds of madness dwell within you*, sounded in his head as if somebody had wired up a loudspeaker system to his brain. "I'm not just like Grandfather," he aid aloud, his voice bouncing hollowly, mockingly, back at him. "I'm an individual, I'm me!"

But when he made a concerted effort to stand, to return to his bed and the lovely young woman asleep in it, his legs would not support him. *You carry the seeds of madness*, the voice said with terrifying clarity in Eric's mind—*madness, and murder.*

Then his eyes closed. He dropped and spilled the second can of beer, and it was no longer possible to stay awake. . . .

* * *

Her arm and hand slapped sleepily at the other side of the mattress and Jennie Spandorff was conscious, eyes staring through the murkiness of the room and reinforcing the fact that Eric was no longer beside her.

What time is it? she wondered, illogically yet understandably, and, raising her wrist before her eyes, tried to make the numbers on her watch restore her customary space/time continuum. There was a feeling of frantic necessity to her desire to know the hour, but it was quite dark in the bedroom now and Jennie had the queer, queasy notion that the face of her wristwatch had gone blank.

Then she was sitting up, throwing her legs over the side of the bed, and wondering, with a total sense of disorientation and horror, where in the hell she *was*. Because this was *not* her apartment and the kid's; this was an alien bedroom, another place and therefore perhaps another point in time . . .

But she remembered, then, and laid back against a pillow that had become wadded against the hard, metallic headboard of the bed, momentarily imagining that everything was fine. She smiled, tentatively, tried to make the mental cobwebs shred to let in the light; but then she recalled that the time was still a mystery to her and a lessened but nevertheless disquieting impression of unreality crept back upon her once more.

I want York, she thought, dully but with wrenching certainty. *I should yell for him but I can't, I don't dare. I could go find him, but I cannot.* The distance from the oversized hospital bed to the bedroom door looked immense, the floor shrouded in shadow and pocked by tiny points of light; the door was ajar, almost like somebody waited silently on the other side of it; and the corridor beyond the door and beyond that lurking someone was black as pitch. She thought, as emphatically and telepathically as she could, *Eric? Eric, come back*!

The bedroom door creaked.

The noises began in the wall again, just loudly enough for Jennie to hear and recognize them: Scrabbling, clawing sounds as if something might be desperate to break through the plaster, pop into her sight and—

Jennie was awake, then, fully conscious and herself. Immediately, the sounds in the wall ceased and she was turning on the bedlamp, feeling how foolish she had been; embarrassed by and for herself. *Daddy would be ashamed of me,* she thought, and stretched. Afraid because she didn't know what time it was or where her lover had gone and because he'd left the door open several inches.

Except that you know this place is hideously haunted, don't you? Jennifer asked herself. *You can't go on kidding yourself, and your special gift. It is a part of you, Jennie Spandorff, whether you like to admit it or not.*

She knew Peggy Porter had, that night, been visited by a force, by some awful graveyard thing no one could see. And she knew Eric hadn't been able to sleep but that he was asleep now, this very moment, in his grandfather-the-killer's offices. And she knew the Baldwin house was haunted, abruptly knew somewhat more of the dreadful things he and his "Offspring" creature had done and planned to do; and also—it was no longer possible to cling to the cherished self-delusion that she was not a natural medium, or sensitive—she knew that Lynn's dark soul still lived, permeating the atoms and the molecules of this sinister house while Lynn also sought control of all the normal, living people who'd made the terrible mistake of going there. And if she thought about it openly, let the communications of the others in the house flow into her, she might even learn why the Offspring yearned to control them all.

I don't want to be a freak, Jennie moaned inside; *I don't want to be a clairvoyant or a receiver or believe in anything metaphysical or occult! I want to learn about Daddy, avenge him, lead a sensible, logical life!*

The chewing and munching began again. Louder. Unbidden, the image formed in Jennie Spandorff's mind of a tiny, improbably powerful, vile thing—furry and a vivid bright yellow of hue—which, more than anything else, resembled a kitten.

Except that it was a fraudulent kitten. Except that it didn't actually *exist*.

Eventually, exhausted, still leaning back against the pillow and half in, half out of bed, Jennie slept fitfully, believing she was still awake. Often, she cried out in the night and thrashed but went unheard by anyone or anything save the clawing, scratching, unreal but menacing artificial cat.

And in the morning, when she awakened with a start, Jennie saw instantly the shoe she'd thrown in a desperate effort toward chasing the wall-thing away.

What scraps remained of the shoe had been methodically, viciously, chewed to pieces.

7

Eric awakened with a start the next morning —on the grossly uncomfortable, cheap plastic couch in the front room!

How did I get here? he wondered, sitting up and, with a groan, gripping his sides. Then he pulled upward, from the ribcage, trying to alleviate some of the kinks in his back. *And what time is it*? Gone frantic, he stared hastily at his Sharp wristwatch, distantly and peculiarly wondering if he would find the face of it blank.

But it wasn't. The crisp, gold hands showed 9:44 against the crisp, gold numbers as the crisp, gold second hand jerked spasmodically in dutiful response to its quartz brain.

And the watch, after strongly implying that

morning had arrived safely, also made Eric yank his head round toward the figure entering from the foyer with crisp, gold spring-style weather at its back. Danny Stanwall, hs arms filled with white sacks.

"How did I get down here?" Eric asked sleepily, getting clumsily to his feet.

"A terrorist hijacked you," Danny grunted, sweeping past, heading for the kitchen. "Maybe you got beamed down by Scotty—how would I know?"

Eric, one foot asleep, staggered after the athlete. "What d'you have in the sacks? Big Macs for breakfast?"

"Don't sound awful to me," Danny called over his shoulder, "but it's that muffin crap—and about six gallons of black coffee!"

"God!" Eric breathed from right behind Stanwall. "I could *bathe* in coffee this morning! I really appreciate you going for breakfast, Danny."

The other stopped on a dime, spun, his face inches from Eric's. "What makes you think I bought crap for anyone but Peggy and me?"

Eric, coloring, took a backward step. "Sor-ree," he said, raising an edged palm and turning away. "My *faux pas* entirely."

"Yo!" Danny exclaimed. When Eric turned back, the basketball player was raising a large container of coffee to him, steam escaping from beneath the lid. "Just fuckin' with ya."

"Bastard!" cried Eric, laughing and slapping Danny so hard on the arm that other containers in the sacks spilled over. "Dammit, I *am* sorry," he said again, meaning it. The two rushed the hot, soggily-splitting sacks into the kitchen—

And found Jennie already there, glancing around at the scurrying young men with the expression of a mother who was getting fedup with the kids' antics. Incredibly, considering the hour, she was nursing a Lite can. When she spoke, she sounded weary and more than a little annoyed. "Living with you two is like living with the entire crew of Saturday Night Live." Her gaze drifted away from them and she seemed small, sitting at the breakfast counter in the huge kitchen Mildred Manning Moag had once manned with such command.

Eric sat across from her, warily, motioning Danny to join them. "We're in a peachy mood this AM," he said tentatively, reaching out a hand to lift her chin and see her eyes. You feeling a trifle peaked this morning?"

"Pekes are tiny little beasts." Jennie mustered a brave smile. Her ruined shoe was in the pocket of her fluffy robe but she was determined not to bring it up—the question of who or what had chewed it into uselessness. "I feel at least dogged, perhaps Dobermanned!"

"Bad night?" Eric inquired gently.

"You should know," she snapped, glaring. Then her expression softened slightly. "Well, maybe you shouldn't, since you got up and never came back to bed." Jennie sighed, touched his hand. "How bad was your night?"

" 'How bad *was* it?' " Eric repeated, doing a Johnny Carson impression. "It was soooooo bad that I wouldn't have turned a knight away on a dog like that!"

"Jesus," Danny sighed and made a face. "It's too early in the day for ol' midget jokes." He looked toward the entrance to the kitchen as if wishing Peggy would put in an appearance.

Jennie, seeing his expression, quickly arose. "Wait! You're trying to be a gentleman and my robe disturbs you, right? You're afraid it'll develop an awful case of gapitis? Well, watch!" Reaching to her waist, she undid the belt and both young men looked at her startled, Eric putting out an arm to stop her. But she slipped out of the robe anyway and was fully clad beneath it. "No applause?" she asked, wide-eyed.

"Well, why the robe then?" Eric asked. "Were you cold?"

Jennie nodded, went round the counter to kiss him good morning. "I'm not sure I'll ever be warm again. Lord, Porter, what was this place like in the *winter*?"

"I dunno," he replied. "Grandfather had me and Peg spend so much time outside, fetching books for Lynn from the library, that I can't even recall what it was like inside the place!"

"Speaking of this 'Lynn' you keep talking about," Danny said. Jennie promptly took her seat, looking expectantly from the athlete to her boyfriend.

Peggy chose that moment to enter the kitchen, also fully clothed. She wore bright-orange jeans and a mediumweight, pullover sweater scooped low in front and back. Surprisingly, she'd swept her blond hair aimlessly atop her head and Eric smiled happily without knowing he did, strongly reminded of the way his little sister had looked as child. "Good morning, people!" she said cheerily. Immediately she'd found the breakfast Danny'd brought and was helping herself before greeting him with a peck on the nose. "And you, *too*, All-Star!"

"Christ," he muttered, "I thought we were here to help *you* feel better, and you look better than the rest of us put together!"

"See how well your plan worked?" Peggy chirped, grinning from him to the others.

And it *did* seem to be doing her good, already, Eric thought, astounded. Peg looked radiant, content, more herself than he'd seen her in ages. In comparison to Jennifer's red-rimmed eyes, Peggy might have been fifteen instead of nineteen. "Both you damsels look as if you're planning to go somewhere," he said, indicating both Peg and Jennie.

"We're going after wood for the fireplace this

morning," Peg said airily, "remember? And *I'm* looking for wildflowers!" She took a huge bite of Egg McMuffin.

"And I am *not*," Jennie put in, applying fresh lipstick and, Eric thought, avoiding his eyes. "If you don't mind, Eric, I'll take the car and drive to the nearest shopping center to pick up a few things." She wrinkled her nose amiably in Peggy's direction. "I don't plan to be the wildflower type again before I'm a grandmother."

"Well, I'll go with you," Eric said slowly, getting to his feet. The coffee had made him feel much wider awake but he had the impression just then of wheels within wheels; of things going on, or moods projected and shared, that were escaping him. "That way, Peg and Danny can have some time by themselves in the woods."

Danny grinned. "I do the coolest wolf waiting at grandmother's house you ever saw." Clawing his hands, he reached for Peggy but missed.

Jennie, loudly, said simply; "I'd like some time *alone*."

"You're afraid," Eric observed, approaching her with concern. "Something happened last night, after I left the room."

"I'm *fine*," Jennie said firmly, stubbornly.

"No, you're not." Eric, who'd looked her over from top to bottom, reached down to raise the hem of her skirt two inches above the knee. "What's that?"

An angry red splotch scarred the inside of her thigh. Anxious, Eric touched it. But Jennifer batted his hand away, turned toward the kitchen door. Obviously, she was eager to be out of the place. "It's Herpes," she said sarcastically to him and to the others who were listening. "Or do people still get that, now that AIDS is a big deal?"

Catching her arm, Eric said, so softly only Jennie could hear, "Tell me. Please."

Jennie's wide eyes blinked several times as if she might begin to cry. She wanted to tell him, all at once, about the clawing sounds in the wall, the way her shoe had been torn to bits, even about her unsought and unwelcome psychic gifts. But not in front of everybody. Bending a knee, she felt the angry splotch with cautious fingertips, as if it might be tender to the touch.

"After you got up," she said slowly, looking only at Eric, "I . . . didn't sleep well." She shrugged, letting him know there was more to be told. "But once, as if awakening only partway from a dream, I became conscious of—of some kind of presence in the room with me. And I was by m-myself." The intensity in her eyes begged him to believe her. "I couldn't *see* anyone, but I knew the presence was there, and I heard it down around my legs and feet, *snuffling*. And breathing *so hard*, as if it were, well, asthmatic."

The kitchen was completely silent. No one else had moved or made a sound. "Go on," Eric urged her.

Tears shone in Jennie's eyes. "It *touched* me, York. Here." Her head twisted appealingly, her mouth crinkling, grimacing. "It laid its . . . hand, or something . . . right *here*, and it was cold, *freezing* cold."

"You should have shouted for me," Eric said softly, holding her.

"Its touch was like *ice*, honey," she wailed; "it was like something that had been on another, freezing planet, or as if it came from—from someplace on earth we know nothing about, where it's winter perpetually and the sun never reaches it."

"Is it still cold?" Peggy asked her.

"No, not exactly." Jennie peered gratefully at the younger woman, glad to be asked for details. She let Peggy touch it, gingerly. "The best way I can describe it is by saying it burns and feels like ice at the same time." Her mouth worked a moment before the rest of it came out. "And I don't even know what *did* it."

Peg turned to her brother. "It's very *warm*," she said, knowing he'd touched it, too.

"No." He shook his head. "It's *hot* to the touch."

"While you two decide whether I was burned or put on ice, I'm booking out of this joint for a while," Jennie declared, hugging the two of them and waving at the still-seated Danny.

"Don't worry about me, I'm fine. I'll be home for dinner."

Peggy had stepped before Eric a pace as they watched Jennie head swiftly toward the front door and a respite from the house's continual shocks, and Eric saw, on his sister's neck, several shocking, red scratches. Already they were beaded with clotting blood. *That must have hurt her,* he thought but said nothing. Danny was in the kitchen with them and he didn't want to mention the scratches in case they were involved with their sex play.

Then, however, Danny needed to "hit the john" before the three of them went out to the woods at the rear of the house. While he was upstairs, Eric, as diplomatically as he could, asked Peg about her scratchmarks.

Lookng surprised, Peg reached over her shoulder to feel the back of her neck. "Ouch!" she cried with a frown, and drew her hand back. Small smears of blood coated the tips of two fingers. "I don't even remember that happening," she told Eric, wonderingly. "You'd think it would have hurt, but I can't recall what happened."

Aloud he said, "You'll live," and grinned. But privately, he thought, *That must mean there's still a lot you don't remember about the things that've happened here.*

When Danny rejoined them, at the front door, he was wearing an old warmup jacket. The Porters had slipped into jackets of their own.

Obviously, Eric realized, Danny was just as anxious as Jennie had been to get out of the place awhile. "Let's do it!" he said.

Which was when every lavatory in the big Baldwin house began to *flush*, one after another.

The incident with the toilets placed a pall on the formerly adventurous mood Danny Stanwall had succeeded in giving them. While it was warmer today and Eric realized Indianapolis might turn steaming hot at almost any time, the morning skies were overcast and glum. Nature's indecisiveness made the back lot of the Baldwin property look simultaneously winterish and like the brief period before day died and dusk fell. There was no sign of any kind of life save their own by the time they'd followed the lengthy driveway and put the street far behind. Eric, who remembered Peggy's kitten Krazy playing in the grass and frightening butterflies, wondered about the lifespan of a house and the lot on which it stood. Perhaps the place, originally rescued from nature, required half a hundred years to pass before nature could reclaim it. *We think we're so special, we're so certain we're the Creator's joy,* he mused, gravel crunching beneath his feet, *but when none of us live there any longer, it's as if we've sucked all the life away for acres and acres—and for years and years.*

He was so enormously relieved to see Peg behaving more like herself that he kept his reflections to himself, even tried to chalk them up to the strange way he'd awakened somewhere other than where he'd fallen asleep. But that troubled him, too; had he sleepwalked or did he just not remember leaving Grandfather's ruined offices and going downstairs?

Danny had ranged far ahead of him and Peggy. Raising his head, Eric saw that the athlete was already adjacent to the old garage. The woods waited just behind it. Funny, the way the dim sunlight gleamed dully on Danny and the garage at the top of the slight rise of earth. Eric placed the thumb of his straightened hand over the bridge of his nose and squinted. He shuddered and stopped. *Two* figures waited by the dilapidated garage. Danny and another, taller, bulkier. While both men were perfectly solid and seemed unapparitional, normal, Danny had not appeared to acknowledge the other man, and Eric knew that he did not want to walk a step closer.

Peg, responding to a gesture of Danny's, started forward at a trot. Eric yearned to call out to her and tell her to turn away, not to go near the pair of masculine shapes at the garage, but the words stuck in his throat. How could he do something like that? Making a great effort of will, he began jogging after Peg.

His sister was still nine or ten yards from where her lover stood when the *second* figure, starlike, winked out. He—it—simply wasn't there any longer. To Eric's dismay, his sister was sinking to her knees and shaking her head, apparently trying not to cry.

"A little exercise get you down, baby?" Danny called. Then he realized how upset she was and ran toward her. He and Eric were with her at the same instant, each stooping to see if she might have twisted her ankle.

"It's the garage," Peggy said, peering up at them through tears. "It won't *let* me go pick wildflowers."

"A garage won't let you?" Danny stood, hands on hips. "What the fuck does that mean?"

It means that the second worse sight we ever saw was in that wreck of a garage, Eric thought, and helped Peg to her feet. "I understand her," he told Danny shortly. *Either she's beginning to remember and piece it together or there was something* dead, *yet returned, which she sensed too.*

"I wish to Christ I did," Stanwall said, glaring. Then he danced back to the old building, jabbed at it and rattled the door, held up the rusted lock. "The damned thing is all locked up—which means *we* can't get in and any relative spooks of yours can't get *out*!"

"I have to go back to the house," Peg said

softly, turning away. Eric had to repeat it so Danny could hear.

"No, you're *not*!" he shouted. But she was already scooting back down the long driveway, blond hair coming undone and trailing after her like a caution flag. "Goddammit, Peggy, you gotta face up to this thing. You're getting goddamn *weird*!" Danny went charging down from the garage, getting angrier by the moment. "You must stay *here*, try to *reason* things through. Dammit, Peggy, I'll help ya!"

Eric leaped into his path, palms raised. "Let her go," he said simply.

"Get outta my way, Porter!" Danny growled, and tried to circle around him.

"I said, 'Let her go!' " Eric repeated it, catching and wrestling with one of Danny Stanwall's arms. "That's *it*. Drop it!"

"The hell I—" Then he stopped. For the first time, the athlete noticed Eric had brought his cane. The head looked weighted, obsidian, and Eric was holding it by the other end as if it were a baseball bat.

The expression on the smaller man's face informed Danny that Eric would not hesitate to swing the cane at his head, if necessary.

The two of them froze that way, Danny crouched and trying to decide whether to charge by Eric or tackle him. In the distance, he saw, Peggy was already back to the house.

From where they stood, both young men

heard the distant, sonorous wail of organ music throbbing in the forenoon stillness.

It took Jennifer Spandorff less than half an hour to see that the city of Indianapolis was in a state of flux. The residential areas of the far northeast side were not very different from those of Dayton, but there was a difference in quantity; Jennie couldn't remember seeing so many middleclass neighborhoods packed into such a relatively limited territory, yet she didn't have the feeling of crowdedness she'd experienced in Boston, Baltimore, or the residential areas of Chicago. Indianapolis, to that degree, seemed to be the community of families with the semireasonable percentage of crime that it had been rumored to be.

On the other hand, during Jennie's explorative drive, she saw more new apartment buildings and complexes than Dayton, even allowing for the difference in population. Whether that meant there were more young people who were having no children or only one or two, or that Indianapolis people were finding it harder and harder to come up with the down payments required for private ownership of property, she couldn't estimate.

But the state of flux was more important in

the shopping centers she toured. While she saw a number of discount stores and small places called Convenience Marts or Village Pantries, along with an adequate number of imposing supermarkets, she was also able to detect the presence of restaurants and variety stores that displayed a more cosmopolitan touch than she had expected to find in Indianapolis. Every few blocks, it seemed, there was a Japanese or Chinese restaurant or take-out in addition to the inevitable fast-food places. To her surprise, she found a plethora of photocopy shops, a costumers, two book stores, exotic everywhere-in-the-world shops, and tobacconists. Most such establishments, she sensed, hadn't existed in Indy ten years back—at least, not in such numbers.

In a shopping center on East 46th street, within a few miles of the Baldwin house, Jennie entered a colorful but quiet store with Oriental writing on the window and realized that the place sold an amazing array of herbs and spices. Apparently, the people in the surrounding neighborhood liked to cook Chinese in their own homes—or Indianapolis had a Chinatown of which Jennie had never learned.

Since it sounded appealing to Jennie to experiment with preparing something different and special for Eric, Peggy and Danny, she hung a basket over one arm and began dropping into it a variety of condiments whose names were entirely alien to her. *God knows what I'll wind up with*, she reflected. *Maybe I'd better go to a bookstore, too, and buy an Oriental cookbook*!

She found herself standing before a display case of fascinatingly exotic things of which she knew nothing at all. Buying one of each and everything represented considerably more expense than seemed reasonable for impulse shopping, but the two clerks in the store—one wearing a kimono, the other shirt and slacks (the former was obviously American)—were occupied with other customers. Again, Jennie scanned the foods in the case: sesame oil, dried flaked bonito, star anise, wonton skins, bean threads, dried kelp, ginger root and more—and felt utterly helpless.

"Pardon me, please," she said with exaggerated care. A small man with faintly slanted eyes and a complexion like flax was also waiting to be helped, a basket hooked lanquidly over one arm. "I wonder—if you—could assist —me?"

His eyes, black as an Ethiopian night, swiveled to fasten compellingly upon Jennie's. She had never seen eyes like his. They glittered as if from some deep, arcane enigma, yet they were also magnetically intelligent. She had the impression that this young man—he could have been any age from his early twenties to thirty-five—not only knew all the answers but the right questions to pose.

"It would be my supreme honor," he replied, closing his eyes and bowing his head.

He's darling Jennie thought. "I'm such a fool about foreign foods," she said, the words spilling out, "but I don't mean to be, I mean I *don't want* to be—and my father was a world traveler. He'd be so ashamed!" She made herself stop chattering, seek control of herself. "*Is* there a difference—a difference of importance—between rice sticks and *somen*? And between plum sauce and . . . and *hoisin* sauce?" The small man didn't reply at once and Jennie wondered if she'd spoken too swiftly; overpowered him. "Should I buy—the Szechwan pepper or the crushed red pepper?"

"*Yes. So.*" His head bobbed once. "You should." Then, as if starting to comprehend, he added, "Rice sticks—Chinese. *Somen*—Japanese." Suddenly, badly startling Jennie, he threw back his mame of coal-colored hair and laughed. "And plum sauce is made from plums, while *hoisin*, I'd guess, is made from—*hoisin*! Whatever the hell *that* is."

"I'm so sorry," Jennie gasped, eyes blinking repeatedly. Sh touched his arm in apology. "You're an *American*—but of Chinese or Japanese ancestry, then, right? Or is it Vietnamese? Or Korean?"

He stopped laughing with difficulty. "I was born in Thailand," he said, "but I've lived so long in this town that I can't even remember what *Thais* eat! Sugar, I don't know from nothing about the crap in the case, and I was on the verge of asking *you*!"

"My God, the *assumptions* I've made," Jennie groaned; "or the *pre*sumptions. God, I'm so embarrassed!"

"Well, if you're as shot down from the experience as all that," he said, smiling, "you have to let me buy you a cup of Chinese tea"—Jennie'd noticed as she entered the store that tea was prepared and left on the table just inside the door—"and tell your fortune."

"Do Thais do that?" She allowed him to guide her to the front of the store. He didn't quite reach her shoulder. "Or am I making another social error?"

"Thais do pretty much whatever *you* do," he said, holding a chair for her. There were two of them and he took the second. "We're a constitutional monarchy—mostly Buddhists, but we're beef-eaters mainly! I'm most proud of the fact that Tahiland enjoys an eighty-four percent literacy rate, one of the best in the world—and that might explain why I'm a journalist by profession." He winked slyly. "If I ever have to go back to the country, there are fifty newspapers for every thousand people. One might say that 'those are the Thais that bind!' "

Jennie laughed aloud at his joke, more freely and naturally than she'd laughed in months. Although this little man's age was hard to figure and there was something rather effete about his gestures and the way he kept periodically opening his black eyes, exaggeratedly, she liked him on sight. "I'm Jennie Dorff, and I guess you know more about Indianapolis than I do. By far."

"Maybe," he admitted. "As much as a member of any minority group is allowed to know members of the majority." She wondered exactly which minority he referred to. "I'm Kasem Chamanan. Don't stew it; I'll *spell* it!" And he did.

"Do you work for either of the Indianapolis newspapers?" Jennie inquired.

Kasem grinned. There wasn't a sign of regret or apology in his sallow face. "I don't work for anybody; not just now. I've been unemployed for months." If there was any emotion in what the little fellow said, it was a certain defiance—as if no one could have the right to feel sorry for or look down upon him if *he* didn't mind being out of work. "Here's a part of that fortune I promised to tell: You aren't sure you're glad you came to this city and something here has frightened you. But"—he put out a short finger to touch the tip of her nose—"you won't get badly hurt. Because you're a survivor!"

"That's pretty amazing," she confessed. "You're psychic, then?"

"All Thais are, I think," Kasem admitted. This time he sounded slightly rueful. "But mainly I happen to be an observant journalist. A button on your blouse is both unbuttoned and broken, but you're clearly a lady—so you were anxious to get out of the house, or you would have changed. You look as if you didn't sleep well last night, but you're much too pretty not to have a boyfriend. And, well, there's *something* in your eyes . . ." He closed his, kept them that way. "Okay, I'm the one who's being presumptuous now, Ms. Dorff; but I believe you're *haunted*." The black eyes popped open, staring, challenging. "Possibly by no more than a loved one's problems. Possibly by the undead."

Jennie couldn't take her gaze from him. "You are right on every point." She took a long sip of her tea, realized with mild disappointment that she'd drained the small cup. "I'm in Indianapolis to help my boyfriend's sister, if we're able." And, dimly recalling that she'd never before said so much to a stranger, Jennie told him about Peggy's problem and her own bizarre experiences of a presence others called "the Offspring." Then she glanced demurely away. "This must all sound exceedingly odd to you, Mr. Chamanan."

"What seems incredible to me," he murmured, "is that a young American female has so readily admitted that she and her companions appear to be haunted. Ghosts don't enjoy the popularity here that they do back home."

"I didn't actually say that we were haunted," Jennie blurted. "It's—"

"Please." He held up a hand, shook his head slowly, smilingly. "You needn't explain. Everyone in Thailand knows at least *one* ghost! We're very *Thaight* with them!"

This clever, odd, gentle little man was so matter of fact! The next thing Jennie said was more a surprise to her than it was to Kasem Chamanan:

"You could help us sort it all out, I think. Can you come to dinner with us tonight? Please?"

8

"Nobody *ever* faced me down that way before!"

"It was probably good for your soul." Eric, straightening, knew it was all over whether Danny Stanwall did or not. But was Peg okay in the house now? Had he imagined the organ music? "Let's fetch the wood the way we planned to do."

"I'm getting really pissed off at you, Porter." Danny raised from his angry crouch, followed Eric toward the garage and the woods beyond it. "And another thing: You know more about what happened here, and why it's driving Peggy off her kook, than any of us."

"What if I do?" He was adjacent to the garage now; he'd promised himself not even to glance toward the old frame building, but he did.

"I think she needs to be told everything you know." Danny danced alongside Eric, his temper under control but his passionate views stronger than ever. "Shit, Porter, it happened to her, too! You don't have a fucking copyright on it."

Something—a wisp of almost-but-not-quite flesh-colored *something*—moved inside the garage. He could see it, detect its gray subsistence, through a window of the building. Then they had gone past the garage. "What you don't get, Danno, is that Peg's better off not remembering unless it comes naturally to her. A bit at a time, maybe she can cope. Which is why I agreed to let her come here at all."

"*You* agreed?" Danny stared at him, jaw slack in amazement. "She was comin' here whether you wanted her to or not!"

"Uh-uh; wrong." They'd entered the woods now. Almost at once he saw several dry branches, freed from trees or partly broken by heavy winds. "If I'd gotten firm about it, put my foot down, she'd have remained in Dayton. She could see it in my eyes that I didn't think it was a bad idea." He stopped, turned to face the taller youth. "You don't get it about us, do you, Danny? That we're closer than most brothers and sisters because of what happened to us, how it was basically Peg and me against the whole world? I protected her then, buddy, and I'll go on protecting her as long as I'm able."

For a moment Danny Stanwall listened, met

Eric's steady gaze and considered what he'd heard. "It's possible, dude, that you can't see past the way she was as a kid. She grew up, Porter. She's a big girl now."

"Just what *is* your interest in my sister, Stanwall?" He crossed his arms, planted his feet in the moist, fertile earth. "I don't mean to come off like an older brother from some James novel, but I want to know: Are you looking for a free ride or do you really care for her?"

Danny flushed but conquered the rise of fury. "I care a lot, baby. I think I love her. And here's the fact you gotta get through your head: *I'm* her protector now, so butt out. You ain't needed."

For a moment, Eric didn't reply. Then he stooped to pull a large branch from its entanglement with others. "It's my opinion, Stanwall, that Peg needs me now as much as she ever did in her life—and I'll be here, whether you dig it or not. Give me a hand, will you? You're the one who claims to be the mighty woodsman."

That afternoon, when the four of them had straggled in and made more coldcut sandwiches, Jennie told them of her meeting "someone interesting" during her shopping expedition. Sensitive to Eric's feelings and the fact that she and Danny were guests in the house, she was careful to make it clear that the Thai, Kasem Chmanan, held no sexual attraction for her; "in fact," she concluded, "he might be gay. But I believe he can help us."

Danny, in particular, looked annoyed and disgusted by what she had said, but kept his place another moment. Eric, hungry after he and Danny had built a more-satisfactory fire in the fireplace, was constructing a tall sandwich with all the variety of meats they'd bought at the grocery, plus whatever else he could pile on. It was Peggy who asked why Jennie believed her new friend might assist them.

"He's very knowledgeable about, well, hauntings, the supernatural." While she was addressing the young blonde, she meant her explanation for the others, too. "It seems that in Thailand there are a lot of people who've experienced ghosts and . . ." Her voice trailed away. "I meant well," she added, giving them a shy smile.

"Cool move, babe," Danny muttered. Wiping his lips with a paper towel, he wadded it and lobbed it toward a paper sack in the dining room corner. "That's really slick, what you're bringin' over." He laughed humorlessly. "Ghosts, gays, and AIDS—all at the same time!" A wink to the other male. "I'll bet Eric didn't know you dug guys like chink homos!"

"I don't *dig* him," Jennie flared. So many misstatements had her reeling. "I don't know that he is homosexual. But what does that have to do with it, anyway? I'll call Kasem and ask him not to come if Eric and Peggy say no, but I'm making Chinese for tonight and it'd be nice to have a guest around who won't be scared out of his tree if something *odd* happens!"

"If he can help," Peggy murmured, "I don't care if he wears a dress."

"I hope he *is* gay," Eric said. He stopped beside Jennie and kissed her wide mouth lightly. He leaned on his cane, grinning. "I'm for free enterprise for everyone but me. I *hate* competition."

Jennie kissed him back.

That evening, Kasen Chamanan arrived at the appointed hour. He presented to the two young ladies meeting him at the door a bottle of saki and a low bow. By the time he was through the door, the three of them were chatting and laughing as if they'd been friends all their lives.

Peggy had pitched in to assist Jennie with dinner and had even remembered a Chinese meal Mildred, the housekeeper who'd raised her and Eric, once taught her. At the dining room table, swearing that it was delicious, Kasem gazed inquiringly from hostess to hostess. "What is it called?" he asked.

Peggy looked at Jennie, who blushed and shrugged. "Wor sho *goop*!" Peggy announced, remembering part of a menu she'd read in an Oriental restaurant.

Eric, who'd asked for seconds, suggested Manchurian mush.

"Peping fairy balls," Danny said quite distinctly, staring at the Thai.

"That would be quite a delicacy," Kasem said after a pause, laughing. He'd arrived in a powder-blue sports jacket that seemed new, well-pressed pants and white tennis shoes. In the limited illumination furnished by the old chandelier that had the duty of bathing the entire enormous table with light, the little Thai looked darker, older, eager to please. "I take it that you would like to know more about the tradition of earthbound spirits in my homeland. After that, perhaps you wouldn't mind telling me what's happened to each of you here."

"Sure, why not?" Danny said flatly. "My experience is simple: I got laid here." His gaze was cool and alert, challenging. "I can tell ya all those details. But I don't believe you'll be interested in them."

Both women looked at him in horror. Despite himself, Eric smiled. Then the girls were turned to him, arguably more shocked that he'd found the athlete's bad taste amusing.

"I'm sorry." Eric jumped to his feet, crimsoning. "Look, Kasem, you're welcome here; I mean that. Stay, and come again soon—not that we'll be here that much longer." His glance sought his sister's but she was frowning in embarrassment at Danny. "Right now, though, I'm not in the mood for folklore or guesswork. What happened here was very, very specific and not like *anything* you've encountered before." He touched Jennie's arm. "If everybody will excuse me?"

Now Peggy turned her head to watch Eric leave the dining room. En route, he retrieved his cane and the steady *tap-tap* as he reached the stairs and mounted them, the gradual decline of the tapping sound until she could not be sure she actually heard or merely imagined it, caused a deep pain behind the eyes. *Grandfather never had time for idle conversation*, she ruminated. A series of images, themselves ghostlike, jittered in mind's-eye until she thought something fundamental to her blockage would break through. When it didn't, she felt drawn, drained, and tuned back into the table talk with a sense of loss and apprehension.

"In the morning," Jennie was saying, "I found *this*." She displayed to them the mangled shoe. "I'm certain it's the same one I threw toward the awful sounds in the wall the night before. What could have done this?"

"You couldn't be sure," Danny argued. He flicked it with his index finger. "They probably made thousands of shoes just like it."

Kasem looked doubtful. "The mystery man you imply, would know, in advance, which shoes Ms. Dorff would bring here?" His black eyes glittered but he didn't touch the shoe. "Lay it there. Please. On the table between us."

"That's cute," Danny said sarcastically. He hummed the old "Twilight Zone" theme song. "Who *are* you, anyway?" He clamped his big hand on the Thai's wrist. "*What* are you?"

"A guy who admires the way two young men, quite ignorant of anything they cannot see, nonetheless feel determined to protect Peggy Porter." Dark brows rising, Kasem turned to the daugher of Verblin Spandorff. "And who looks out for *your* safety, Ms. Dorff?"

"You told me I wouldn't be hurt," she replied with a smile. "That I was a survivor. Remember?"

Kasem nodded. A strain of some unspoken contact, not necessarily with anyone present, flashed in his somewhat slanted eyes. "I told you that you would not be *badly hurt*." He paused to disengage Danny Stanwall's fingers from his wrist. "I'd rather, Jennie, that you were not hurt at all."

"The dude's good," Danny growled, slumping in his chair at the table. "I'll give him that." He looked at Kasem from beneath half-lowered lids. "But you didn't answer my question."

As if delighted to be reminded, Kasem told Danny and Peggy what he'd said about himself to Jennie that afternoon. "Since I am unmarried, and I have the habit of saving what I earn, I've been in no rush about finding other employment." He shrugged. "I *am* concerned about the fact that I just got tossed out of my rooms. The owners sold the house and I'm temporarily homeless."

"Oh, Kasem, what a shame," Jennie said quickly. "When will that happen? When do you have to be out of your rooms?"

Kasem grimaced. "Day before yesterday," he said wryly. Then, as if realizing he had virtually asked permission to stay with them in the big house, he adriotly changed the subject. "But you wanted to know about my country's preoccupation with the dead."

"The girls did," Danny said shortly. "I can go whole days without wanting to know about dead folks."

"Ignore him, Kasem," Peggy suggested. She'd slapped Danny's arm and elicited a somewhat apologetic smirk. "Please. Tell us."

"To begin with," the little journalist began, "in Thailand, there's a weird mix of people, beliefs, education. Most of us came from southern China in the eleventh century and roughly fourteen percent of Thais is still Chinese—so we are at once an advanced, informed people and a people with roots in the past." He hesitated, scanning their Occidental faces before speaking. "There are *millions* of haunted houses in Thailand—or we believe that's what they are."

"Fascinating," Jennie breathed.

Chamanan had paused to withdraw a

gleaming cigarette case and a book of matches. When he saw that nobody objected, he offered long, nearly brown-colored cigarettes around and lit one himself. "I don't mean the homes in which natives of Thailand reside. Theirs, all too often, are ramshackle; little more than huts. The haunted houses I mentioned"—his dark brows raised—"are built for the spirits themselves."

"Full-sized buildings," Peggy asked, "for ghosts?"

"No, not as a rule," Kasem said smilingly. "These are exquisite, miniature castles somewhat along the lines, structurally, of birdhouses. And no backyard in my country is considered safe without one." Kasem allowed trails of very white smoke to drift from his fine nostrils. "The houses are made of teak. The concept itself is logical enough: if the souls they've passed to the other side have a home of their own, they won't become so forlorn and lonely that they will return to living people's homes to moan, howl, and destroy."

"Logical?" Danny scoffed. "You're making this crap up, right?"

"No, Danny, I'm not," Kasem replied. "Where I grew up, *two* kinds of ghosts must be appeased, satisfied: *Chao*, which is good; and *Phi*, the evil spirits. Together, they share the small homes made for them. And to keep them in balance, the tiny house of the haunted is placed in such a way that no shadow falls upon it." His smile was slow, suggestive. The women found him a source of fascination. "When the house is not turned just so, the ghosts, good or bad, may wish to move into the home of a Thai—and that is not desirable."

Jennie asked, "But what happens if they do?"

Kasem looked off into space. "Marriages are ruined. Children become disobedient, or worse. Ill health. Misfortune of great variety." He pulled on his brown cigarette a last time and put it out. "This is true whether the good *Chao* or the evil *Phi* invades the house of the living. We are raised to believe that those souls which haunt have no place among the carnate, the people of flesh and blood. I, myself, have burned incense and brought the sweet fragrance of jasmine to the home of my family to discourage restless spirits."

"I agree with Eric," Danny commented, heavily. "I don't see what any of that crap has to do with this place." He added, hastily, "Not that it's haunted."

"But it is," Kasem murmured; "quite horribly. I sensed that the moment I passed into the house. And the spirits here do not belong, either." He gave Danny Stanwall the sweetest and gentlest of smiles. "Besides, I have yet to tell you the rest of my story."

Climbing the stairs, alone, Eric Porter was both irritated and anxious. Jennie had had no right to ask a complete stranger to the house. There were important things happening there, matters that did not concern outsiders. Already, he tended to wish that he hadn't brought Jennie Dorff and certainly that Peg hadn't asked the Neanderthal along. Point of fact, he thought broodingly, he should have had the foresight to come here years ago with nobody but his sister. The two of them could have dealt better with the unseen, eerie forces in the old house—he'd begun quite recently to wonder if it wasn't simply stained by *psychic traces,* the way an Englishman named Lethbridge had believed hauntings operated—and he'd have had the opportunity to bring Peg gradually back to normal. To the level of ability and confidence she'd evidenced as a little girl.

And what made Eric nervous, as he leaned on his cane and limped heavily from step to step—*must've twisted my ankle or calf somehow—* was the realization that ol' Kasem Hopalong, or whatever his damned name was, might exacerbate the situation, not help it. If the Offspring's spirit *was* restlessly roaming the house, and its spirit had lost none of its living vindictiveness, any interference on the part of strangers could put them all in terrible peril.

Tapping his way unhurriedly along the poorly lit second floor, Eric wished he could move Jennie's and his own sleeping arrangements to some other room, even if it meant using cots instead of the inexplicable, enormous hospital bed. But that would bring up his total recall of their childhood experiences; everybody'd be at him again to say exactly what had *happened* in that room, that house. Yet now it seemed quite improbable, even impossible, that the people he'd contracted to make the house semilivable had "coincidentally" installed the same kind of bed Lynn had used—had even put it in the same room. Maybe they'd been possessed, somehow. Eric pondered the problem. Or maybe the bed wasn't what it seemed to be! That could be it! Considering Lynn's incredible, living skill at projecting long-range power of suggestion—hypnosis from the Offspring's bedroom to anywhere in the house—maybe Jennie and he only imagined . . .

He stopped in the center of the hallway, frozen in place, clutching the cane, holding his breath. Movement, there was movement, at the end of the corridor. Someone was emerging from a room, breathing heavily, as if from unknown exertion. The door whispered shut behind the person.

I'll be doggoned! Eric thought, relieved, delighted. It was the delivery boy who had brought the housekeeper, Mildred, the huge quantities of meat that the bed-bound Offspring consumed. "Eddie, *yo*!" he called, happy to see him again. They were approximately the same age. They'd attended the same school. "Eddie, it's Eric here!"

But I am not twelve years old any more and he is, Eric thought. The realization and sight of freckle-faced young Eddie drifting expressionlessly down the hallway toward him scared and alerted Eric. *It's Eddie, but he should be in his twenties, too*!

Shivering, skin crawling, Eric pressed himself against the wall to allow the unchanged, unchangeable delivery boy to pass without touching him.

Only *half* of Eddie existed. Below the waistline, there was nothing.

Nothing at all.

9

Behind him, down the hall, *footsteps*, pounding their way up the stairs! Panicky, Eric, who had started toward the stairway and the quickest possible descent, spun and ran in the general direction from which the delivery boy's shade had emerged. When he realized that he definitely did not *want* to go there—not now, not *yet*—he felt trapped, stopped, and froze helplessly where he stood.

Instantly he felt that he was surely freezing. His teeth began to chatter, the fine hairs on the back of his neck stood up, and his arms went involuntarily around himself in a desperate, heat-seeking bearhug. Looking down and to his sides in fresh alarm, Eric realized that it was this exact place—where he was half-standing, half-crouching, wholly shivering—that was cold. Glacially, killingly cold perhaps; as if he had stepped through a gap in space and now found himself stuck in some unmapped, arctic clime. Shimmering walls of apparent ice crystals rose around him on all sides; he could see no farther than inches in any direction. Badly frightened and making a noise in his throat, he lowered his head to run once more.

But Danny Stanwall stopped him, held him hard even as his feet and legs pumped, sought escape. "What'sa matter, Porter, you see a mouse or something?"

Dimly, it dawned on Eric that the running steps on the stairs had belonged to the rest of his companions and, as his vision cleared and he saw Jennie, he sobbed with relief. "H-How did you know I needed you?" he asked the others.

"You screamed," Jennie said. She went close to him, smoothed his hair.

"I never scream." Eric denied it, shaking his head. Just then, heat was returning to his body. Then he glanced back to Jennie. "Did I?"

"Like a little girl," Danny answered for them. Then, relenting, he slapped the older man's arm. "You jokers who have your nose in a book all the time get pretty spastic at times."

"What did you see?" Kasem Chamanan stepped toward him soundlessly, his sallow face fixed in a grave expression. "What did you experience?"

Haltingly, miserably aware of Danny's presence, Eric explained.

"Christ, you people have such wierdo imaginations you'd make a big buck writing down this shit," Danny sighed.

Kasem, who'd vanished from Eric's field of vision, reappeared. He held something in the palm of his small hand. "The power of suggestion is akin to the psychic sensibilities," he admitted. "It can be difficult to differentiate between the two, even with the best of will. This, however, is not imagination."

Eric and Danny peered into the journalist's palm where a white sliver of bone rested.

"What Eddie delivered," Eric said softly, "was meat. Lots of meat."

A sudden, sharp yelp of pain made them all turn.

Peggy Porter had been last to climb the stairs and advanced slowly up the corridor toward them, elbow jutting out, her gaze on her forearm. "It *hurts,*" she moaned.

Even yards away, Eric was able to see red welts forming on his sister's arm. "What happened, Sis?" he called.

She was almost running by the time she reached him. Danny squeezed between them, reaching for her arm. "*Ow*!" she cried, tears in her eyes. She raised her arm so that they might see it clearly.

Five impressions had been made, so painfully and penetratingly that it seemed surprising that no fingerprints were visible.

"It grabbed me at the bottom of the steps," Peggy said, trying not to sob. "There was nothing to see, no shape of any kind, but I felt, well, *jostled*. So I knew something was there. When I nearly fell, it . . . sort-of caught my arm with its h-hand and the pain was excruciating." She peered from one to the other of them, searching for belief, for an answer. "I didn't make this up."

"*Lourdes*," Danny Stanwall snapped. Startled, the others looked at him. "I'm sayin' it's *still* power of suggestion—'cause people who go to Lourdes usually believe they're healed." Belligerently, he folded his strong arms across his chest. "Look, if folks can make themselves believe paralyzed legs hold 'em up or that cancer goes away because of some crummy statue, folks can also leave imprints in their arms!"

"What of the bone?" Kasem asked, showing it again and then putting it in his pocket.

"What the fuck about it?" Danny demanded. "It's picked clean, like it's been here a long while. You guys said workmen were here several years ago." He shrugged, almost laughed. "Shit, can't you see? It's part of a goddam Kentucky Friend Chicken!"

From the spacious living room the sounds of organ music began again. Peggy glanced at Jennie in alarm. "I hear it," Jennie confessed. "I heard it the first day." All of them listened, transfixed. What had sounded more or less like an actual melody was growing twisted, distorted. The sonorous strains became louder, the notes veering off to meaninglessness, mindlessness, and got louder again.

Kasem, with no word to say of them, broke from the group in the corridor to run with astonishing speed toward the stairs. Then he was gone.

Peggy stared at her lover, Danny, without saying anything; but her expression conveyed a question anyway: Is that imagination?

The Thai journalist was back in moments, trotting. Although he did not look frightened nor filled with ready answers, he looked utterly fascinated. The organ sounds had ceased. "I felt the vibrations," Kasem said quietly, reaching them. "They fairly gushed out of the wall, the air. Alternately hot and cold, alternately the sounds of someone who is lost, and unhappy and someone who"—he hesitated, looking from Jennie to the brother and sister—"someone who is virtually the personification of evil."

"Lynn," Eric replied, supplying the name. *And Mama*? he wondered.

"I thought you were going to protect us," Danny growled. He looked embarrassed, because of his own fear.

"I didn't see you racing to accompany me," Kasem retorted. He tried to ease out the sting of his accusation with his ready grin. "Besides," he added, "the noises stopped, didn't they?"

The Thai guest had insisted upon sleeping on a cot in the room from which Eric had seen Eddie, or Eddie's spirit, emerge. It was quiet again in the Baldwin mansion and Eric, promising he wouldn't leave Jennie again that night, had retired with her to their bedroom. Theirs now, but once the Offspring's, Eric recalled as he left Jennie to undress and went to the adjacent bathroom.

Jennie, glancing at the wall behind which the unnerving chewing sounds had occurred, prayed they would be allowed to sleep that night. Increasingly, her loss of real restful sleep was leaving her vaguely ill and edgy, and worst of all, unable to control her tendency toward unsought psychic impressions. Because Eric was nearby and the room was presently silent, she removed her dress and shoes and paused to stretch. She couldn't remember when a bed had looked more inviting in her life. Oddly, however, she also really wanted Eric tonight. Not only did she need his arms around her but she yearned to be sexually transported from the disturbing Baldwin house and all it seemed to portend.

Naked, Jennie heard what she took for the

sounds of Eric's ablutions in the bathroom. Smiling, she turned in expectation of her lover's return.

A floating, mammoth head *seemed to fill the whole bedroom*, bobbing in midair like a hideous child's balloon.

Jennie danced rapidly away from it, the best she could, but it was still expanding, growing larger, discernibly, by the moment. She tripped, sprawled on the oversized hospital bed.

And the upper half of the bed shot up, locked in place with a snapping sound, thrusting Jennie toward the head. Because it was continually growing, it moved closer and closer even while its core stayed put. There was nothing of a child's balloon about the swelling, weeping, feminine eyes or the protruding, pouting lips which now appeared to stretch, to *reach* toward Jennie in the mockery of a kiss. Drool poured from the puckered mouth as it began a taunting smirk. And at the moment when she felt the moist lips and the rest of the bulbous face distend until it brushed against her, Jennie felt her mind being invaded by thoughts and images of alien nature. Forceful, penetrating, cruel ideas and visions spun in her brain and impinged themselves upon her consciousness. "*Get out*," she cried, aloud. "Get out of my mind!"

A door carommed off a wall. Further frightened, desperate, Jennie craned her neck, saw Eric staring from the bathroom, his lips moving as if uttering her name, or a warning, but *no sound reached her.* It was as if the gigantic head were spongelike and absorbed human speech, soaked it up and kept even that much help from being granted her.

Yet when her terrified gaze switched back, to the slobbering head, it was gone. Gone as if it had never existed. Jennie curled herself into a tight fetal ball and the bed slammed back into place with a noise like thunder.

"Is something wrong?" Eric asked mildly. He'd rushed to her when she hadn't heard him and hadn't replied. Now, he held her in his arms, close to his bare chest. "Tell me, Jen, what is it?"

"LYNN—HERE." She felt her lips move, but she hadn't willed them to do so, hadn't *wanted* to speak. And her voice, what was wrong with her *voice*? "LYNN SAYS—STAY OUT OF IT." While still a female voice, while her own vocal chords were being used, Jennie heard herself fairly boom the words at Eric. Horrified, she sensed the floor beneath the bed vibrating because of the way her voice thundered at him. "LYNN SAYS—BE *GOOD* AND NOBODY HURT. LYNN SAYS—REMEMBER WHAT HAPPENED TO YOU—AS *BOY*. CAN HAPPEN . . . AGAIN."

Eric pulled away from Jennie, bodily, although he continued to hold her hands. He stared at his girl, his woman, in memory and in acceptance. What he remembered was being a boy in a room up the hall from this very one, watching the most infamous monsters in history and in literature scratch at his window to get inside and, once there, attempting to drive Peg and him insane. He recalled Mama, after she died, reappearing in his room as something not *quite* his mother any longer—a fiend, who wished to take him to hell with her.

And for the first time, truly, he accepted the fact that the Offspring had survived death and dwelled in the long, stealthy shadows of the only home Lynn had known in life.

I can't keep it from them much longer, especially Jennie and Peg, he thought, his mind racing. *Even if it harms instead of helps her, and the others, they'll have to know in order to defend themselves.*

If any of them could.

The Offspring had almost succeeded in fulfilling Grandfather's plans. It had been almost impervious, invulnerable, in life.

What any of them did now, to survive the being, Eric had no idea.

Kasem Chamanan lit the incense he'd brought with him in his sports jacket pocket, then perched quietly, and alone, on the edge of his cot. Only a single, naked bulb in an old ceiling fixture provided him with light as he also drew from his jacket pocket a small spiral notebook and an inexpensive, red Papermate pen. Tapping the end of the pen thoughtfully against his snowy white teeth, the Thai began writing down a faithful, factual report of what he had seen and heard that evening.

Little of it surprised him. Some of it did, but that might be easily explained in terms of a far greater power than he was accustomed to rather than a specifically *different* one. The noises pretty Jennie Dorff had heard in the wall, for example, even the chewed and mangled shoe. They were reminiscent of the *hantu loceng*, a ghost that often troubled the residents of Muar, in Malaysia. Its presence was usually announced by a howling or muttering sound, heavy thuds, a belllike tinkle—and a noisy racket of *clawing* sounds from inside the wall. With the exception of the fact that Ms. Dorff had not made mention of a tinkling bell, the similarity was striking.

Kasem chewed on his Papermate, considering. What his host, Eric Porter, had seen was commonplace, not only in Thailand and neighboring Thailand and neighboring Malaysia but throughout the world. It was generally supposed, by parapsychologists, that such an apparition reflected the failure of the spirit to know *how* to reveal all of itself, or that the psychic energy charging the residence's house was insufficient to create what spiritualists once had called ectoplasm. Quite conceivably, Chamanan reflected, the boy Eddie did die here in the Baldwin mansion but was no knowing part of the phenomenon these people were calling "Lynn."

As for that principle entity, despite their statements about the person's murderous and magical conduct in life, Kasem had seen nothing yet that implied anything worse than what Malayasians and Thais alike called "Momok." Tersely described, the Momok was a supernatural bogeyman with scary faces, bulk, and a rather uninspiring assortment of noisy tricks. It would not be beyond its power to make discordant sounds on an organ that had once existed, as had the organ downstairs. By and large, even clever spirits seldom showed much originality and tended to be limited in shock value to what they'd done, alive, and what traces existed of articles that once were present in the residence.

Kasem stretched, yawned, reclined. He allowed himself a slight smile. The large one, the athlete named Danny, was such a skeptic that he was a prime candidate to be earthbound after his death—and it would serve him right! Only fools ignored what they experienced with their own senses, and more times than not it was the agnostic or atheist who found himself stranded in his house when he passed away. He'd met Stanwall's kind often enough, Kasem thought. Born bullies and ignoramuses—the kind American journalist H.L. Mencken had called "yahoos"—who added to the clutter of their feeble wits something that went well beyond healthy skepticism to adamantine mental immobility. The Thai grimaced and sliced one palm sharply with the cutting edge of his other hand. Whether the ball player believed that Kasam Chamanan knew what he was doing or not was of little importance.

Or should be, Kasem added to himself, sighing. *They've Americanized me more than I ever intended,* he mused wryly. *Because I care too much, now, what they think of me. It's sickening, but it even matters to me when that functional illiterate, Stanwall, questions my masculinity.* Just then, he wanted very much to tell Danny of being married before he was eleven years old—the first time. That he was the father of a fully-grown man.

Yet there *was* a way to prove himself to all of them and a very practical reason why Kasem meant to attempt to do just that. The local newspapers, particularly in the south and the midwest, did not believe him when he cited newspapers on which he'd worked in Thailand because they'd never *heard* of them, any of them. And whether Kasem or anyone else cared to discuss or admit it, they sought more and better credentials from him because he looked clearly more foreign than they would have a man with an American face. It was becoming impossible to find work, at least as a journalist. And that meant, eventually, willingness to endure privation or not, he would have to think seriously about returning home unless good fortune finally found him in this "land of golden opportunity."

It was such a paradox. "I live in the most advanced and charitable country on earth—it's called 'mankind's last hope' and the freest nation on the planet—yet *I* am not free to pursue what I was trained to do." He'd spoken aloud, making a face, and now he recorded his thoughts in the little notebook. "But if I succeed in impressing them all, by understanding or even exorcising their spirits, they may let me spend my entire summer here!"

It was better, Kasem decided, then going "home" to Thailand. He was proud of his country's accomplishments—in 1983, the Thai forces had even repulsed an invasion by the communist Vietnamese—but he'd made a second mistake in addition to learning to care what people thought of him.

He'd fallen in love with America.

It was about to get her, it was going to succeed this time and tear her to shreds or drive her hopelessly forever mad; and the dreaming Peggy Porter fought with all her courage to propel herself up through the many mists in her mind to consciousness, and escape. She was backed, instead, against the front door of the old house and Mildred wasn't there. The old housekeeper had disappeared, along with Grandfather Baldwin, and she was helpless. Now the Offspring was rolling unhurriedly toward her, the fang-lined mouth opened wide, the foul, fetid breath spreading over her face like rancid coldcream. But then someone was shaking her. Peg couldn't see him but she *knew* it was Danny, she blue-skyed her mind across a dense decade of partly perceived time and stunted growth to remember him, to *know* that her own silly-sweet muscular Danny was drawing her out of the killing nightmare, just in time.

Peggy's eyes popped open. Although lingering scraps of her remained in the terrible past, her heart chirruped with relief, with anticipation, and she willed her vision to clear and to focus, to let her *see* her anxious, caring, brave Danny Stanwall.

But all she saw, sprawled flat on her back as if drugged, was a wide, moon face in self-made shadow, two fluttering-lashed great eyes, and a skulled baldness so vast and so unnaturally white that Peggy started screaming even before unbearable coldness took a frigid grasp on her arms and daggerish nails kneaded into her flesh with indescribable power and pain. Distantly, she perceived Danny's voice, shouting for her, begging her to be all right and safe. She clung to the inflections of his ordinary human tones to allay the terror, to hold at bay *another* feeling that ran so deep it might have been a counterpoint to everything she had ever feared: the feeling of a loss so onerous and embittering, so debasing and soul-stealing, that her heart broke as if in response to the loss of a loved one.

He had come out of a funny, half-asleep state that was an admixture of coziness and warmth of well-being, of distant loneliness and a sense of absolute apprehension, to find himself lying atop the unresponsive body of his lover, yet simultaneously crouched in sexual readiness in some boundless aerie of vacant sky. The next instant he'd found himself several feet in the air above Peggy, suspended yet supported, able to see her tortured features beneath him but incapable of reaching her. It was rather as if they existed then in two quite separate universes that touched every twenty centuries, the drifted apart for millenia.

A moment later, Danny's hand, arms, chest and belly flesh registered the refrigerant frigidity of an unseen mass directly under him. He felt it buck, and spasm; then he was falling off and away, driven hard to the floor of the bedroom. He hurt. He'd been shouting, calling Peggy's name.

Now all Danny knew definitely was that he ached everywhere and footsteps were pounding up the corridor to their room. A second later, they were hammering on the door, yelling Peggy's name and his. But he was unable to make himself think and stood stockstill, stoop-shouldered, pathetically naked. One further instant and they were crowded inside the bedroom, gaping at him and toward his girl in a tableau of terrified anticipation.

"Why do you look so worried?" Peggy was asking. Danny, swaying, turned to her and was astonished to see that she was smiling, relaxed, and wide awake—apparently unharmed. "Did we make too much noise?"

Eric crossed to her at once, drawing a sheet up to his sister's chin. When he stepped back, the sheet, untouched, dropped back into Peg's lap. "You both screamed," he said, temporarily afraid to go near her.

"You must be mistaken, Bro," Peg replied smilingly. "Everything's fine, now. It's better than it's been for years."

"Why, Peggy?" Jennie asked, slowly starting toward the bed. "Why do you say that?"

Peggy cocked her head, and smiled as if thunderstruck by their lack of perception. "Because my nightmares are over, at last."

"How do you know that?" Danny frowning, still in a daze, sat beside her on the bed.

"That's easy!" Peggy exclaimed. She peered, bright-eyed, from one to the other of them, the flaming scratchmarks and bites on her arms and breasts of no apparent concern to her. "*It* said so." Her head swiveled to face her brother when he whispered the single word, "*Who?*" And Peggy touched his cheek sweetly. "It!" she repeated. "The *Offspring*!"

Kasem Chamanan said distinctly, to no one in particular, "Her nightmares may be over but I fear ours are only beginning."

PART TWO
SLIPPING BY

And I lie here warm, and I lie here dry,
And watch the worms slip by, slip by.
—Dorthy Parker, *Epitaph*

1

Blistering summer heat came rushing at the tarrying quintet of terrified youngsters like a dully witted but powerfully bullish creature. It poured out of the walls of the old Baldwin place as if it had been hiding there all along, waiting for the secret signal of a hot day in late July to emerge and sweep over them. Jennie thought it felt "like heat that's been stored up, sweltering heat from the past." She said she sensed something musty about it, "like old clothes that were washed briefly and then hung in the closet so long they're like decaying bodies."

Eric said nothing. Peggy agreed, but smiled sunnily. Danny Stanwall grunted and went outside to a makeshift basketball backboard to take shots with an inexpensive ball he'd bought.

Kasem nodded, eyes gleaming, appreciative of the mature brunette's imagery and insight.

August was around the corner. No one had suggested that they return to Dayton, nor had anyone, even Chamanan, wondered aloud, to the others, why they lacked the initiative to leave. God knows, nothing about the house or the way they were reacting to it seemed normal to him. He had stayed because he needed a place, had begun to wonder if he might get a book out of the legend of the Offspring. Nobody had quite told him to leave or to stay, so Kasem had taken silence for assent and privately went on wondering why the four Occidentals remained. Although the pledge which the Offspring had supposedly made to Peggy had been kept—no *overt* horror scaring all five of them had developed—the way that his friends had settled into a routine left Kasem less than sanguine. Most of the time, they slouched in the paradoxically modern plastic front room furniture, seeking the security of companionship but seldom speaking in more than spasmodic outbursts. Worse, the Thai thought, was the nature of that conversation, including his. What each of them said amounted to reminiscing, and ceaselessly dredging-up the past was not his idea of normal discourse among the young. By now, each of them knew the other four better than they'd ever known anybody else.

Kasem often tried, in the month-plus since

Peggy's last nightmare, to figure out just why they'd stayed in this old horror of a house when returning to the campus surely must have been attractive to them. Then it occurred to him that, in a way, they weren't as free to go as he'd believed. Jennie and Danny might have managed it, but they'd aligned themselves with Eric and Peggy who, unsettling as it was, were taking part in a homecoming. Additionally, something definitely had happened to the Porter girl the night she'd made her amazing comment about the nightmares being over, and that something must have its natural conclusion in this place of her *genius loci*. On an emotional plane, that was understandable, even logical. And it wasn't illogical for Peggy to have stopped being afraid of the house since her nightmares *had* ceased; Danny said he was no longer awakened by the girl's sleeping terror. Fact was, Peggy was by now the only one of them who seemed cheerful or behaved spontaneously at all.

Which probably meant, Kasem Chamanan reflected, that Peggy was being told or forced, to relax, to see life sunnily. This was the point at which he began to feel slightly out of his depths. Unless it was to lull him and the others into a sense of false security, even cause them to leave the Baldwin house and Peggy behind, the end of the worst haunting, didn't add up to him. Young Peggy's air of nearly jaunty cheerfulness, her constant childlike prattle, seemed incongruous to him, and nervewracking. This was not a typical summer vacation; even if the collective nightmares had stopped, this was *not* Grandpa's summer cottage on a lake somewhere. Periodically, all of them but Peggy were irritable and jumpy, especially the Stanwall moron. Yet after an outburst, each of them subsided into moody silence, apparently unable to sustain any emotion that might motivate them to snatch Peggy up and flee.

It's this simple: we're waiting, Kasem concluded. *Waiting until something unforgettably hideous happens.* He tried then to think of abandoning the others himself; then he lost his train of thought, frowned, and refocussed upon his hosts.

Eric's behavior was becoming an increasing concern to the observer from Thailand, particularly now, in the last week of July. While he spoke sparingly about it, he exhibited a number of quite peculiar but significant symptoms: numbness in the limbs (once, he'd stood and almost fallen flat on the front room floor), periodic difficult in swallowing his food (followed by loss of appetite), shakiness, excessive care to make each remark perfectly understood, and a tendency to drop whatever he was doing at the time and run full tilt for the closest bathroom. Sometimes he confessed to feeling nauseous, or short of breath. Even before the thermometer began its summery climb, Eric was sweating constantly. *The term for it,* Kasem thought, *is agoraphobia—usually the fear of being alone but also the terror that comes from knowing one's avenue of escape was all but sealed off. People with agoraphobia felt undesirably different, and misunderstood; at the root of it was an unreasoning fear of losing their minds—or dying.* But in Eric Porter's case, in this house, Kasem knew, such fear was not necessarily 'unreasoning.'

In the last analysis, the little journalist eventually decided, he was probably making no effort to find another place to live because the Baldwin place was endlessly intriguing. *He* was surely not on the ghostly Offspring's hit list!

Eric hadn't told the rest that he'd begun keeping a journal and those small, frightening but not collectively horrifying experiences he was quietly trying to survive went into the journal in a format that he knew suggested his long-standing, unvoiced urge to write fiction.

"At first, or if there ever was, there wasn't much to see, and I was too nearsighted to observe it in the dark. With my heavy glasses removed and insomnia keeping me awake once again, all I made out at first was the smudge of sheer blackness by the window. Even that wasn't easy to discern until the late night curtains gusted back and I realized that shadows stood where no shadows should, or could, be.

"No one has written down what you're supposed to do about such moments. Most of the events in life were choreographed, years ago, and I suppose the content person is he who continually goes through the prescribed and proper motions with a measure of grace.

"There is no minuet of manners to organize and direct the dance of horror. There is never music on the air to assuage the emotions of a person who knows that he is terribly haunted. And considering what happened here, before my sister's last nightmare and the promise she was given, one routine haunt seems scarcely worth mentioning.

"Even though it is terrifying me.

"The first nights of my own, special haunting, I simply lay in bed and watched, trying to convince myself that I was a spectator of nothing whatever—to persuade myself that it is only an optical illusion. With my feeble eyesight, that should not have been too enormous a task. But by the third night there was further substance, and I knew the shadows were starting to gather, as if the spirit at the heart of the unmoving blackness had gained in thickness, presumably weight, at the precise pace it was gaining confidence.

"By the last night of that week early in July, the shadows had blocked-out the window in its entirety. I should not have been able to detect the difference between the darkness of the bedroom and obsidian dark of the constantly developing shadows. But I could, God help me! Just as there are degrees of evil, levels of malice, of madness, there are degrees of darkness; and regardless of how mightily I squinted to sharpen my myopic vision, I could not quite penetrate the leaden wall of motionless Something.

"Without seeing, *I saw through* to it, to a great, thick, substance.

"I've thought a lot about terror since we came here. Terror, like love, or laughter, is like death, perhaps, a matter of the moment. It passes with the unlocked hours and becomes a matter of haunting only when its residually clinging awfulness begins to cake one's daylight soul. Still, *still,* it wasn't what one discussed in the morning; not to a woman glad for the appearance of tranquility and deceit of the commonplace. Terror makes man a willing conspirator. Certainly, *I* could not whisper to Jennie, or to my sister, that while they slept in the tender yet vulnerable grasp of sleep, I remained awake. Endlessly awake. Awake, and shuddering in my own nightmare horror which itself kept apace of the shadow's continual growth.

"No, I thought each sun-clamoring morning, a woman wishes to believe her man is content, full of her food and of her love. She likes to believe him ready, at the first sound of unidentified footfall, to vault from bed to do sweet battle for her.

"Any woman strives to believe that her man is sane . . ."

* * *

By day, Eric kept his fears to himself, and kept himself, more than ever before, to himself. One afternoon, Jennie showed him her scratch marks on her legs. They'd been there that morning but he'd slept—when he slept at all—on the front room couch. Why did she wait until then, after lunch, to show them to him? "I w-wasn't sure you'd care," Jennie whispered. He'd wept with her, they had made love on an unused cot on the second floor, he'd promised to be less aloof from her—and kept his word fewer than twenty-four hours.

Danny, too, had been passingly marked. He'd surged up into morning like a swimmer breaking water, his belly and buttocks freezing cold. Although he'd not been able to see his posterior, he knew it matched the angry red splotches on his abdomen. And he'd showered for well over an hour, thinking, "Power of suggestion power of suggestion," until he'd found the courage to join the others.

Part of Eric's problem, or a reason for his agoraphobic mental state, involved the way he had been forced to relinquish the hope that Lynn, the Offspring, was truly and forever dead. As he could not flee from the house, while his sister continued to behave like a preteener in a young woman's body, he could no longer escape the most petrifying fact of his life: fire, and death, hadn't stopped his kinsman's reign of terror. Having emerged as an independent adult, the winner of a valiant fight he'd waged for years against his own remembered horror, he was newly reduced to the state of an impotent child. Eric hated it even worse than he feared for their lives. If he could not find a way to recapture his rather cocky, self-assured and wholly defensive approach to life, he couldn't be certain of leaving the Baldwin place sane. It was all so unjust, so much a case of the cards having been stacked against Peg and him since their earliest years.

So, by day, Eric believed that the real target of the Offspring remained his sister and the faint measure of relief that gave him left him afloat in guilt. The anomalous cold spots on Stanwall's stomach and ass, the scratches poor Jennie had to endure, even the stealthy incidents of nocturnal hauntings with which he himself was afflicted were to Eric cruel pranks—no more and no less. If they could be tolerated somehow while Peg really began to pull herself back together, then he believed that he might learn to live with the threat of insanity which seemed to run in the family.

In Eric's thinking, his responsibility to his sister was ongoing. He accepted that, completely. Now, however, he questioned whether or not he was up to defending her with his life, the way he had when Peg and he were small and Lynn had assailed them with mental projections. It had something to do with growing up, realizing that one's days were limited and wanting more of the good things that life offered. A child did not know the wide range of his future options, did not doubt what he'd been taught about heaven, even the terror and possible pain of dying. Maturity, Eric decided, created lesions in one's faith and self-confidence; certainly he did not doubt, as an adult, that there were innumerable ways to meet sudden, unexpected death. And with Lynn's spirit around, those ways became larger in number and more terrifying of scope.

And Jennie, whose psychic ability was such a surprise to him, as it was unwelcome to her, didn't make it any easier when she whispered to Eric—they were in bed at night, he'd been almost asleep and felt a huge, resentful anguish when drawn from sleep's cozy cocoon—something *else* she had intuited: "The . . . spirit . . . in this house," she said close to his ear, as if afraid she'd be overheard, "this Offspring that you won't tell us about . . ."

He groaned, "Yes, go on. What about Lynn?"

Her fingers against his bare shoulder had seemed freezing cold and she moved her mouth even nearer to his ear. "I'm not sure Lynn is dead. Or—not *exactly* dead." And she'd confided no more, incapable of interpreting her own psychic impressions.

But when Eric had eventually fallen asleep, the shadows once more gathered in the corner by the window and he awoke in time to stare forlornly at them until sullen daylight crept into the room.

During the first week of August, because Eric had explored the woods and reported finding succulent-looking berries ripe for the picking, Peg Porter agreed to conquer her fear of the old garage they would have to pass to reach the woods, and complete her long-planned expedition. It even seemed strange to Peg that she had been stopped by sight of the garage before. She felt like a girl again and utterly dauntless. Jennie, Eric, and Kasem Chamanan promptly agreed to accompany her.

Danny, however, had a birthday coming up in a few days and said he needed "to get in touch with civilization again." He planned to drive to a neighborhood shopping center to rent a few movies. One of their few pleasures, since June, had been derived from a VCR they'd rented and weekly films which seemed to tuck the spirits away in shadow so long as John Candy, Eddie Murphy, or Richard Pryor were making them laugh. But it was obvious to Peggy that her lover felt both bored and neglected. Probably, he was hinting for her to remember the need to buy him a gift or two. Hoping to find the courage to leave the house later for just that purpose, she let Danny drive away. They were having a cook-out that evening and she wanted him to be in a better mood. Increasingly, Danny was at Kasem's throat and she was afraid the little Thai might get hurt.

The foursome passed the garage without incident and Peggy's sunny pride in her accomplishment gave them each a welcome lift. Then, three of them half-running into the woods, Kasem paused before entering to drop to one knee and lower his head. Jennie noticed that he closed his eyes and that his lips were moving as if in prayer. But then he was bouncing after them, laughing, and the moment was forgotten.

The woods were deeper and thicker than Jennie Spandorff had expected. Several yards into it and sunlight was choked off, the day turned to dusk. It seemed to her, when she glanced up, that trees here went on growing higher and higher into the air. She had the impression that the foliage which blotted out the sun was an unnatural, even purposive, accomplishment. She felt that branches were bent far above them to touch and unite with others, thereby inverting time. Humankind could not physically withstand confusion of that sort, people depended upon the natural rhythms of the sun and moon, the formal ritualization of week and weekend, the slow but reassuring turn on the seasons. Immediately, she wanted to go back. Even that old house seemed preferable to a wooded land that mumbled its own mysterious questions and retained secrets human persons could never answer. Eric might have gone with her, too, because he whispered—none of them but Peggy had spoken in a normal tone of voice—"it feels *different* in the woods today. Almost like we're invading a place we aren't supposed to be." *But I think it wants one of us here,* Jennie thought. And Peggy, after a pause, was seizing Kasem's small hand and dancing deeper among the stoic, stalking trees, innocent and unafraid as a little girl.

Reluctantly, Jennie and Eric tagged after them. Neither spoke, but the archaeologist's daughter clung to her lover's arm, freshly reminded of her diminishing feeling of independence and confidence, and shaken by the realization. *Half the time I forget why I even came to Indianapolis,* she thought. She almost tripped over undergrowth that clutched at her feet and groped at her bare ankles as if meaning to do so. The women had donned shorts for the expedition and Jennie's calves were already a maze of scratches. *This damned woods is nothing more than an extension of the house. Old, unused, mysterious and dense—always on the verge of showing us something terrifying, or revealing the truth at last.*

"Eric!" yelled Kasem's voice, filled with excitement. Jennie's fingernails dug into Eric's arm but he glanced at her, then dashed after the little Thai. "We've found something over here!"

Momentarily alone, Jennie felt the motion of the towering branches, almost black against the sun they resented, and shivered. She started forward and was struck by what she imagined to be a violent arm, reaching for her waist. But a low-hanging branch had snapped back and she brushed awkwardly past it, last on the scene.

The other three stood in a clearing, forming a rough circle, and were peering down. At first, Jennie couldn't see what had excited Kasem. She edged nearer, tentatively, and saw what they were looking at:

A very wide patch of ground, barren except for several scattered shoots of grass and weeds. At first glance, a recently excavated patch of ground somewhat hurriedly filled in. At second and third glances, quite an old mound, because the replaced dirt was clearly, permanently hardened. And at each and every glance Jennie and the others gave it, it looked very much like a grave.

"Are you thinking what I'm thinking?" Eric asked Kasem.

Kasem nodded. "That's what it looks like," he said, and each man knew the word neither of them uttered.

"But . . . *whose*?" Jennie asked in a whisper.

Peggy, without speaking or crying out, was running back the way they had come, eyes wide and her hands pressed over her mouth. She dropped the straw basket as she ran and the few berries she'd picked skittered over the face of the grave like capsules of blood.

None of them wanted to discuss it when they had all returned to the house. Instead, as if nothing had happened to mar her sunny new serenity of spirit, Peggy enlisted Jennie's aid in planning for the evening's cookout. All remained tranquil, if strained, until Danny Stanwall's car was squealing to a stop out front and they heard his footsteps trotting eagerly up the front lane. Entering, he held a white plastic sack containing three videotaped motion pictures, and a surprise the others found stunning.

He had met a fan of his in the video shop and asked her to dinner at the Baldwin place, as if the house wasn't at all different than any of the others in Central Eastwood. He told them about the girl as ingenuously as a small boy asking a friend to stay the night. "Her name's Corey Livingstone and I met her once when Dayton was here to play Badler U during my frosh season." His eyes were bright, almost feverish, as he followed Peggy around the kitchen. "She remembered how many points I got and even a key assist I made to start the second half. Ain't that somethin?"

"It's that, it's 'something,' " Peggy replied shortly. She put a pot on the stove to boil potatoes for potato salad and one of them almost popped out as she slammed it down. "How gorgeous is she? Is she a real groupie?"

"A groupie?" Danny's face clouded. "Shit,

girl, you ain't turnin jealous on me, are ya? Besides, she got me a deal on the movie rentals—her old man manages the shop!"

Eric, looking into the sack with the movies, silently shook his head. Was it possible that a potential brother-in-law of his was *that* obtuse? It occurred to him for the first time in over two months that while Stanwall had seen certain strange phenomena in the house, he'd been saved by it once and was the least effected of them. Additionally, he was the only one who continued to attribute the hauntings to the power of suggestion. Was it a case of the stupid being protected by their own ignorance, or lack of imagination—or was Danny not quite the ordinary guy he certainly seemed to be?

After eating a late and very quiet lunch during whih not even Kasem Chamanan had anything much to say, Danny motioned to Eric to follow him and led the way out front.

"Look, I'm crazy about your sister," he told Eric, "but this joint gets on my nerves. A guy like me has to have a little action now and then."

Eric nodded, frowning. "A 'little action' usually refers to smoking dope, behaving like a turkey around the sorority houses, or chasing women. I think you could have asked Peg if she minded." He noticed Kasem exiting the front door, a yard or two away. "Or had the commonsense not to bring another girl here, period."

"I get it." Danny straightened, his hands

fisted. "What you're reminding me is that this ain't my house, right? Or was I supposed to ask *your* permission?"

Eric sighed. "Maybe I just expect too much of you, Dan," he said, turning to go back into the house. "Sometimes I forget that bad manners go hand in hand with stupidity."

Enraged, Danny shot out an arm, caught the smaller man around the neck and turned him, off balance, until Eric was facing him. He pulled back a fist to hit Eric.

And Kasem Chamanan was stepping nimbly between them, his palms raised. "It's the weather," he said quickly; "it has us all on edge, Danny."

"You want it, do you?" Danny shouted. Red-faced, he stared furiously at the little Thai's composed features. "You wanna fight me, huh? Right?"

Kasem shrugged, smiled, looked away. "I think that is probably inevitable, Danny," he said softly. Patting Eric's shoulder, he guided him back toward the house. "When the time of unavoidability arrives, you'll have your chance."

"Damn right! damn right!" Danny muttered, nodding and wiping sweat off his forehead. He followed the other two men. "Whenever you want it, Peter Pan, you can have it."

With the humidity soaring to new record heights for the date, they left the front door open all afternoon, holding it that way with one of the cheap plastic chairs. After finishing their work on the cook-out food and leaving it in the refrigerator, Peggy and Jennie joined the men in the big front room, drenched with perspiration. Danny's guest was scheduled to arrive before long and the women intended to clean up and change clothes before she got there, but neither of them had the energy to spare just now. Eric was setting up a card table in case anyone wanted to play games that evening when they heard the chair spin away and the front door slam shut.

"Horseshit," Danny growled, going out to the foyer and, through it, to the front door. He crammed the chair back into place, tested it and saw that it was properly fixed.

Satisfied, Danny turned to walk back through the foyer into the living room.

And again, the chair slipped free. He looked around in time to see it carom out the front door and watch the door slam violently closed. The sounds had brought Jennie and Peggy, who peered inquisitively at the athlete.

"Shit *fuck*!" he exclaimed, embarrassed. He rushed outside to retrieve the chair and, with exacting care, jammed it between the door and the doorframe. He rattled the chair, couldn't budge it. "There!" he said. "That'll hold it!"

Behind Danny—and no one felt the slightest

gust of wind—the chair simply self-destructed, crumbled into a twisted plastic mass, and the door clapped shut with a great, cracking retort like that of a cannon going off. On the floor of the foyer the wrecked chair quivered like a beaten animal. Danny Stanwall gaped at it, then the closed door, immobilized.

"It . . . doesn't *want* anybody else here," Jennie said in a whisper.

"Only us," Peggy said in simple agreement, her eyes enormous.

"Well, gawddammit," Danny answered, coming to life, "it let that faggot of yours in!" Almost as frustrated as he was angry, he reached out to open the door—and couldn't. It held. He locked both strong hands on the knob, tugged. Nothing happened. "*Please*," he whispered and, crimsoning, he braced one large foot against the foyer wall and yanked on the door with all his might.

It didn't move a fraction of an inch.

But at the moment, rapping sounds came from the other side of the door. "Danny?" called a highpitched feminine voice. "Is something wrong?"

"It's her, Corey," Danny exclaimed, and tried one last time to pull the door wide. He stared at it, marveling. It was as if the door was a part of the wall. There was no suggestion that the door had been separate from it, or even that the door would ever open again. It wasn't stuck. Something had willed it shut. Outside, Corey knocked again, louder. "Am I too early?"

She's gonna book, Danny thought. That second, the petite redhead who loved dating athletes seemed to him the most necessary person in the world. She became a way to remain sane and healthy, a means of continuing to scoff at the others, continue to pretend that he'd never once been frightened by what had happened. Going livid with fury and frustration, Danny turned and raced back through the foyer, rushed through the house, toward the back door.

Eric, who had remained in the front room, dusting off the card table, did not know precisely what was wrong but ran after Danny, trying to piece it together. He was two yards behind Stanwall after they'd reached the back yard and the athlete was cutting nimbly around the side of the house.

There was *motion* on the roof of the Baldwin house—Eric heard it, broke stride long enough to glance up. What he saw shocked him into silence.

Gingerly dipping its all-but-weightless yellow paws in the roof's gutter, noiseless as the grave, a *cat* was prancing above Danny Stanwall's head. And it was readying itself, crouching.

Sailing off the roof, it plummeted just as Danny passed beneath it. Belatedly, Eric cried, "*Look out*!" But he was much too late. The cat—scarcely out of a kitten's stage—landed squarely on Stanwall's head and, as if astonished by its own daring, dug its claws piercingly into Danny's temples, for balance. What made the moment worse for the staring Eric Porter were other factors, among them the alarming, almost human shriek the cat emitted, and the snarling, virtually curse-bestowing yowls it went on making as it clawed Danny's cheeks and forehead. *It's trying for his eyes*, Eric realized with further horror.

Now Danny was staggering toward the driveway, perhaps the busy street; his hands and the animal's evilly rending claws prevented him from seeing where he was going. The cute, petite girl with red hair who stood at the front door gaped at the sight open-mouthed. With no idea where he was but blessed with an athlete's sense of impending risk, Danny stopped, crying, and sought to pry away the feline claws.

"Get *out* of here!" Eric yelled at Corey, gesturing frantically. "*Move* it, for God's sake! You're gonna get him blinded if you stay—or killed!"

At once, the redhead turned and scurried toward her car without a backward glance.

And when Eric again looked at Danny, he saw that the cat had disappeared. *Vanished.*

Peg, who'd watched the terror through a window, easily threw the door wide and rushed outside toward Danny, who had sunk to his knees on the paved driveway in agony. But Peg was looking now at her brother.

"That looked just like the cat I had when we

were kids." Her tone was one of mixed wonder and frightened disbelief. "I think it *was* ol' Krazy." And only her awestruck eyes added, *But that was more than ten years ago.*

2

They had the cookout anyway.

First, Eric rushed to the nearest People's drugstore for medication, Band-Aids, and gauze. Meanwhile, Peggy and Jennie bathed Danny's wounds. By the time they'd disinfected and dressed him, Danny was ready to play the Mummy in any film production. Refusing to comment in any way whatever about the cat's attack or the girl who had been frightened away, he did rouse himself from a confused blending of pain and fear to proclaim himself "fucking starved," and added that he didn't "wanna be a party pooper."

So the outing in the massive, moody backyard of the Baldwin estate went on as scheduled, even though they started later than they had planned. By now, no one was in the right frame of mind for any kind of party and Jennie noticed, with a shudder, that darkness was coming fast. What bothered her, when she gazed toward the garage and the woods beyond it, turned the bite of hotdog in her mouth to lead. The ebbing day's light seemed massed above the old garage and shot with electricity. Behind it, the woods looked already cloaked by night. Instead of individual trees stretching against the lowering sky, she saw a further massing, a bristling huddling together. It was hard not to believe that the woods were edging toward them, menacingly, militantly.

Humidity had their sparse garb sticking to their skin in that queer, clammy way that makes one feel naked, exposed. Above the backyard where the five of them spoke in nervous spurts but otherwise languished, consuming more beer than food, the peculiar weather conditions worked brooding and unwelcome magic. Anything they uttered sounded strangely garbled, yet harsh, pointed. When they arose to fetch another hotdog, more potato salad, or a fresh can of beer, the slighest motion seemed simultaneously obtrusive and apparitional, as if they had become homeless ghosts whose speech or movement was the breaking of some inwardly acknowledged sacrament. When, at last, they'd lapsed into frowning silence and were left within themselves, individually, it was, Eric thought, as if they were turning into a neatly framed surreal painting. And when it was hung, they'd move and speak no more.

"The cat that attacked you." Kasem Chamanan's rather high-pitched, melodic voice sounded sinister in the way that it insinuated its way to each of their ears. He was, of course, turned to Danny Stanwall and in the growing gloom of the yard only his gleaming eyes were apparent. "Feline creatures are part of the lore of almost any culture."

"I don't wanna talk about it," Stanwall grunted. He glanced only briefly at the Thai, almost rigidly erect in a plastic chair they'd moved outside. Danny was sprawled on a blanket.

Kasem ignored him. "The curious point is that we assume ghosts are apparitional projections of formerly living people—people with *souls.* In Western civilization, animals are not thought to possess that ultimate gift of the Creator." He smiled and his bond-white teeth flashed once, then vanished. "But reports of such beings as ghostly cats continue, unabated. Do you know about the Killakee cat?"

Silence greeted the question. The women stirred, briefly. Eric's voice sounded in the stillness: "No. Was this a recent haunting?"

"It occurred in 1968," Kasem said softly. "At Killakee House in the Wicklow Mountains, near Dublin. An old house, built in the eighteenth century. Then it was the headquarters of the Hell Fire Club, all those years ago. The Earl of

Rosse loathed black cats. Once, he doused one in whiskey, set it afire, and frightened the townspeople who saw it screeching down the hill with his shouted cry that it was the Devil itself."

"Do we have to listen to this shit?" Danny demanded.

"Rosse held the black mass, using a cat when Satan did not materialize," Kasem continued as if the athlete had not spoken.

"I thought you said the hauntings occurred in 1968?" Jennie asked, rather more sharply than she had intended.

"I did," Kasem said. "Killakee House was abandoned, much the way this house was left to stand, left to its own devices until the late sixties. When a Mrs. O'Brien acquired it as a center for Irish artists and sculptors to show their work, she heard rumors almost immediately of a black cat the size of a large dog which haunted the old place." The Thai's eyes glittered. "The cat had been haunting Killakee House for more than fifty years."

Danny cursed. Peggy whispered, "What happened after Mrs. O'Brien bought the house?"

"Three men, including an artist, were working in the front hall. It opened onto a ballroom. The artist, named Tom McAssey, had just locked up when the door opened again, of its own accord. They knew the lock and bolt were strong, in good working order. Upon approaching the open door, each man saw a figure draped in black, waiting outside the door. Tom welcomed it, said to come in. But the figure replied, 'You can't see me—and leave this door *open.*' " Kasem paused. "Scared, the artist slammed and bolted the door, turned to run after his friends, who'd already headed for the interior of the house. But Tom glanced back when the door was thrown open, again, crashing against the walls, and saw a monstrous black cat crouched in the hall, its red-flecked amber eyes fixed on him."

"Knock it off." Danny said. Now night was upon them, elongated shadows stretching vertically across the backyard as if the trees in the woods had advanced and had hesitated fleetingly before converging upon them. "Just knock it *off*, and I mean it!"

"Other reports continued," Kasem said. Now he spoke so quietly that the others were forced to strain in order to hear him. "A champion pole-vaulter came forward to say that he'd seen the immense cat many times, usually lurking in the garden. He hunted it, with its 'terrible eyes,' but never managed to corner it. A seance was held at Killakee House shortly before 1970. Large furniture was thrown about as if a giant hand had tossed it; one chair was left in 'tiny slivers.' Rosary beads were found separated from their string. Knockings were heard frequently. At last, a shallow grave was found, containing the skeleton of a murdered dwarf with an enormous head, the brass figurine of a horned devil, and the remains of a great, black cat . . ."

Danny Stanwall loomed up from the ground like a corpse leaping from its grave, growling like a dog and hurtling his athletic body toward Kasem Chamanan.

But Kasem was no longer seated, no longer there. Anticipating Danny's attack, he'd jumped with amazing alacrity from his chair, side-stepped Stanwall, and was snaking out one arm and hand in quest for the perfect grip. Finding it, he whipped Danny around in a circle and bent him to one knee; there, the little Thai held the much larger youth, at the full extent of one arm, Danny's nose inches from the ground.

Danny's scream of pain and surprise carved the oncoming night like the summoning call of a crusading trumpet. Eric, only feet away, saw that Kasem could, without much expended effort, dislocate Danny's shoulder and perhaps his wrist. "Let him go," Peggy cried, rushing toward the little tableau "Please, Kasem, don't hurt him!"

"I won't," the Thai promised. But he didn't release Stanwall. Instead, he applied pressure and Danny instantly cried out again. "You will lie on that blanket, quietly, trying to be civilized." He'd leaned his own upper body over the forcibly-crouched athlete and was making it clear that this would be his only exercise in mercy. "You're so *spoiled*," he said scoldingly.

"You felt free to call me names but you had the nerve to demand that I shut up. You don't even understand what makes your country great but you threaten its freedoms every time you open that unpleasant mouth. Now: will you do as I ask?"

Danny didn't argue, didn't even swear. Tears squeezing from his eyes, he nodded.

Kasem let him go. "Friends?" he asked. A hand was outthrust and his smile was as sweetly innocuous as before. "Is that possible?"

Danny massaged his shoulder, said nothing as he glowered as the small Thai for a moment. Then he turned toward the house, gripping his arm.

"Stay with us, please." Kasem indicated the blanket, grinned. "We value your companionship."

Danny's gaze met Peggy's and fell away. Silently, he dropped to the ground on his blanket. Facing away from the others, he touched the Band-Aids on his forehead and temples and rocked miserably to and fro.

"This is a manifestation of what's happening here." Jennie was on her feet, spreading her arms to include everyone and everything within range. "We're being constantly challenged. All of us—can't you see that? And we're losing every time, doing just what that damned Lynn wants us to do!" Her face was fierce with something close to embarrassment. "We're providing entertainment for the Offspring while time passes until—" She stopped, unable to finish it. "We've living like *movies*, like films rented for the VCR, to amuse Lynn." She touched Eric, looked pointedly at Danny Stanwall. "Let's not be so cooperative. All right? Let's not bring any further amusement to that bastard!"

Peggy rose to her bare knees, her vivacious face pale in the new flood of moonglow. "Do you know yet why the Offspring wants us here?" With the others, Peggy had learned of Jennie's developing psychic powers.

"No. Not yet." Jennie spoke slowly, carefully. "But I *am* getting—"

Her hands abruptly reached for her inner thighs and she gasped. For a second, the listening Eric Porter thought that mosquitos were stinging her. Then Jennie covered first one breast, then another, with her frantic hands. "What's happening?" Eric asked her, jumping to his feet. Even Danny turned to see what was wrong.

"It's *groping* me," Jennie choked out her answer, slapping now at disembodied hands that no one could see. Red-faced, embarrassed and frightened, she squeezed her legs together. "Get *away*!" she shouted, edging away—and both Eric and Kasem saw that she was being driven toward the house. "Leave me *alone*!"

Usually placid Peggy ran toward Jennie, protectively, put an arm around the older woman's shoulders. Crying out, almost sobbing,

Jennie backed farther away, moving awkwardly, pawing at something none of them was able to detect. Then she broke for the house at a run, Peggy hurrying after her with solicitous words.

Kasem watched them go. A moment later, the door slammed behind them and he muttered something in a language Eric and Danny didn't understand. It could have been a curse. He sighed deeply but his dark eyes flashed anger.

"Right back into that foul house," the Thai said softly. "Just as it wanted them to do." His voice sounded disheartened. It rang with frustration, along with a note of reluctant admiration. "So they will be there again. For the long night."

They fell silent while each man was left to his own thoughts.

Then Danny Stanwall snapped open another beer and drank deeply. "It's nothing but imagination," he said. It was the first time he'd spoken since his own furies had been forcibly quelled. "Just suggestion."

Danny's comment seemed hollow to all three of them, but neither Kasem nor Eric bothered to correct him. It was apparently Danny's way of letting them know he didn't want to be isolated from them.

Above the garage, which was now all but indistinguishable from the glowering woods, the gray light remained like an aura that refused to blink out. None of the men could discern an entity of any kind with their eyes but each man sensed a presence, watching them. "This . . . *Lynn*," Kasem murmured wonderingly, "enjoys far-ranging powers. What just happened to Jennie reminds me of another kind of spirit in my country. It's called *orang minvak*."

"What does that mean?" Eric asked.

"It means 'the greasy man,' " Kasem replied after a pause. "It attacks young women and little girls. *Paws* them. For the sake of terrifying them." He glanced toward the Baldwin house. "But I think Lynn wants more than that."

Unwilling to leave Jennie alone and wanting to be physically nearer his sister, as well, Eric went into the house moments later and found Jennie sitting on the edge of the immense bed, fully dressed. She seemed especially young and vulnerable to him with her feet and legs dangling and the way she scarcely glanced up at him when he entered the bedroom.

"I don't think I can stay here much longer," she began. Her gaze was fixed on the wall from which she had heard the scratching and chewing noises, now apparently caused by the cat Peggy'd called Krazy. She was perfectly still, her limbs immobile, as if she would not be able to run or to defend herself if anything more occurred. "Not until you tell me—tell *us*—precisely what happened to you and your sister. Tell us everything you know about Lynn."

Eric, who'd begun unbuttoning his shirt, stopped. "You know how I feel about that."

She raised her face to his and he was startled by the lines he saw in it. Lovely Jennie was starting to age, in a matter of months. "Do you know what it feels like trying to survive when you don't even understand the nature of your attacker, your enemy?" Her fists lightly pounded the mattress once. "Isn't it more than a little selfish to be the only one who *does* know what he's up against?"

He started toward her, palms wide, begging her to see his reasoning. "Honey, you just don't get it. I—I'm afraid that if I describe Lynn to you, it will be like letting Lynn come all the way through, like providing added *power*."

"Describing?" Jennie repeated, looking sharply at him. "What do we care what Lynn *looked* like? What does that have to do with anything?"

"Believe me, you'd care," Eric retorted. He'd stopped feet from where she perched on the bed, afraid she would rebuff him. "In a way, what Lynn looked like is the key to . . . everything." He hesitated. "And what Lynn *was*."

"Go on." She caught his gaze, held it. "You've begun, at last. Please. You might as well go ahead with it."

"I can't," Eric replied, and shook his head. He

turned part way toward the bedroom door. "Not just now; not yet." He glanced at Jennie from the corner of his eye and saw tears welling up in her wide, striking eye. "I don't dare."

When she rolled over on the bed with a groan, Eric left the room and eased the door gently shut behind him.

Sometimes, for some people, weeping is so close to the content of dreams that misery leads to the brink of sleep. But nightmares seldom surface or are recalled in that bleak state. Intead, obliviousness is generally the matching, rather maudlin reward.

But for Jennie Spandorff, quietly sobbing and drifting toward an unconsciousness of despair, nightmare—*real* nightmare—was on tap.

Sound so slight it was like the wings of butterflies rubbing occurred when Jennie was alone and, sufficiently self-pitying that instant that she felt inaccessible and apart, she turned onto her back to identify the source of the sound.

Smoke swirled and ebbed near the high ceiling of the old room, coiling and chudding in a weighty, ponderous way that was simultaneously serpentine and like the wriggling of porcine things. For only one second did Jennie doubt its supernatural origin. Then her senses were automatically seeing to become attuned with the vast, complex brain at its nucleus and bounding away, repulsed, with the suggestion that the thinker behind the cloudy apparition didn't mean to reveal itself this time. It reminded Jennie, as she flattened her palms on the mattress and sought to push herself away from the somewhat slimy and greasy smoke-mass, of what she and Eric had seen on the stairs when they first came to the awful house. While it wasn't touching her, it also carried with it the same impression of substance, of bulk, along with a quietness that seemed furtive and sinister. Her heartbeat accelerated. She mumbled somebody's name, uselessly, on her grimacing lips.

Now the smoky quality was clearing and the ectoplasmic mass at the ceiling was achieving an image of rank corporeality, to Jennie's staring horror. An instant later and she realized she was looking up at a great mass of naked, floating *flesh*, armless and legless and without a head, but *becoming*. Jennie twisted her head from side to side, strove to look away from it, couldn't. It was as if perverse nature had effected enough pale, puffy flesh for two human beings or more and, like a lunatic sculptor, was starting to *mold* it—to carve away the surplus until a grotesque body would be left. A belly, then massive buttocks, took form.

And Jennie knew that moment with her whole heart that she did not want to see the mad sculptor's creation when that foul, pasty blob of surging flesh became a recognizable mockery of Man, or Woman. "*Eric*!" she screamed as loudly as she could, at the moment the clawing sounds in the wall started afresh and the sobbing cry like that of a bizarre human infant worked its way into her ears and consciousness. "*Please* come, Eric—*please*?"

Sitting on the floor in Grandfather Baldwin's laboratory on the third floor, Eric withdrew the journal he'd been keeping, and which he had hidden away, and continued his most recent entry. It was a record of what he'd experienced last night: the outcome of his strange, silent, nocturnal haunting; and anyone reading it would have known why he was quiet and uncommunicative that day:

"It was my good fortune that I wasn't the kind of man who felt a nightly urge to visit the bathroom. Small blessing, I suppose, probably attributable to my youth—even if all I have left of that is only physical, not mental or spiritual. To reach the bathroom, by day or night, meant passing directly by the partly shaped shadows at the bathroom door.

"But we'd been drinking and I'm not accustomed to that. When Jennie and I retired last night, I was pleasantly surprised to find myself drowsy and I fell asleep almost immediately, then slept quite soundly.

"I awakened at three-fifteen, however, to an insistent and pressing need for personal relief, and saw that dark *Something* beside the bathroom door. It was much larger but pressed against the wall, as if intuiting my needs and wishing to accommodate them. Perhaps I imagined it, I thought, and, if not, maybe it could not *help* seeming menacing and had the soul of a black lamb.

"It seemed to take forever merely to rest my bare feet on the peculiarly icy floor, then begin padding my way toward the door in a crabbed, creeping pace. When a person is frightened, he has the tendency toward silent, even stealthy movements. Perhaps that rises from a racial memory of what our ancestors found it advisable to do . . . to edge away from fanged and wolfen creatures, to emulate their very secretiveness in the mournful hope of borrowing a measure of their might. I recall closing my eyes involuntarily when I passed *It* and, when I'd thrown the door wide and darted into the bathroom, it was with a feeling of release I had never known before. My relief was unrestrained.

"Despite a terrible fact elicited from my little stroll: the Something between the window and door of my bedroom found it necessary to *breathe*. Laboriously, raspingly—and I thought it the sound of a being which was itself . . . *out of place* in the room of living persons. For one cheering moment, alone in the brightly-illumined bath, I hoped that the Something was as much a victim as I, perhaps as alarmed by what had befallen it as all of us were terrified.

"I so relished my regained security—splashing water on my face and hair, applying fresh deodorant, even a dash of aftershave—that it wasn't until I took a close look at my face in the mirror above the washbasin that I realized my travail was not at an end.

"Because I had no choice but a return trip to bed, and Jennie.

"I saw my chin nod, my face paler now. Then I sought to reason it out and concluded, trying to believe my logic, that light has always been the foe of darkness. It won't kill the monsters of the night but it will hold them at bay. With that in mind, I left on the light, brought the door open.

"And *exulted*, my heart filled with joy! In the puddle of light through the bathroom door, I saw that the shadow was *gone*! The old magic still worked! Stepping back into the bedroom, I ran my trembling fingers over the window curtains, finding nothing bizarre or untoward. The relief I'd experienced previously was as nothing!

"So I fairly danced back to bed, inadvertently sprawling on the mattress. I was immediately contrite knowing that I'd surely jarred Jennie from her sleep. Meaning to caress her arm, reassuringly—to indicate by my silent touch that all was well for another night in the damned house—I put out a hand in mute apology.

"But when my fingertips came in contact with her cool shoulder, I withdrew my whole hand in terror and felt my heart begin to pound as if it might burst from my chest.

"From my lover's side of the bed—although she did not move so much as an inch—there came, quite distinctly, the sound of labored, rasping, entirely out-of-place unfeminine breathing."

Eric raised his pen, peered round his grandfather's old rooms, and shuddered. A moment later, the gasping sounds had ceased and Jennie herself had turned on her side to him, frowning as she sensed the light seeping in from the bathroom. All the glorious feelings of relief he'd already enjoyed paled to comparison with what Eric had known at the moment.

But before he'd quite slipped safely into sleep, the door to the bathroom had slithered shut and the massed shadows between the door and bedroom window were back, more ominous, more substantial, than before.

He found a shovel in the basement, tarnished with rust on the big blade and the stout yellow grip ensnared by ancient spiderwebs. Brushing them away with a rolled-up newspaper, Kasem Chamanan drew the shovel out into the solitary illumination—one bulb dangled at the center of the basement, producing narrow moving shadows—and inspected it. The handle hadn't rotted through.

"It'll do," he said softly, aloud.

When he was climbing the basement steps, holding the old shovel as if it were a weapon, the little Thai paused, startled by his thought.

Perhaps, he reflected, *this is the very shovel that was used to bury it.*

ERIC! she called again, but this time Jennie wasn't sure whether she had shouted aloud for him or simply tried to convey her desperation telepathically. The mound of pale, molded skin—it was working on producing an arm, now, but it was unimaginably too enormous and the sausage fingers that had popped into view were ludicrous—was against the wall now, above her, and she had the impression that it was using the outsized ectoplasmic fingers to try to crawl down the wall toward her. Again, she probed with her mind for the consciousness behind the blob, informing and willing it.

This time she *was* allowed inside long enough to have her oldest, private fears visually confirmed: Senator Adam Baldwin *had* brutally, intentionally, shot her father, Verblin Spandorff, to death. It had occurred in an Iraqi mountain range and there the aging professor/ politician had left Spandorff to rot. For a flash of a moment, Jennie saw the shooting, the murder. Through the sadistic permission of the haunting brain which motivated the prodigious apparition suspended over her head, Jennie was able to see a glimpse of the towering and dignified Baldwin and the carefree little genius who had been her father—saw, as it surely happened, the revolver discharge and the bullet burrow between Verblin Spandorff's eyes and into his brain.

She even saw, in the background of the astoundingly vivid scene, a figure swathed in bandages, or tape, and heard, not with her ears but with some arcane corner of her own fine senses, the words *mumia* and, in a furtive wail as distant as the ancient winds howling over Egypt and Babylon and Sumeria, *Mother*.

The bedroom door crashed open! Jennie, gasping, saw a figure framed there. Then she recognized it as Eric Porter. Simultaneously, she heard a shocking, erupting noise and turned her head and gazed back at the mass drooping down from the ceiling. It had exploded; now, slimy, viscuous slabs of what looked like human skin were running down the wall like melting flesh, like mortal flesh turning to liquid but adhering to the wall. Disgusted, revulsed, Jennie pointed at it for Eric to see.

Then it disappeared and left no stain whatever. All that remained of it was the worst odor Jennie'd ever smelled. But then that, too, was gone.

Eric, indicating that he would believe anything she had to say but that she did not have to say it, lay down on the bed and held her comfortingly, whispering soothing sounds and kissing her. "I know, I know," he said repeatedly, caressing her cheek, her throat, the swell of one breast. "But it's over now. It's gone again."

"I want out of here," Jennie chattered, eyes wide and mouth working. "I want to be where there are ordinary things I understand, where I don't need to figure everything out, where I can *enjoy* life a little, where there *is* life! I want—"

"Sh-h," Eric murmured, helping her out of her blouse. He palmed her naked breasts with his two hands, his lower body across hers now. Almost without knowing he did it, or why, he kissed her lips, her neck, each rising nipple. "sh-h-h . . ."

"And I want *you,*" Jennie cried, suddenly and openly. She licked her lips as if they were dry or she were hungry, starved. Her hands reached, searchingly. She found his zipper, tugged at it and felt inside, freeing him. "And I don't want to *lose* you."

He gasped, surprised by the warmth of her holding hands, amazed by how hot he was in every sense of the word. She wrestled his pants down to his ankles and he kicked them the rest of the way off, then tore at her snug-fitting shorts until they were removed. While she was cooperatively kneeling, he eased away her panties, kissing her small navel and beneath it, anxiously, then, he tugged the undergarments from her eager legs and feet. When she was lying on her back, urging him on, she reached behind her for the bedlamp and Eric slipped slipped out of his encumbering undershorts. He was afire with the heat of his need and, when he fell lightly atop her, her hands and fingers once more reached down to cluch at and manipulate him. He stopped long enough to switch the light back on a moment after she'd turned it off, wanting to look at them in the throes of intercourse. She'd fallen quiet now, as if attempting to command and direct her desire, yet her one hand cupped and the other continued to move feverishly up and down. The light came on and he glanced down, almost ravenous for her.

Beneath him Eric saw a great mass of obese flesh, surging like the sea. Fluttering eyelids with long lashes. The coyest of expressions. It giggled madly and its cold hands squeezed hm remorselessly, painfully.

"*Do* it," Lynn said, bucking against Eric. "*Do* it to me!"

3

Although he searched his memory furiously, Kasem was unable to remember the exact Thai prayer for use when one man, alone, wished to enter the woods at night—and disinter a grave.

It definitely was not the same plea for permission merely to walk among the spirits of stones and trees which he had uttered in the company of Jennie, Peg, and Eric Porter. Then, they'd intended only to pick berries, or flowers; to be one with nature for a while, in friendly communion.

If a man planned to desecrate an unhallowed grave after midnight, he was wise to do everything in his power to propitiate the woods spirits—and the stoic, wise, powerful god who controlled them all. Trees had played a prominent role in the lives of men everywhere, from earliest times: anyone who cut off the branch of a certain tree growing in every woods was certain to part with one of his own limbs. The leaves of the aspen were said to quake because the Christian son of God had been crucified on its wood and aspen had trembled in horror ever since. And in Europe, the spirit of the yew was the guardian of the dead for miles around.

But Kasem Chamanan, fervently anxious to repay his hosts for their hospitality, had left the Baldwin house after midnight to learn who, or what, was buried in the grave they had found and he retraced their path of the afternoon with determination and apprehension.

At first, the going was rough for the little Thai and the flashlight he'd brought seemed entirely inadequate for his frightening task. The beam extended so narrowly that Kasem imagined subtle motion on either side of it, and the beam's range appeared foreshortened, as if black night itself devoured the end of it and might be methodically eating its way toward he who held the flashlight.

Then, as if an accommodation had been strangely granted, the beam widened, its farthest illumination seemed to vault forward among the trees in a penetration that was ravenous, and Kasem felt himself pulled forward more and more rapidly. *I'm a fish,* he thought in a queer mixture of whimsy and terror, *and I'm being reeled in.* Lurching forward, almost running, a question occurred to him: to find . . . *what?*

He came to a stumbling halt in the clearing they had found and, gazing first around and then up, Kasem considered the advisability of turning to run. Fear in the presence of the dead, whether recently made so or, as in the case of the grave at the center of the clearing, a matter of years ago, was unfamiliar to him. But he remembered with a certainty he cursed that the boughs of the trees rising above him like gaunt, gray soldiers had intermingled, not left a generous, capacious gap through which the full moon could shed its luminosity so shockingly. *It's like day here, now,* he thought, but corrected himself. It was like the dawn of the first day of time.

Kasem nodded. He hadn't noticed, in the afternoon, but two trees were nearest the rocky mound of earth. The elder and the willow. Judas, it was said, hanged himself from an elder and people who believed still in the traditional ways knew that lightning could never strike it, or good fortune come to the person who burned it. The willow, he recalled, had been the emblem of misery and grief for centuries.

But what disturbed the journalist even more was the clear presence of crumbled stones strewn on the far side of the plot and a huge, oval rock lying almost as a headstone near one extremity of the grave. He shook his head and raised the shovel he had brought as if in defense or from his own independent, idiosyncratic need. The ancients of his and other nations believed that stones literally *grew* from the earth, that they received nourishment by means of a percipient vein connecting stones with spirits that muttered or cackled in soft crevices of the earth. There were other, less cheerful traditions involving rock, stone, planet. Kasem shrugged them off by applying the tip of his implement to the ground rising slightly above the grave and willing himself not to think of such beings as ghouls again, not when he was in such a woods at night.

Digging was difficult. It was so not only because Kasem continually met with hard-packed dirt that stubbornly resisted his efforts but because—always when he was on the verge of halting his labors—the earth suddenly gave, muscular gouts of obstinate dirt dropping away beneath the shovel as if pulled down into the ground. Kasem was momentarily falling toward the pit he was creating with heart-stopping suddenness. *What I'm going to find was burned to death*, Kasem reminded himself; *it won't be pretty*.

And when he reached a huge, largely disintegrated carton suggesting how hastily the body was buried, he had steeled himself. Parting the crumbling lid of the container and stooping to his knees to look inside, Kasem made ready. Even the sight of the massive skull, whiter than sheets and picked clean by time, or worse, did not cause him to flinch.

He paused, however, when he realized that the great skeletal body which stuffed the carton from side to side had been buried *face down*.

Still, once more guarded and in control of his nerves, Kasem reached for and began turning the enormous skull over with aplomb, unshaken even when he saw a toothy smile on the fleshless head's mammoth face that seemed to extend from east coast to west.

He didn't panic until he saw the hellish red light glowing deep in each of the hollowed eye sockets and the skull began to sing to him—cooingly, crooningly, the high-pitched ethereal voice intoning in minor a child's lament of mayhem, malice, and the joys one took from murder.

The shovel in Kasem Chamanan's hand dropped into the carton when his unnerved fingers unclenched. The blade struck the bones sickeningly with a sharp *crack*! For one moment Kasem was sure the folded white hands would stretch up for him, and he closed his eyes, frozen in place because his brain told him there was no point in striving to run away.

When he opened them, however, looked back into the moist, reeking, submerged container, the bones of the Offspring were gone and what remained—what, in truth, lay in the decade-old carton—was almost as terrifying and even more dismaying.

Two skeletal bodies—the remnant of clothing sticking to the skeletons indicated a man and a woman—appeared for an instant to be a *single* corpse with more arms, legs, and heads than it was entitled to. Blinking repeatedly, cold sweat from his sallow forehead raining down into the wounded earth, he finally understood that what he was seeing was two dead people who had been burned to death and now lay, forever, fused to one another.

"I'm *sorry*, gosh, I didn't mean to scream that way!"

With Jennie at his side, Eric stood on the second floor just outside their bedroom, trying to apologize to his sister Peg and Danny Stanwall and simultaneously explain what had happened. It wasn't working for him. He'd stammered his apologies three times and hadn't found the words to describe what it was like to believe he was having sex with a dead monster.

"Well, shit, dammit," Danny protested, yawning. "Is there anything to be worried about or not?" He'd pulled on a robe that ended well above his knobby knees and the styling of the modern bathrobe gave him the look of someone who was both slightly effeminate and almost musclebound. Two of the Band-Aids protecting his scratched face had come off and the skin on one cheek and temple made him also appear flushed, or embarrassed. Worst for him, he detested being awakened and looked punch-drunk.

"I must've just dozed off and dreamed it," Eric said. Abruptly, he seemed to realize that he still hadn't said what happened. "I, well, I thought I was in bed—making love to Lynn." He glanced at Jennie to see her reaction.

"What a dumbshit thing to dream!" Danny retorted, half-turning to head back to his and Peggy's room. He stopped to wink boldly at Jennifer. "Not the greatest compliment *you* ever got, lady!"

"Did you see it?" Eric asked her, desperate. "Were you at all aware of what was going on?"

"All I remember is falling asleep, just about the time you got into bed," Jennie replied. Clearly, she was as mystified as the others. "I didn't see Lynn. Just you."

Peg rested her hand on her brother's goose-pimpling bare arm. "It . . . wasn't really just a dream. Was it, bro?"

"Fuckin-A, it was," Danny broke in. "Lynn's dead, even if you won't fill us in about the son of a bitch! So how could you see him in your bed, Porter?" He sighed his disgust. "You all have enough frigging imagination to become basketball referees!"

Jennie, who'd found herself standing behind Eric, gasped and pointed to his naked back.

"Danny, he didn't imagine anything," she declared. Firmly, she turned Eric so that the others could see his back. "Something did that to him—and before you make another smart remark, Stanwall, we're not into S & M!"

Even Danny gazed in surprise at Eric's bare back. "Oh, bro," Peg sighed sympathetically. She started to touch him but stopped when she realized she might hurt him further.

Shockingly deep scratches had been virtually carved into Eric's skin over the shoulder blades, at his sides, and above on buttock. They were seeping blood, as if he had been literally clawed.

Eric, as if the identification of the gouges triggered his sensitivity to pain, winced and cried out. Then he turned pale with alarm and revulsion. "I'm going to grab a shower with water as hot as I can stand it," he said, and jogged of up the corridor. "Lord knows what that thing had!"

The power of suggestion. Danny didn't speak the words aloud but he said them, anyway, in the expression he turned sneeringly upon the two concerned women.

Then, at the sound on the stairs, he crouched in fear as if readying himself for a last-ditch race.

But the newcomer trudging slowly down the hallway to join them was only Kasem Chamanan.

"You have your clothes on," Jennie called,

surprised. "Weren't you sleeping?"

"You're all *dirty*!" Peggy added. Then she and Jennie noticed the haunted gleam in the Thai's somewhat slanted eyes. "What happened? Where *were* you at this hour?"

"He's been in the woods!" Jennie exclaimed before Kasem could answer. She looked deeply frightened and her own wide eyes were slitted as if peering into two worlds at once. The truth about the Thai's activities had vaulted into her troubled, intuitive thoughts with no shadow of doubt. "He was . . . digging out there. That grave we found." She stared closely into the little man's newly distant, frightened eyes and penetrated to the terror in them. "I know that's where you've been, Kasem. Who was buried in the woods? Did you find anything in the grave?"

He paused, deciding whether to mention the apparent illusion of an enormous skull and supernaturally shining eyes deep in the sockets, or if he should only describe the truth that followed the illusion. *If it is the truth*, Kasem thought, more unsure and scared than he could remember. "Bones," he said simply, and inhaled deeply. His intelligent eyes focused and refocused on each of their young faces. "The bones of two people, except they were fused together as one." Inadvertently, his gaze settled on Danny. "They'd been burned to death."

"You're scared shitless!" Danny yelled, bouncing with delight and shoving a finger in the small man's face. "You're out of it, man.

You've gone and got the Baldwin syndrome and you're just as fuckin' neurotic as they are!"

"Danny," Peggy murmured, "please . . ."

"Please nothing!" he shot back, laughing openly at Kasem. "This little geek comes here like a know-it-all, full of fancy goddam theories and weirdo crap from some third-rate country that believes in greasy men who attack girls and pussycats that rise up outta their fuckin' graves, and he's no different than *any* of ya!" He looked from Kasem's impassive expression to the women and seized Peggy's arm. "Well, your nightmare's ended, baby, and I've had enough of this late-movie bullshit! I say we book outta here!"

"Dan, we don't *dare*," Jennie said with urgency. "Maybe it would let the rest of us go, but it wants Peggy to stay—and we can't abandon her."

Stanwall glanced nervously from one anxious, pretty face to the other.

"*You* go home, Danny." Peggy peered up at him and gently took his arm. "It's all right. I'll . . . be fine."

He looked down at her in consternation. This was his way out and opening practice for the new basketball season would be starting before long. He was out of condition. He hadn't even stayed in touch with the coach. Maybe this would all be wound up in a few days and maybe he was stuck here for weeks, months. Suddenly, he bent down to kiss the tip of Peggy's nose.

"We'll *all* be fine," he said softly. " 'Cause I'll be here and make sure of it!"

I pray you're right, Kasem Chamanan thought, suddenly exhausted and badly in need of sleep. From the first floor, the organ that was no longer there began to play sweetly, sanely, as if the musician approved of the decision to stay and was rewarding them with a nice little medley of old favorites. None of them jumped at all or even registered surprise.

But Kasem, slipping out of his smudged jacket and shirt, traipsing toward his solitary bed, stopped at his bedroom door and shut his eyes tightly as the clairvoyant thought took shape in his mind: *Not all of us will go home, ever. And one of us is going to die . . . soon.*

4

Following Kasem's appalling discovery of the burnt, buried bodies, which Eric morosely announced were, in all likelihood, his and Peg's long-dead cousins, Bernard and Sue, he grew moodier and more withdrawn than ever. Sleepless now, Eric had taken to prowling obsessively through the old house by night, the *tap-tap-tap* of his cane an ellipsistic comment on the peace of mind which had been finally excised from his existence.

By day, Eric seldom initiated a conversation but tended to spend his time in either Grandfather Baldwin's ruined office, writing in his journal, or alone in the fire-scorched old breakfast nook. There, he consumed pot after pot of black coffee, as if he longed for the protection of Mildred, the housekeeper who had raised Peg and him both in the Baldwin house and in Dayton. Even his sister elicited little response from Eric when she expressed her concern in that same, peculiar, everything-is-surely-all-right fashion that had been her way since her nightmares ceased.

Eric told her, monosyllabically, that he'd been unable to forget the revulsive moment when he had imagined himself sprawled upon the sexually excited bulk that was, or had been, the Offspring. Even though it was a psychic contact, it had been physical, and such proximity to the gross and repugnant being had traumatized Eric. It was that simple, and that pervasive. He made no further romantic overtures to Jennie in the weeks ahead and appeared to age by the day. Jennie, who'd tried to reach Eric, to draw him out, thought that his behavior was similar to that of a prisoner in jail who'd been homosexually raped—or for that matter, to that of any rape victim, since he sometimes seemed not only silent and uncommunicative but strangely ashamed.

And with Eric's apparent surrender to the dark forces manifested in the house of his childhood, and Danny Stanwall's loss of both face and customary peppery vigor, no living person present had the courage either to urge that they go back to Dayton or to suggest a course of action they might take against the house's evil haunts.

Except, early in September, Kasem Chamanan.

"I believe that a seance may be our only way of learning the truth," he told the rest of them at lunch one wet, foggy day. Although he did not make a conspicuous point of it, his lively, often-sardonic eyes turned to Eric, the one among them who might have explained much of the mystery. "Between Jennie's acute sensitivity, however much she hates it, and mine, I feel confident that we can convince Lynn and the other spirits—if there *are* others—to appear. And to tell us what they are trying to accomplish."

Instantly, Jennie stared at Kasem with alarm. She'd never become accustomed to her developing psychic gifts and had no intention of encouraging them. "I don't know anything about conducting a seance!"

"But I do," Kasem said quickly, winking at her and grinning.

"I think it sounds fascinating," Peggy said with a smile that further distanced her from the clear danger to the others. Eric, turning to watch his sister's little-girl vivacity, knew that something had to be done soon or Peg would surely be locked forever in the mold of vague cheerfulness and detached but sunny apathy. She seemed like someone dependent upon Valium. She glanced at Danny and squeezed his hand. "Finally we'll know that the house means us no harm, just the way you've always believed, Danny."

"What can we expect from a seance?" Eric asked, somewhat interested, even optimistic.

"Who knows?" Kasem shrugged. "No two seances are alike. Some produce levitation, with articles of furniture, even people, raised into the air. Other physically dominated seances generate mysterious happenings, like roses that materialize from nothingness, or growths of ectoplasm from the medium's mouth." He laughed. "Since I'm going to be the medium, I rather hope that doesn't occur. It's always sounded gross to me."

"The whole thing sounds gross to me," Danny remarked. "And like the biggest excuse for the power of suggestion yet!"

"Past seances have reported the miracle of heavy objects becoming light as a feather," Kasem continued as if he hadn't heard the athlete's comment. "And the actual appearance of the haunting entity, either looking very filmy, or cloudy, or revealing just pieces of itself. Then there's table rapping, the writing of spirit messages, and—this is what most people attending seances privately wish for—those times when the ghost *speaks* to those present, frequently through the mouth and vocal organs of the medium."

"Isn't that potentially dangerous?" Jennie inquired, recapping a bottle of milk and returning it to the refrigerator.

Kasem hesitated. "Well, *any* contact with the

other side is potentially dangerous, Jen. Whether the visiting spirits are intentionally harmful or not. We're talking two different dimensions, or parallel universes of existence." He grinned. "But I'm a pretty self-possessed, disciplined sort of person. I'd never permit a spirit to assume *complete* control of me. My will is strong."

"If we go ahead with this," Eric said slowly, "when would you want to try it?"

Kasem's brows rose. He looked questioningly at each of them in turn. "What's wrong with tonight?" he demanded.

The five of them sat around the dining room table, in the dark except for the placement of a single candle. Outside the Baldwin house, while there was no thunder or electrical lightshow, rain dripped and drizzled at a rate that appeared coolly calculated and the day-long buildup of fog pushed and huddled against the dining room window as if straining to listen.

Each of them wore black or navy blue, at Kasem Chamanan's suggestion, as much to put them in the mood—another purpose of the single, silent candle—as anything. He'd learned enough about seances to know that it was hard for spirits to come through if everyone approached the rites skeptically. While it was undoubtedly true that most mediums over the years had been charlatans capitalizing upon the vulnerability of the needy and griefstricken, attempting to create a receptive, impressionable atmosphere was just as important to the sincere sensitive. And since this would be Kasem's first attempt at communicating with the dead, he needed as much assistance as he could obtain.

And, for that matter, as much proof as the others required. He knew that if he succeeded only in bringing *apports* into the room—flowers, fruit, anything real that wasn't present now—he'd have truly proved the existence of the other side to himself. Because he'd rigged up nothing, made no attempt to deceive any of them, especially himself.

In a way, it occurred to Kasem as he began to explain the ritual to everyone, he'd almost rather he materialized something than succeeded in making the mysterious Offspring speak to them. Apports wouldn't help them in the least, but a bouquet of chrysanthemums or a pretty bowl of oranges, apples, and bananas wouldn't put anybody at risk, either!

The Thai had prepared for this night the best he could, since they had elected to attempt the seance a matter of hours before. He'd consumed nothing except water, as much water as he could drink; it was part of the ancient preparation technique. During dinner, he'd eaten nothing and had been particularly careful to touch none of the others. In a way, he had come to regret volunteering to conduct the seance and knew clearly now how Americanized he had become. While that change was desirable for many different reasons, he had momentarily forgotten the immense risk he was assuming. Should he literally enter a trance, that xenophrenic state was capable of raising his pulse rate to some one-hundred-thirty beats per minute, which was customary with female mediums, or to the frightening two-hundred-thirty beats of male sensitives. He wouldn't have told the four people whom he was loyally trying to help, but tachycardia was a definite possibility. His pulse could race with such violence that it amounted to beating oneself to death. Ancient Egyptians referred to the pulse as "the voice of the heart itself." And in China, from whence his own people of Thailand had come in droves, the major diagnostic method for millenia had been taking one's pulse.

Now that the hour of the seance had come, and the dining room was darkened, Kasem Chamanan was surprised to discover that, for the first time since his seemingly coincidental arrival at the Baldwin house, he smiled privately. Kasem knew there was no such thing as happenstance. He was able to detect the auras of the other four temporary residents. With practice, he thought, he would be able to detect every pulsation or fluctuation of the dark band one-quarter inch wide, which wound all the way around each living mortal. For the most part, his recollections of what each color of the aura indicated were dim after years in America, away from his native land. But the ill had pale auras, which seemed contracted, and Eric's aura was rather pale this night. Kasem was worried about the youth.

But he was more concerned about the impression he had of persons whom he could *not* see in the room, yet sense: entities that gave off what were called psychic rods, suggesting a horrifying conflux of shapeless evil.

"Four sitters and the half-done medium," he joked, aloud, rousing himself from uncharacteristic anxiety, "isn't the optimum number. It's really best if it's twelve sitters plus the sensitive."

"Look, man, I could buzz over to the shopping center and see about scaring up another eight neurotics," Danny offered sourly. *Jesus*, he thought, *what the fuck have I let myself in for this time*?

"Come on, Dan," Eric grumbled.

"Danny, you promised to behave." Peggy, across the table from Stanwall, spoke in a bizarrely childlike fashion. She shook her finger scoldingly.

"What can we do to help?" Jennie asked Kasem. She had noticed that the little Thai had insisted upon a specific seating arrangement: He was at the head of the table with the women on either side of him, Eric and Danny the farthest away. Under ideal conditions, Jennie sensed, there would be an alternation by gender.

"After Eric says a prayer, as I have asked him to do," Kasem replied, "I would like us all to form a chain. Lapponi's method is what I'd recommend: each of us will touch our own thumbs together, while also touching the little fingers on each hand to the little fingers of the person to our left and right. That includes me. Now, if I've done it okay up until then, there should be a fairly early *response*. From the ghosts in the place. Rappings, as a rule. Or the table could be raised, slightly; tilted."

"What about the need to be careful not to break the chain?" Eric asked, worriedly. "I've heard that must not be allowed." He peered closely at the Thai, a Bible that had been Mama's clutched tightly in his hands.

"Oh, bullshit," Danny muttered, making a face.

"You're absolutely right!" Kasem exclaimed, and smiled at the athlete. Danny looked back at him, astonished. "It *is* bullshit, Dan. Obviously, since our hands won't be locked or linked—just our fingers will be touching—almost any peculiar thing that occurs might cause us to forget and separate our hands. But it will continue." He turned to young Eric. "What you've heard came out of a lot of old movies, Eric Porter. Now. Would you honor us with the prayer you chose, please?"

"This is from *Samech*, in the Psalms," said Eric, clearing his throat: "Thou art my hiding place, and my shield: I hope in thy word. Depart from me, ye evildoers: for I will keep the commandments of my God. Uphold me according unto thy word . . ." Eric glanced around at the other youthful faces, crimsoning slightly because he wasn't used to reading, aloud, from the Bible. "Thou puttest away all the wicked of the earth like dross. Amen," he added.

"Which," Jennie murmured, "means, so be it."

"Amen," Kasem and Peggy said simultaneously, the latter's eyes like blank moons.

Then they all bonded little fingers and turned their heads to observe Kasem Chamanan.

For moments, he seemed simply to have shut his eyes and allowed his chin to droop upon his thin chest. When another half-minute passed, it looked to Dan Stanwall as if the Thai had gone to sleep. He wasn't certain that instant whether he was rooting for or against Kasem.

At the second when the rain began to be harder, when it snapped against the unlit dining room window and the fog seemed to become thicker, Kasem's head went back and he was talking—although no one was sure whom he was addressing: "Cold, I'm very *cold*." All color had seeped from his cheeks and his skin was nearly translucent. "I am . . . traveling . . . I am . . . out of my body, making sufficient room." The closed eyelids were pinched together now; despite the coldness he felt, a fine line of perspiration was forming across his wide forehead. "I am . . . traveling *in space*, alone, *so* alone . . . and cold. Stretching, I'm *stretching* to make contact."

The organ in the front room began to play. No melody; a discordant wail, as if something were dragging an invisible hand mournfully across the keyboard. Elsewhere in the dark house, bells tinkled distantly, eerily. Eric remembered his boyhood experience but shook his head because *this* sound of bells ringing was a remote, unpleasant clamor lacking all musicality or beauty.

"I see," Kasem groaned, "I see . . . clouds. Clouds like the sun, ablaze with light." He appeared to be trying to avert his inner gaze and his face twisted into a grimace. "They pass . . . they're going, *gone* now—the red clouds that signified ill fortune." Kasem moved spasmodically in his chair at the end of the table, frowned. "Clouds," he rasped, "clouds are black, now—black as bad news, dark as *terror* coming . . . or death . . ."

A toilet flushed. Then a second; and a third. Interspersed between the disquieting sounds was the almost subliminal noise of feet running, scrabbling and scuttling from one to another room and onward.

Kasem was on the verge of speaking again . . . when the *fires* began.

Four fierce fires, springing up in the corners of the dining room—miniature red leaves of angry flame that crackled like small bones breaking. Danny started to leap to his feet, to run to put out the fire before it had a chance to spread.

But Eric, knowing all this for show, for prologue and preliminary, clutched Danny's wrist with desperate, remarkable strength. And when each man looked back into the otherwise darkened corners, the fires were *vanishing*. Not going out because of a lack of fuel, but disappearing. As if they'd never existed.

The long-obliterated organ's sepulchral sounds resonated from the cathedral-style living room—in the booming, bass reaches of its supernatural career, then squealing like souls on a dead-run as the treble keys were attacked by unseen, maniacal hands. The organist was pumping the pedals madly, furiously, extending the nightmarish screech of the instrument and making it louder, *louder*, LOUDEST, starting to deafen all of them with its violently discordant cry.

And little Kasem Chamanan was doing his level best to *exceed* the orgasmic organ's volume of terror as, half-rising from his chair at the end of the table, his eyelids momentarily sprung back and he was demanding their attention: "LISTEN!" he shrieked, and the noises from the front room ceased. "LISTEN—TO *ME*!"

They did, Eric and Jennie and Peggy and Danny, they turned to face a man they'd known who now looked unfamiliar, alien to them, as if certain of his features were distended or swollen and a smell issued from his tiny body like that of ozone. Behind and around and seemingly from within Kasem Chanaman, small sounds like voices shouted from the stars—or a black world in the center of their own planet—tittered and growled menacingly and bitterly quarreled. At the nucleus of all that, Kasem was straining from his chair with his eyes tightly sealed shut and a spume of electrical flashes and dashes darting every which way around him. The air around him, his chair, the portion of the table where he sat, quivering, was a cloudy gray now with splotches of black smudges and arrows of red flame burning into and mingling with the flashes and dashes.

"I MEAN YOU NO HARM." Kasem's voice; *not* Kasem's voice. Had he ever shouted, even once? "I—FRIEND." Kasem's head shot forward onto his chest but he forced it back, held it stubbornly, bravely erect. "He's *not*—he's your enemy, he's *evil*!" The Thai's eyes opened, bulged with internal strain. "*Go*, everybody, get *out* while you can!" Kasem's neck twisted, tight as a coiled spring; the veins stood out at the temples. At one and the same time, it seemed that *two* beings stared out at them: one from each eye. "Losing, I'm losing it,"

Kasem gasped blood appearing at the corners of his mouth. "Too *much,* I *can't control* it . . ."

Danny, who'd despised the little Thai, found himself on his feet, moving from the far side of the table toward Kasem. He meant to slap Kasem's face, try to bring him out of it.

But he halted in his tracks, staring in horror.

Ectoplasmic growth was beginning to geyser from little Kasem's straining mouth. A moment later, they saw with still greater horror that tiny streams of it were starting to pool out of Kasem's pores, then from his ears. The journalist made noises midway between garbled speech and a throaty, liquidy gargle; he lifted one weak hand, batting at it as, just for a moment, the essence of Kasem showed in his wounded eyes. The stuff issuing from him was greyish, somewhat more substance than liquid, and it undulated as it puddled his chest and oscillated down into his shirt collar. Danny dared to stick his index finger under Kasem's right ear and then withdrew it hastily, gasping at his finger as if it had been burned, or frozen. Instead of that, he whispered: "It's like p-putting your finger in a spiderweb." But as all of them watched, the psychoplasmic growth started to solidify where it went on curling, gradually covering almost half of the little Thai's body; now, it appeared stickily adhesive, because it glistened in the candle's wavery glow and began to take on the appearance of a beast's recently-chewed-off umbilicus.

"It's horrible," Jennie choked, looking away.

"Look!" Eric cried, shaking her arm and pointing at Kasem. "Oh *God*, Jennie—look at *that*!"

At the point where Danny had unwisely touched it, the vile growth was beginning to dissolve—but the rest of it was first rolling and then snapping, elastically, back into the apertures and pores of Kasem's body from which it had originally issued. It was retreating like something alive.

And while they were trying to adjust to that, to the expression of excruciating psychic pain on their friend's knowing face, something far worse—something infinitely worse than any of them had ever witnessed or experienced in their most fiendish nightmares—started to happen to him.

Kasem's flesh and his frame had begun to swell.

As if his internal organs had elected to begin growing again for the first time since childhood, obliging his body itself—and his limbs—to furnish much greater room, Kasem Chamanan's chest and belly were expanding until he seemed to be carrying a nine-month elephant fetus inside him and his shirt and the top of his pants tore away with a shocking sound of ripping and rending. Even worse, his passive, amiable face and his head also were starting to bulge—from the now-beetling, lunatic's brow and thickening animal nose to the puffball, distended cheeks and a mouth that was swallowed into the ascending, rolling hummocks of fatty tissue.

"LYNN—NOT WANT—*STAY* DEAD. IN LIMBO." The booming, stentorian message surged out of a mouth like vaginal lips. "THIS—FOOLISH FOREIGN PERSON—INTERFERES. CANNOT BE CHANGED. NO ONE —DISTURB LYNN—REMEMBER, PORTERS? *NO ONE*."

Whatever glint of Kasem's very own that had remained in those piggish, crazy eyes had gone out. What illumined the submerged eyes, the constantly-swelling face, was now the color of dried fishblood. The skin of Kasem's face had become so impossibly tight and taut over the burgeoning internal pressure that it began to crack, first along the plump arc of temple, then one entire cheek and jaw. It split free, then, laying back flaps of sallow skin with a sickening sound like that of a zipper being yanked down and the spraying of fine, crimson droplets.

"Get *out* of him!" Danny demanded, feet away from the incredible, ruined thing in the chair. He was seeing himself proved wrong and he didn't care for it. Fists doubled, he stared into the dreadful jigsaw puzzle face from close range. "Goddam you, you fuckin fat freak-show—leave him *alone*!"

Without warning, stunning everybody but the Offspring, Peggy giggled. She put the tips of her fingers over her mouth, regarding the dying

Thai and her lover with big, child's eyes filled with awe, and awful delight.

Jennie, unable to stand it, her gaze moving in horror from one daunting phantasm to another, turned white, then fainted.

Eric couldn't stop gaping at Kasem, or what remained of him. He was as helpless as a spectator at a six-car crash. The top of the Thai's skull chose that moment to open and a gray, mushroomlike substance flowered into view like growing califlower. Above the bridge of what had been a small nose, a line like a razor slice appeared, turned bright red, making the little journalist seem surprised. Incredibly—revoltingly—Kasem's hands suddenly lifted from his lap and locked over the tumorous stomach just as it broke in two. Tubular stuffs like blood-flecked liver sausage surged up, and out, streamed between Kasem's desperate fingers.

"DO WHAT—LYNN SAYS. YOU ALL—REMAIN." The cacophonous words were almost visible, painted in the air in human gore. Kasem was seeping blood now from almost every pore and turning red. The blood washed down over his tree-stump legs, bare in pants torn up to the thighs, and bloated feet. The latter had forced their way straight through the tennis shoes and enormous toes wiggled in the gaps like lizards seeking sunlight. Eric looked helplessly back up the protuberant and grotesque body to the eyes and realized they would pop from their sockets at any moment. "YOU—WON'T STOP ME.

LYNN . . . IS *COMING BACK."*

When Kasem was vacated and his freshly emptied body slid to the dining room floor like a suit of clothing which was far too large, it was Eric who said: "Nobody would believe us. We can't tell the police. We'll have to bury him; in the woods."

5

If there was the smallest quantity of justice in God's master plan for humankind, Mildred Manning Moag knew that she would not be seeing Lynn in the hereafter. Because they wouldn't be going to the same place, not if a mite or morsel of what Mildred had tried to live by all her life was true.

And that made it not only easier to accept the fact that she was surely dying, but pleasant to anticipate. *Maybe I'm no saint,* she thought, in her hospital bed in Dayton, Ohio, *but the most vengeful Maker couldn't be confusin' the likes of me with the likes of . . . It.*

Not that the quiet, expressionless doctors and nurses tending to her had promised her a release in death. They'd spoken contrariwise, mumbled optimistic nonsense meant to cheer her, to bring her back to her feet one, last time.

It was a case of a body knowing the truth once she'd experienced such an "episode"—that was what Doctor Barnett, the old fool, had called her attack—and felt everything inside starting to turn to mush. To slow down, polite-like, as if obligingly giving her a chance to get used to the idea.

Well, Mildred Manning Moag was used to it, all right, and goin' to her reward would be a precious blessing now that she knew she'd never be able to live again as she had before—except that the naked, disgusting, smirking image of the Offspring she'd seen atop that vehicle was surely a warning. A warning, a tease or a threat, that with her own expiration, Margaret and Eric Porter's lives were about to be put to the test by that *monstrosity*!

During her partial recovery when she couldn't communicate with the nurses or doctors anyway, her sound, strong mind had searched for the truth about Lynn's terrifying, unexpected materialization. That the Offspring was dead Mildred could not seriously doubt. Bedfast the fewer than twenty years of its accursed existence, Lynn had been swallowed by flames and no amount of mental hocus-pocus could have conceivably kept the creature from burning to death. That seemed a given, to the aged housekeeper. What she had seen, then, had been either its ghost—or one of those thought-projections of the Offspring's spirit, the sort of terrifying images poor little Eric and Peg had experienced when they were kids. What made the former possible, Mildred had reasoned, was the divine promise of afflictions being removed after death, so that the lame and halt among the living were enabled to rise and frolic when freed of earthly flesh.

But a thought-projection of Lynn's evil soul, somehow able to remain in the Baldwin mansion instead of going to its "reward" in eternal flames, appeared to be much more probable. Everything she had read about haunting revenants over the decades argued that the earthbound were, more specifically, bound to a *single location*—generally that place in which they'd spent most of their fleshly lives.

And the only swift, unerring way the Offspring could have located her, thought the dying Mildred, fiercely concentrating, was *not* as a ghost but as an astral traveler.

What horrors that implied, if she were correct, occupied the old woman's tortured thoughts through much of the summer.

Years ago, when Senator Adam Baldwin had returned from his travels and brought the infant whom he called "Lynn" for Mildred and his own daughter to raise, it had seemed wise, to Mildred, to add a great deal of reading about occult matters to her rather haphazard and romantic study of numerology. Among the topics about which she'd read was that of astral travel.

And while the young people she had raised were, to Mildred's horror, spending several perilous months in that damnable house in Indianapolis, Mildred was dredging from her remarkable memory the details of her study—beginning with the theory that the astral form was the vehicle for the *pathemic* or feeling self, and acted as a sheath for the immortal soul. Sometimes, the ancients had called it the *perispirit*.

For countless centuries, those who knew that reincarnation was a fact had believed the astral body was susceptible to attack by forces of evil; that was why believers rarely instructed the public at large in *how* to leave one's body and travel anywhere at will: it was too dangerous for those who lacked the proper training.

But in Lynn's case, demons coming into contact with its dark soul would have been greeted by the Offspring—recognized as kindred spirits, even enlisted as aids! It would not have surprised Mildred (she realized with alarm) if the Offspring had not only welcomed and enlisted such evil powers, but commanded them, dominated them, to do Lynn's bidding.

And that meant that her Margaret and Eric were probably not only imperiled by the astral-traveling spirit of Lynn, but by other malicious, menacing entities. The house probably seemed overflowing with them—and she was helpless to go to their rescue, as she had when the kids were little!

Once, she had demanded a telephone, called long distance, striven to contact her former charges. But no phone had been installed in the Baldwin mansion and she'd been left to think the rest of it through with a patience she had never succeeded in summoning before in her busy, industrious life.

After dying, the astral body was to emerge on the other side. At that point, Mildred remembered, it would become a thanatic body, from the Greek *thanatos*; for death. But the more Mildred contemplated everything she knew about Lynn, about the strange origins and birth of the Offspring, the more she reached the firm conclusion that Lynn had managed to stop, midway between death and the hereafter.

And how bizarrely appropriate that seemed, considering the kind of being Lynn had been in life: neither fish nor fowl, now and forever.

But how much sense did it make that the Offspring, with such an incredible intellect, with its variety of horrifying abilities only amplified by life as an astral body, would be satisfied to remain what it was? Alone in that foul house for more than ten years, wouldn't it have formulated some sort of plan to free itself from all that had restrained it since its inception millenia ago?

Today, well into a September that announced

itself with dampness that the hospital heating could never quite handle, Mildred was finally able to answer those frightening questions that she'd been putting to herself for months. The realization of the likelihood that she had discovered the Offspring's plan, that she knew the diabolical intent of monstrosity and believed Lynn had aleady begun to act upon it, brought her to her unsteady feet and sent her wobbling across the hospital room to the closet. For her clothing.

She knew that leaving the hospital, now, would surely finish her off, end her mortal days, but the love she felt for the children she had raised overpowered Mildred's own need for survival. Because she had remembered that reincarnationists long ago evolved the well-reasoned theory that a person who came back to life on earth, reincarnated, would have a different astral body but retain the same soul. Did it not seem likely, then, that rebirth, for the Offspring, also meant a new physical shell, an opportunity for Lynn to exist again in flesh but in a far more normal, more mobile body than its soul had ever known?

What that alone implied to the aged housekeeper galvanized her into a teeth-gritting, courageous impression of the Old-Mildred-in-Action. She hadn't dressed so rapidly in years, even if her fingers felt like gnarled stumps of wood.

Because the rest of what she had pieced together was by far the overwhelming worst of it; and twofold. If, to be reincarnated, the Offspring relinquished its astral body in which, ghostlike, it was sadistically influencing the lives of the people present in the Baldwin place, in order to return to the Source of all life, no kind Creator to whom Mildred would ever pray would permit Lynn's warped soul a return to human existence. Not until it had been punished or instructed or reshaped for the sake of simple decency.

But what, Mildred had understood with an enormous maternal obligation to save Eric and Peg Porter at all costs, what if the Offspring had the incredible gall to try to bypass even the will of Almighty God?

She wouldn't put it past Lynn. And there was, Mildred perceived, moving away from her room and tottering up the hallway, one way Lynn might be able to do just that. And if *she,* an ordinary human being, could perceive it . . .

The walls of the antiseptic hospital corridor shimmered, moved, swept upward—up, dizzingly *up*—and became the ceiling. The pain that struck a sick old woman was deceptively less than it had been before, when it had put her in the hospital. Really, it was different this time; there was a warmth to it, a cozy caterpillar feeling at the middle of her being that spread like the hot toddies she'd sometimes fixed for herself to summon and encourage sleep, and the wriggling digits along the sides of the fast fanning-out spider warmth were almost as much tickling sensations as those of ultimately annihilative, killing pain.

There was nothing in the grave at all, the one disinterred by the man whose corpse they'd carried to it in the dark, and while it didn't even strike Eric Porter as strange, he was beginning to accept anomalies the way he'd accepted rain that seemed to come from the clear blue skies, or sixty degree temperatures in February, and only marginally did he still understand that insanity lay in that kind of acceptance—it struck him as a good thing. *Lynn kills one of us and then has the good manners and kindness to leave us an open grave for it, already dug,* he thought in a rattled, bemused fashion as he and Danny lowered Kasem Chamanan's body. He made a small tittering sound, realized he'd let go of his end too soon and the little Thai's head had bounced off the floor of the pit.

"What in Christ's name are you laughing about?" Danny growled. His eyes flashed white from the other side of the grave.

Eric considered the question, couldn't remember. He said what came into his mind: "instant weight reduction." When Stanwall looked perplexed, and angry, he added, "Kasem discovered a sure-fire way to lose weight."

Another bemused sound, part-giggle and part-snort. "He's light as a feather."

Danny started to snap back, but forgot what had annoyed him. "He was like haulin' a empty suit of clothes around," he agreed. A blade gleamed in his grasp. "Look. A shovel." Wonderingly, he hefted it into the air, saw the way the business end of it was framed against moonlight. "Guess he left it here for us to use." He began to cover the little dead journalist's body with the dirt Kasem had excavated.

Eric nodded. Wordlessly, using his hands, he began sweeping dirt back into the hole in the ground. "You're scared now, too?" he asked. Actually, he'd said it flatly, with no hint of a questionmark.

"Never been so scared in my life," Danny admitted, and he sounded more normal than since they'd left the house.

It was infectious. "Then you agree with the rest of us that we're haunted?" The fine edge of challenge was in his voice and Eric felt his head begin to clear.

"Yeah, I have to." But Danny paused in his labors, rubbed the small of his back where digging pains were beginning. "No," he said, changing his mind. "Horseshit, Porter, I don't know. It could be that our own fear has made all this crap happen, in some way."

Eric took the shovel from the other young man and finished the work. He started to pat the dirt down but realized if he did that he might continue slamming the shovel at it until he dropped. "One thing sure," he said, at last, clapping Stanwall's shoulder and motioning for him to return to the house. "Whether we're imagining it or not, Dan, Chamanan's dead. That's close enough to reality for me."

On their way through the dark woods back to the Baldwin place, Eric, manning the flashlight, nearly dropped it. When he'd glanced back, deeper into the stygian woods, he'd seen what Kasem had called a *golek*. Another of the numerous Thai spirits. At a glance, it was a bed-sheet hovering above the earth and moving with unnatural, unbelievable alacrity between the trees—as if it knew every growth in the woods, or needed to fear nothing; nothing at all. Periodically, however, the *golek* went head over heels in a white blur as it rolled on, and on, until it disappeared from Eric's sight.

Is that Kasem himself? Eric wondered. When he heard a shockingly clear hooting sound, and the rustling of cloth moving covertly toward them, Eric began to jog back to the house and Danny Stanwall followed him, occasionally glancing over his shoulder to see if they were followed.

Breaking out of the black-cotton mass of woods, however, both Eric and Danny slowed to a quick-paced walk and, hurrying back down the driveway past the garage, halted at the very normal-looking city street at the front of the Baldwin estate. They looked left, then right; like two little boys being careful to follow Mother's instructions. But they wouldn't be crossing the street, couldn't be leaving the place or leaving the young women behind. Like it or not, fear of spending another minute in the house or not, they had to reenter it.

"That street goes in two directions." Danny sounded emotionless, spent. But he kept on looking left, then right, then left again. "Both of them are away from here."

Eric nodded, said nothing in reply for another count. "And they intersect with other streets, eventually with other roads. Going . . . everywhere but here."

"It did something to Peggy, you know that. Right, Porter?"

"Or it's going to," Eric said softly. The taillights of a passing pickup truck flared as it disappeared into the distance. A block and a half away, an elderly man was carrying garbage out to the curb, presumably for a trash pickup the next day. A puppy, somewhere, was yelping in puppy excitement and enthusiasm. "You're right, Dan. It's about time."

"I ain't goin' until your sister's ready to leave."

"I know that." Eric gave him a sympathetic and appreciative smile. "I meant that it's about time I explained . . . about Lynn, and what happened here, what Grandfather Baldwin was trying to achieve." His chin bobbed as if he were answering a question. "And I *will* tell you all. I'm ready for that now."

"If Lynn doesn't object too much," Danny said, heading back up the walkway to the house.

Eric nodded, and followed. His gaze rose, attracted by something in the distance.

A shape stood at the door to the abandoned garage, many yards from where they stood. Eric thought he knew what it was, and who it was.

Then he was following Danny into the house and there were enough problems there without attempting to deal with the other horrors waiting for all of them elsewhere on the lot.

6

Days passed, and Eric could not force himself to tell the others the story of the Offspring, and the constantly threatened youth spent by his sister and himself. The start of the fall semester at Dayton had also passed, and been forgotten or, at least, went unmentioned by any of them. The bleak, rainy September of Indianapolis was upon them like something damp and disposed to seep into the house, but nobody suggested leaving the city, or the terrible house, behind.

They did not dare to after what had happened to Kasem Chamanan. And after what the Offspring had said through Kasem even while his frail body was blowing up like a balloon.

But Danny Stanwall hadn't forgotten Eric Porter's pledge, and he hadn't allowed twelve hours to pass without reminding Eric. While unread and too physically charged for reflection or unscheduled study, the althlete was blessed with sufficient shrewdness, an uncanny sense of how to get under other people's skins, and he had reasoned that harping on Eric's promise would simultaneously remind Eric that he considered himself a man of principle. Such a verbal attack would never have worked on Danny; he knew that himself. But self-analytical sorts like young Porter, he'd reckoned, could not withstand pressure combined with guilt.

Without any clue of any kind that he'd decided to do it, then, on a Friday night when the VCR stores they'd joined had nothing to rent that they hadn't already seen, Eric asked the rest to join him in the high-ceilinged front room and began, without further prompting, to reveal his deepest secrets.

"I was scarcely old enough to remember having lived with Mama, at all, and couldn't clearly remember Dad," he started. "From what I pieced together over the years, Peg's and my father was only around 'til I was three or four, and Peg was on the way." Eric glanced around at the others, all sprawled in the center of the living-room floor, companionable and "tight." He and Peg were separate. When Eric had begun speaking, his sister had moved quietly to the couch where, without comment, she'd taken a seat facing him. "Our housekeeper, Mildred, assured us that Father was a good man. But we never really got to know him and eventually we heard from Mildred that his father-in-law—Grandfather Baldwin—ordered our dad from the house. When he refused to leave, ol' Lynn gave him an encouraging push. Since Dad didn't contact us even after the fire and Grandfather's death, when it was in all the papers across the country, I assumed that Lynn, well, killed him. Maybe even Grandfather didn't know."

"And the reason Grandfather brought us home, to this place," Peggy said so softly they had to strain to understand her, "was partly because Mama begged him to and partly 'cause he needed kids to run errands for him." Everyone stared at her as she spoke, unsure whether she'd remembered this all along or if it were returning to her mind. "To get all sorts of tough, technical textbooks in a lot of disciplines, from the library. For Lynn to read, and grow." Anger flickered in her eyes. "Grandfather didn't want anybody to get suspicious about the way Lynn could read and memorize five or six books a day, and more."

"I've thought about that a lot, Sis," Eric put in. "I think there was another reason Grandfather had for wanting us here. No one suspects little kids of masterminding an attempt at taking over or reshaping the whole government of a nation. True. But I think the old man was also aware that he looked suspicious. He lived in this big, old house with no one but his daughter—whom everybody thought was, well, crazy—and a housekeeper slightly younger than he. I believe he felt that he needed a better cover, all around." Eric stared soberly at his sister. "I think he wanted us to appear to be a real family."

"I wanted that, too," Peggy said somberly, gazing at her hands.

"Listen . . ."

Everyone turned to look in surprise at Jennifer, who, staring across the half-darkened room, had called out to them in a tone midway between a hoarse whisper and a gasp of shock.

The rest of them, at first, saw nothing. But they *heard* it . . . the mournful, lugubrious, sustained but beautiful strains of organ music. From an instrument that had burned up well over ten years before and which, as they continued to gaze at the place where it had once stood, began casting a deep, quavering, fearful shadow on the distant wall.

"Don't you see her?" demanded Jennie, frozen by attention and by gripping fear. Her arm raised slowly, almost without her own voluntary guidance, the finger pointing at . . . something else, starting to assume rudimentary shape. Peggy made out a bench, dangling legs. Jennie glanced back at the others, her wide eyes enormous. "Don't you *see* . . . the beautiful lady?"

"Mama," Eric said huskily, half-rising. But he

did not dare edge nearer. And he saw—almost nothing.

"It *is* her," Peggy whispered, partly delighted and partly terrified. "It *is* Mama!" For one instant it seemed possible to her that the dim shadow-figure whose ghostly hands moved upon the keys of the transparent organ would keep developing, achieve complete human form, and Mama would be with them again in life.

"I get," Jennie said, barely audible, "loneliness . . . and sickness, of spirit and remembered body. I get . . . guilt; haunting guilt." She closed her eyelids. One tear emerged, wended down a soft cheek like cooling lava. "And—guilt, terrible *guilt*. She feels responsible."

"She needn't!" Eric exclaimed, gaze riveted to the strangely, dismally distant, moving form. "She isn't guilty."

"Responsible for *Lynn*," Jennie finished, and the apparition was gone.

"She said," Peggy quoted, ashen but thrilled, "she loved her precious Margaret and Eric."

Eric gaped at the blank, unprepossessing front room wall where, again, nothing at all remained in evidence. "Mama," he said in a whisper, sinking back onto the couch with Peggy.

"Even the spirit of your mother," Jennie said when she was able, "seemed frightened by

Lynn, so deeply wounded by what was done by Lynn in life that she remains afraid of the monster." Mental pictures of her own father, the Verblin Spandorff she had never gotten to know, came to mind, speaking to her of the reason she had come with Eric to the Baldwin house. "York, where did Senator Baldwin find Lynn? What *were* Lynn's origins?"

Eric observed Peg's gaze as it drifted butterflylike from his face and became distant, hazy. But she went to sit beside him, as if sensing that her failure now to hear him out would leave her always in the dark about their shared sibling past. And he also noticed that his girl Jennie's interest had become passionate fascination; as if she'd waited much longer than their three months in the old house to learn the truth.

"It took me years to pry enough out of Mildred and to read everything written about the famous Professor Baldwin," Eric started afresh. "Plus, matching what I remembered about Lynn with what Grandfather told Mildred." He paused, sure just then that the Offspring was somehow eavesdropping on them and deeply, privately frightened by what Lynn's resentment could do. "Our grandfather, Peg's and mine, was a genius who loved the fresh discovery of knowledge as much as he loved power. I don't know how anyone could be more ambitious." He paused and glanced at the cane leaning against the nearest chair. "And he was so brilliant that he was capable of learning anything. One of his major interests was archeology. I think he felt that, if he knew enough abut the past, he might discover how the rest of us became so dumb!"

"You're your grandpa's grandson," Danny Stanwall snapped.

"I know that," Eric replied, soberly. "I've worried for a long while that I was taking after him, that I might even be, well, possessed by him." When he shook his head, it seemed almost regretful. "For good or evil, I don't seem to have enough drive, enough ambition, to want to dig into every kind of fact in order to improve myself. I s'pose I waste too much time wanting to have fun, and normal relationships."

If you'd been more like Baldwin, Jennie Spandorff thought, keeping her expression blank, *I might have been able to avenge Daddy at your cost.*

"Well," Eric continued, "it appears that Grandfather had a brilliant ex-student named Spandorff who made a really exceptional find in Iraq, before Peg and I were born. And our grandfather realized its importance and decided to take it away from Spandorff."

"I never heard any of this," Peg Porter murmured.

"Yes, you did," Eric corrected her. "Some of it. But you blanked it out. You always believed in family, Sis. On top of everything else, you couldn't accept the idea that Grandfather was also—a murderer."

The girl went pale. Eric grasped her arm, squeezed it. "Go on," Peg said after a long pause. "I'm a grownup now. I can handle it." She gave them all a sad, sweetly optimistic smile. "At least, I *hope* I can."

"It was," Jennie said suddenly, spontaneously, "a mummy he found." It wasn't a question, but a statement. She had seen it and the cave in which it had been placed in an image that bolted before her mind's eye.

Eric's brows raised. Nodding, he said, "The cave which concealed the mummy was atop a mountain that overlooked the cities of ancient Sumer; they had wonderful, mysterious names such as Umma, Sippar, Enki. It was in the Mediterranean basin that civilization was born, and it was Verblin Spandorff's claim that civilization did *not* develop, but was *the product of a single event*." Eric smiled. "He'd notified Grandfather because he wanted to brag, to prove his claim was correct. Apparently, Spandorff was in some ways the kind of man Grandfather was."

"No!" Jennie exclaimed. "He wasn't the same kind at *all*!"

The others, startled, looked questioningly at her. Then Eric nodded. "Okay," he spoke for everyone, "if what you see psychically makes him different, I'm wrong. The point here is that

Spandorff was proving there was *no* missing link between *Homo erectus* and *Homo sapiens*, which is what we are—that *erectus* was, in a way, shocked by a single incident and influenced in astonishing ways by that one event. Since then, just in recent years, a scientist named George Michanowsky has proven that the event took place." Now Eric was afoot, pacing, his keen intellect stimulated and his youthful desire to tease them, to make them all wait for an explanation, again reminding Peg of their monomanical grandfather. Eric's hand reached for the cane, but he startled her by drawing it back, rapidly, and spinning to tell them the rest of his story. "Consider: *before* that astonishing event, people much like us had done nothing to put down roots; they'd invented nothing of the slightest importance. But research and carbon testing show that shortly *after* the supernova called *Vela X*, people stopped being nomads, invented a written language and movable type and rubber stamps —*printing*!—and agriculture! Sumerians devised a progressive system of math, the first laws and schools, a pharmacopoeia! They invented a cosmology, electric cells, even— according to Sir Norman Lockyear—*electric lights*!"

"What was this supernova, Porter?" Danny asked. He was more serious than Eric had ever seen him. "Something like Halley's comet?"

"It was," Eric said, turning to the athlete,

"the most brilliant explosion of light ever seen in the skies. Ancient Chinese credited a sighting of the Crab nebula with inspiring them to structured thinking, but Vela X was four times nearer earth! To the people of Sumer, Dan, it must have been like the world's biggest UFO, but they had nothing whatsoever to compare it to! It's believed that anyone seeing it probably went into religious ecstasy, or went mad, or—not knowing it wouldn't ever happen again—began trying to understand the ways of nature: at an *instant* in time, more than six thousand years ago!"

"What does all this have to do with . . . with *Lynn*?" Peg asked in a whisper.

That second, Eric knew with all his heart that others, unseen, were listening. A shiver of terror turned him cold inside, but he went ahead, too caught up in it to pull out now. And what he had to tell them was incredible: "The mummy"—he leaned toward his sister with his eyes flashing behind the thick-lensed glasses—"was *pregnant*. What Verblin Spandorff called our grandfather to see—which is why he was shot to death—was the mother of civilization. That's the term Spandorff used in his notes that Mildred found, in which Grandfather quoted his former student. And Lynn, six thousand years later, was the first Offspring of civilization—a being who was ready to be born when the mother died and was mummified, not in the way of the Egyptians but those of

Sumerians, who kept the mountain caves perfectly cold and humid for that purpose."

"And Lynn," Jennie said, understanding, "who was supposed to have been born all those centuries ago, became the product of the ancient world, *Homo erectus*, and our kind too."

"Right!" Eric said, plopping down on the sofa. "As Mildred used to put it, 'poor Lynn was neither fish nor fowl.' "

"How the hell was the fetus kept alive all that time?"

"Hold on," Eric told Danny Stanwall. From his billfold, he withdrew a crumpled sheet of paper. Clearly, he'd owned it for years. "Spandorff quoted a thinker named Benjamin Walker as saying that scientists used to believe in a force known as *bioflux*, which influenced both the bodies and minds of animate objects and could be transmitted from great distances. And Spandorff says, 'The energy is diffused uninterruptedly throughout the universe. When it permeates living beings, it emanates from tissues, cells and organs with properties of magnetism and electricity, including polarity. Hippocrates called it *dunamis*, for "power and virtue." Polynesians called it *mana*, Moslems *baraka*, some Indians *orenda*. But Paracelsus named it *mumia*, to describe at once the impulses emanating from mummies and the very essence of life in man.' "

"So much has been lost," Jennie murmured, "that is only being regained."

Eric beamed at her. "What a terrific thing to say! I agree."

"So this *bioflux*, or *mumia*, sort-of sustained the fetus and was an explosive influence of the Vela X supernova—that right?" Danny demanded. He watched Eric nod. "Okay, I can see how a kid born after the longest goddam gestation period in history might be a little weird! But—so evil?"

Eric shook his head. "Dan, I'm not sure anyone is left who can tell us why combining the genes of the past with a modern birth would turn anybody bad—but it may, partly, have been frustration."

"Frustration?" Jennie repeated. "Why that emotion?"

"Because the Offspring was an invalid." It was Peggy, surprising them. As she leaned forward to them, her eyes were saucers. "A lot of it is s-starting to come back," she said excitedly. Then her eyes were clouded and she slumped back against the sofa to bury her face against her brother's arm. "It *stopped*—just like that! As if someone made me stop. I nearly knew, then, what Lynn looked like; but I could only remember that—"

"Yeah, right!" Danny exclaimed, himself excited. "You're always hinting how fat Lynn was, Eric. Wasn't that it?" He wrinkled his nose and upper lip into a perplexed frown. "There must have been more to it than that. He wasn't an invalid because he was a butterball, was he? And was he frustrated only because of his bulk?"

Eric's smile contained warmth but not humor, not levity. He glanced up, toward the high windows of the cathedral-style room, and saw that night was upon them the way it always came in this house: covertly, as if it had secrets to conceal in darkness. It was raining, again; autumn had come once more to the city and Eric understood then why it was called *fall*. So much fell, collapsed, for so many then, or slid into nothingness once summer was spent and the sun hid its hopeful face. Easy to see why, before Vela X, people worshipped the sun. But fall was the prologue to winter—middleage of a year's short life—and it whispered to all who were obliged to listen: "It's ending. It will be over, soon."

"I don't believe," he told Stanwall and the others, rousing himself, "that I have ever referred to Lynn as 'he' or 'she.' " He felt Danny's and Jennie's surprised eyes watching him, an insight of inkling gleaming. He slipped an arm round Peg, who was trembling as her slowly ascending memories rose like graveyard dust to meet the drenching rain of autumnal truth. "Sis and I tried for months and months to learn who or what, Lynn was. But we never had a clue until—when Grandfather was ready to set the Offspring loose upon humankind—he took us up to Lynn's bedroom for the first time."

The room on the second floor reeked, of old sweat and a tart sweetness like garbage left too long at the curb, partly eaten through torn sacks. It was like an operating room, brilliantly bathed in glaring white light, and stacks of books grew in corners like paper trees. The children, Eric and Peggy Porter, saw a complex recording system against one wall along with IBM computers and video display units. The girl-child loathed the way a computer hummed incessantly to itself like a doddering human professor lost in senility or the triumphs of a destructive past.

And there were, the young and gaping eyes discovered, meat bones left upon trays even dependable Mildred could not swiftly enough remove. Bones picked clean and, now and then, nicked by great beastly bites.

There was also a massive bed, draped by an oxygen tent. For a moment, it was partly hidden by the tall, powerful figure of their famed grandfather and some human unwillingness to believe. Then he stood aside and, with a gesture of unexplainable pride, he announced the creature which lay upon the bed: "Children, allow me to introduce . . . Lynn."

It was unforgettable, save when one's memory was mercifully eclipsed. Peg started a scream, quickly stuffed most of one small fist into her mouth—a gesture of automatic courtesy. Eric first saw the creature in its entirity but no adult could have accepted Lynn in that fashion. So he and Peg moved nearer, to look, to perceive.

It lay upon its broad back, legs sprawled, twitching with each intake of oxygen.

And the ambigious, recondite Lynn, wholly naked, seeping sweat everywhere, looked back at them.

They saw more and, in queer ways, less. Picture a circus Fat Man; think of another, and another, another—and combine. Globular toes and swollen feet like pillows; calves the thickness of a man's hips, doubled; Eric's visual tour of horror slowly moved up the enormity of Lynn. He saw tree-stump thighs, was awed that taut flesh could contain it all.

Was revolted by the hairless, baby-pink melons of Lynn's testicles and the absurd incongruity of a tiny infant's penis, three-fourths of an inch of parodied maleness.

And the boy's hypnotized gaze worked upward, swept from side to side in order to experience the totality of the titanic belly and hillock hips lacking any line of separateness—that abdomen spread out like a world, oozing over the edges of the mammoth bed, scarred by road-map stretch marks as capacious as moon craters. The creature's navel was positively imbedded in gross fat.

And just above the cosmic belly were the full-blown pair of perfect, undeniably woman's breasts, ideally proportioned and tipped by petite, pink nipples . . .

What shocked young Eric Porter that revulsive, embarrassing, bewildering moment was that he still did not know WHAT LYNN WAS—especially not when he'd peered closely at the Offspring's Saturn-sized bald head with its quadruple chins, its gash of a mouth with razor-sharp incisors flashing when It grinned at Eric, its cupid's-bow crimson lips, fruity blob of a nose, and above all, Lynn's eyes. Eyes of terrible, impossible beauty, with blistering blue pupils fairly popping from fat-packed sockets, luxurious long dark lashes, and a positive blaze of naked knowing—encyclopedic, unfathomable, emotionless knowing that rocked an ordinary person's mind and soul and threatened to plunge him, drowning, into cerulean seas of merciless, murderous menace.

Then, the Offspring had spoken, briefly: "*I*—WANT—*THEM,*" *it said.* "*TO*—EAT."

"It wasn't just gay, then?" Danny Stanwall demanded, grimacing with repugnance.

"No." Eric shook his head. "It was a hermaphrodite. Which, Grandfather told us, had always fascinated other people. Here in America, Crow and Sioux Indians had *berdache*, boys who had visions and were raised as females. Nomads in Siberia thought hermaphrodites were blessed with the power to control supernatural forces. The Latin sort-of complimented them with the phrase, *utriusque capax*—meaning 'capable of both.' And while Lynn was a virgin, Lynn seems to have believed that and, after dying, to want to prove it!"

"Why was . . . *it* . . . so obese?" Jennie asked softly. She knelt at the foot of the couch on which Eric and his sister sat, needing to be close to them.

It was Peggy who answered, haltingly. Inside her own long-stifled brain, she fought for freedom. "Grandfather used a bunch of scientific terms, but it was a problem with the chemicals in Lynn's brain; something called CCK, which led to pathological overeating."

"Great, Peg!" Eric encouraged her. "Hyperphagia, it's called. I guess it happened because of Lynn's gestation period. During it, the Offspring learned breathing techniques that blocked the neurotransmitters which regulate the breakdown of food." He paused to study Peggy's expression. The look of quick-thinking, exceptional intelligence, which he hadn't seen there for long years was returned along with a flow of information, and he exulted for her. Now it seemed he should have told her, told *all* of them, everything he knew months before! "The Offspring, in some ways, was a marvel, and had the finest brain the world has ever known."

"Fuck, why *not*?" Danny asked, disgusted. He'd climbed to his feet to stretch and to go out to the kitchen for a beer. "The bastard had thousands of years in the womb to do nothin' but think!"

"But is it a wonder that it went half-mad?" Peg said, reaching up to touch Danny's arm. "Think of it! Total isolation!"

"That's right," Eric agreed, sitting again, "but it was an isolation without any kind of education or information. Since it had never been outside its mother, it hadn't even seen another living being. Our grandfather pointed out that all it heard, at first, were the screams of people who'd witnessed Vela X—then silence for all that time. Lynn had to think without language or any points of reference, which made it totally independent and without any emotion for another creature. So it developed telepathy. It heard voices at impossible distances. Grandfather mentioned that the mammoth whale can hear sounds at frequencies from sixteen to one-hundred-and-eighty-thousand hertz!" Eric looked at each of them in turn. "But all it really had to think about was itself. Of course, it was utterly selfish!"

Now Jennie stood, staring miserably down at her lover. "I'm here," she said, "under false pretexts. Eric, I lied to you, from the beginning." She swallowed hard. With difficulty, she met his startled gaze. "I met you on purpose, tried to get to know you, because I wanted to learn why my father was murdered. And I've . . . used you." Tears welled up in her wide, intelligent eyes. "I'm so sorry, now."

"What does that mean," Eric asked, stunned, "that you lied? Who was your father?"

Swiftly, she leaned down to kiss him, then straightened. "My name isn't Dorff, it's Spandorff. Verblin Spandorff was my father."

Eric reached up for her but she twisted away and ran silently across the immense front room, toward the foyer. "Jennie, wait!"

"Give her some space," Danny said quickly, restraining Eric. Awkwardly, he patted Eric's arm reassuringly. "You can work this out."

"She said she was *using* me," Eric said ruefully, but did not pursue Jennie. "Dammit, what does that mean?" He turned to his sister. "I thought she *loved* me!"

"Danny's right," Peg told him, taking his hand. "Let her have some time alone and you'll be able to patch it up with her. Besides," she added, "I have something I must tell you and Danny."

"Is there more of it?" Stanwall demanded,

interrupting. "Because once we wind this up, we can book outta this joint. Looks to me as if Peg's gonna be fine now!"

Eric sighed. "Well, there's just a little more to explain." He started to light a cigarette but, instead, picked up his old cane and leaned heavily upon it. For the first time, he looked as if he needed its support. "My own interest in learning—in trying to better myself—began when I started researching this entire nightmare while I was in high school. I found that in time of Plato and before, many persons felt that the soul was not only alive but free before it entered the womb. Free in the sense of being unfettered by age, or space, or human obligation. If Jung was right and we all possess a common, collective past that can influence us millenia after evolution, Lynn's parents were close to that dawn of humanity, that common pool of influence. Ancient Egyptians, who really came after Sumar, believed that the womb communicated with the rest of the body, and when it was *occupied* by the fetus, it could communicate with its bodily parts and its mother's. But Lynn's mom was mummified! Whenever the fetal Lynn cried out, it was answered only by its own bodily needs—and complete, terrifying silence. But it was kept alive; sustained. It—"

"Eric, Danny," Peggy interrupted them, incapable of keeping her secret for another moment. She looked anxiously from brother to lover, unsure of their reaction but having to confide her great surprise. She reached up to take their hands. "I'm about three months pregnant."

7

"You irresponsible son of a bitch!" Eric exclaimed.

Immediately, he charged Danny, swinging both fists wildly and inexpertly. The athlete ducked, bobbed, and weaved, held up his palms to demonstrate that he didn't want to fight. Without hesitation, Eric jabbed with his left at one open palm and connected with a crossing right to Danny Stanwall's chin.

The punch caught him offguard and Danny dropped to one knee, shaking his head and drooling claret spittle. "Hold it, guddammit," he said, trying simultaneously to clear his head and control his innate eagerness for combat. "I didn't rape your sister, Porter!"

"You knew she hadn't been herself for years,"

Eric snarled, throwing another punch that glanced off Danny's temple but mostly landed on his desperately waggling palm. "It was up to you to take precautions, you contemptible creep! You've been nothing but a nuisance since you got here. Now this!"

"Yeah, well maybe she'd have been all right a lot fucking sooner if you'd used your bossy yap for something other than givin' people orders!" Stanwall was on his feet now, just discovering that he was bleeding from the mouth and genuinely surprised by it. He looked at his blood-stained handkerchief, then at the furious Eric, with admiration. "Now, back off before I take you apart!"

"Kasem already proved what a phony, what a wimp and marshmallow, you are!" Eric taunted him. "Now we've learned just what kind of a man you are! Come on, dammit, fight back!" He flicked out a stinging left that hurt even though Stanwall quickly moved his head away.

"*Stop* it, please—*stop it*!" Peggy strove to move between them, to restrain her brother. "Eric, listen to me, *now*!" She saw his outraged gaze drift toward her frantic face and made her other announcement before either young man could connect with another punch. "It's not exactly Danny's. I mean, not *just* his."

"What the hell does that mean?" Eric demanded. Abruptly, he dropped his arms and turned to his sister with an anguished expression. " 'not *just* his?' Peg, you aren't a dog!"

Now it was Dan Stanwall's turn for fury. "Who else, Peggy?" he asked irately, towering over her. "Who's the other dude? And how can there be somebody else—unless it was the chink?"

Peggy shook her head and her wavy hair shifting was like the motion of golden clouds. "I can't explain it," she said dolefully, honestly, almost in tears. The two sets of masculine eyes were filled now with something close to contempt for her and it was nearly more than Peg could bear. "That night in June when I . . . I felt so peculiar. As if D-Danny and I were not the only ones in our bed. And then, afterward, I knew somehow that my nightmares were ov-over—as if I'd fulfilled my part of some bargain." She allowed her voice to trail away. She was incapable of explaining it better than she had and the childlike inflection returning to her voice alerted and warned both Eric and Danny.

"Let it go for now," Eric said, sighing and shaking his head. He resumed his pacing and his psychosomatic limp and his bespectacled eyes raised inquiringly to the ceiling, in a look of frustration and vast annoyance, reminded Peg instantly of expressions she had seen on Adam Baldwin's grizzled face. *What was it Jennie said*? Eric pondered, and remembered his own remarks about the Offspring and astral travel. *It was as if Lynn wasn't exactly dead. And considering that monster's capabilities, and all that time there was in this house alone, it is also as if Lynn returned to the mother's belly faced with still more isolated years and this house a replica of the womb. So how many new horrifying marvels did Lynn figure out during its second gestation period?*

"Jennie," he said aloud to them, going pale. "Where did she go?" He looked from Peg and Danny toward the foyer. The athlete, taking the handkerchief away from his seeping mouth, saw the reason for Eric's concern at once. "Dammit, she's gone outside . . . and alone."

Eric rushed through the foyer, Danny hurrying after him, and they discovered the front door of the house standing wide open. When Eric took two swift steps forward, he had to throw up one hand in protection. A vicious autumnal wind gusted through the open doorway, and distantly—whether she had spoken aloud or he were receiving her call in some queer telepathic way, Eric thought he heard Jennie's voice, uttering his name.

"Jen, I'm coming!" he called back, as loudly as he could, and realized that moment that she would not have gone out into the rain voluntarily, and that whether she had deceived and used him or not, he loved her. And was terrified for her safety.

Then he and Danny were rushing outside, the

drenching downpour of rain battering their heads. A crosscurrent of vicious wind whipped water across their foreheads and cheeks like stinging lashes from a cat-o'-nine tails. Where in heaven's name had Jennie gone? He and Dan Stanwall shouted her name, again and again; they craned their necks for just a glimpse of her through the lacing sheets of violent rain that came at them abnormally, unnaturally, as if supernaturally summoned. Automatically, they'd headed toward the rear of the lot and, as Eric rounded the back of the house, his nervous glance lit upon the place where something utterly fiendish had happened years before—on another dark night when the Offspring's mesmerism had reached out to decent human minds in order to destroy them.

"Ready?" Bernard asked. He'd helped his wife dress, and pack.

Sue, one breast completely out of its bra nest, gave him a covert, confused smirk. He'd butchered her zipper, torn the material of her dress. "Ready!" she replied. Each of them giggled as if they meant to do some madcap, enjoyable thing together.

They took the stairs to the first floor, moved conspiratorially out to the kitchen and through the door leading to the dark cellar. Aside from them, the house was silent but not all the other occupants slept. Finding what he sought, Bernard nodded in satisfaction and returned to the foot of the cellar steps where Sue seemed to have fallen. Her lovely, ripped frock was also filthy, now; one knee was gashed and it was bleeding copiously.

And for one brief moment allowed by pain, her face raised to Bernard with a look of bewilderment which the husband who loved her was quite unable to read. They had the glint of baffled terror gleaming from their souls, through their dulled eyes, but neither of them was quite himself tonight.

Bernard reached down to lock his fingers in her hair and yank her to her feet.

And Sue smiled, limped after Bernard gladly as he mounted the cellar steps. She trailed small red spots from her cut knee.

Back in the kitchen, Sue even did her part. She located a small box they needed just inside a cabinet door and, chuckling, they left the kitchen and went through the silent house and foyer and thence outside.

It had snowed heavily and their legs were swallowed up to mid-calf. Neither had a topcoat but Bernard was whistling, softly, as they paraded around to the side of the house.

They stopped beneath the Offspring's window. Here, they were out of sight from the street but no one was attempting to negotiate the untended neighborhood streets anyway.

They glanced up with expressions of utmost respect. Neither spoke, but the question was on their faces: "Are we doing this properly?"

Immensely relieved by what they intuited, close to delight that they were behaving in a pleasing fashion, both Bernard and Sue sat down in the snow and wriggled their buttocks in it to get comfortable. Next to the young wife's wounded knee, the snow began turning pink but they didn't notice, or care.

"Ready?" Bernard whispered, again; and when Sue nodded, he lifted the two-gallon can he'd found in the cellar—right where it was supposed to be!—and poured its strong-smelling liquid contents partly over Sue's head and partly over his own. He tried hard to make sure it came out even, that he didn't get more of it than Sue did. Dutifully, he shook out the final few drops above Sue and it ran down one soft cheek to her long throat.

Sue smiled at him, even though some of the gasoline had gotten in her eyes. They were, she knew, an adorable couple; petite midwesterners with a sense of family obligation, civic duty, and never an inclination to stir up trouble until they'd come to Indianapolis to visit cousins Eric and Peg and their mother. It was only right that they pay for intruding, it was only proper, and Christian, to accept their punishment with a smile. Besides, they'd been told how much fun this would be!

"Love ya." Bernard watched as Sue rubbed the

gasoline into her bare breast, her arms, the wound on her knee, and felt distantly intrigued, aroused. But that moment of normal desire slipped away at once and what was left was this ancient ritual of anointment he'd been asked to perform, with Sue. He knew it was a fine, proud chance and his heart filled with joy as he reached out to exchange a kiss.

"Love you!" Sue said promptly, almost curtly, the way she did when there were things she was busy doing. Bernard nodded and watched as she opened the box she had removed from the kitchen cabinet, sharing another busy little smile with her.

But the culmination of Sue's fun-punishment and Bernard's ritual honor wasn't as easy to achieve as either of them had believed. Sue found that gasoline was greasy and, despite the fact that she labored with intent, mindless concentration, spilling things from the box into her lap and Bernard's, she began to wonder with panic if she'd ever succeed in striking a match.

"Come on, darling," he prompted her, keeping his voice low so he wouldn't disturb the individual in the bedroom above them. "Time's a-wasting!" His eyes gleamed with the affectionate but patronizing gaze of husbandly tolerance.

Then Sue was breaking into a smile as she realized, dimly, that she'd located a dry one. "There!" she said exultantly, and the kitchen match flared.

A face as wide as a human chest appeared at the window above the swiftly incinerated couple. It appeared, among many other things better undescribed, pleased, and proud. The last two Christmas ornaments in town were burning brightly and not making the slightest annoying sound.

The abundantly lashed, rather beautiful eyes stoically regarding the terrible scene in the melting snow belonged to the first sensate creature to recommend human sacrifice; it had merely never had the opportunity to do so until now.

Did Jennie's unannounced departure, her rush from the house as if propelled by guilt over her own deception, mean that the Offspring still had such power to seize the control of living persons' minds, and destiny? Eric didn't know, as he jogged with Danny through the downpour and toward the abandoned garage, but it began to seem that way.

And if Lynn *could* direct them against their own will, where would it end—who could defend himself, or herself, against such power? How would he or any of the others be able to perceive the difference between fact and horrid fancy, grim-enough reality and the worst of fantasy?

Even this cannonading wall of rain into which the two of them were running to find Jennifer Spandorff might, Eric realized, be nothing but illusion. For all he knew, perhaps they were all still sitting in the front room, or lying in their own beds, and this was a punishment for the way Eric had finally told the others the truth. How would he be able to tell otherwise? Maybe Kasem Chamanan was still with them, and had not died at all. Maybe it was still June and they had just arrived at the Baldwin house; *maybe anything at all that Lynn chose for them to believe if the Offspring not only retained, in death, the same powers, but had increased them—multiplied them to the extent that maybe Lynn intended to pick up where Grandfather Baldwin left off in attempting to overthrow the governments of the world, and this was mere practice!*

Such notions, Eric saw as he sought to penetrate the pouring rain with his myopic eyes, were self-destructive, ultimately worse than anything the Offspring could do to people whether It was dead or alive, or somewhere in between, because believing that one was damned, or doomed, led to total inaction; and inaction was what truly caused the breakdown of both civilizations and individual lives, regardless of what anyone else thought. The people or the person who let things happen, without raising a finger, under the assumption that defeat was already certain, were fulfilling their own dark prophesies, acquiescing to the victory of whatever dark forces wished them to accept such nonsense.

It could all be traced back to the difference between reality and fantasy, and Eric knew, then, that it should never be a case of preferring one to the other but a case of stressing the ultimately vital need for a balance between the two. Madness might be the product of an imbalance, might not, but evil was certainly its product, and it began not with mistaken actions or deeds but with the inability to act at all.

Now the constant spray of rain was piercing and coming at the two young men almost horizontally, as though fired at them from one nest of diabolical water guns trying to drive them back, and away. It hurt when it struck their faces, it seemed almost to burn and blind, and still they'd seen nothing of Jennie Spandorff. "Dammit, Jennie," Danny Stanwall wailed, himself a streaming, shadowy image at Eric's side, "where in Christ's name are you?"

"*There*!" Eric stopped, dragging at Danny's arm to pull him to a stop, too. He pointed—

At the deserted garage where a slight female form, coatless but standing upright—as if other-motivated and having no need for normal human sight—was paused at the door to the garage, apparently waiting for them.

"Jennie!" Eric called, his voice snatched-up and whipped across the remaining distance to the woman he loved. "Jennie, we're coming!"

"We'll be there in a minute," Danny grunted, starting to run toward her. He wasn't moving as quickly now as Eric and grabbed at the latter's arm. "No need t'kill yourself gettin' there. The garage is locked, remember? She can't get in."

Nodding, Eric matched his pace to that of the athlete.

And the two of them saw Jennie Spandorff reach out to the garage door and open it, effortlessly!

Eric reached the garage a step ahead of Peg, gasping. "Shit," he swore, "there's a new padlock on the door! We can't get in."

"There's got to be a window!" Peg, pert, bright Peg, joined her big brother in trying to find one that was unlocked. "try this one!"

Pounding over to her, Eric hefted mightily and reddened. "Aw, it's locked too," he said with disgust.

Little Peg heard his note of despair. They'd run out back to hide from Grandfather, who would surely punish them for breaking ol' Lynn's window with a snowball. "Try it again."

Eric did. With a screech, the window rose several inches, the interior of the garage instantly smelling musty, old and unused.

Peg was inside first, boosted there by her brother's cupped hand. Despite their heavy winter clothes, each child was miserably cold. Eric dropped to the garage floor, glad to be in from the terrible Hoosier winter.

To their surprise, it was flooded with light when Peg flicked the switch—and what they saw before them was an old four-door Chevrolet, deserted and badly rusted out. Their father's, they guessed; but if so, how had he left when Lynn ordered him from the house? "If it was Dad's," Eric said thoughtfully, rapping on the hood and fender, then kicking a tire, "it'll be ours someday. Still in good shape."

Peg was peeking into the closest car window. It was frosted but her brother, joining her, mopped at the window with the elbow of his overcoat. "What is that?" Peg asked.

She indicated the backseat. "What?" he inquired.

"A blanket. It looks lumpy." Peg's eyes became round, bright buttons. "D'you suppose it's something Daddy left for us to find?"

With no answer to that, or, as it was commonplace between them, Peggy Porter's insatiable curiosity, he decided to work his arm into the scant few inches of open space in the car window and seek the vertical lock release.

Suddenly, there was a tiny snapping sound and Eric was glancing back at her with pride and delight. "You wanted to see what was in the car, didn't you?" he demanded.

Then he ignored his sister, opened the rear door, and reached out to pull the blanket away.

Little Peg's view was completely blocked by Eric's back, but she felt him tense, from head to foot. He began making small, strange sounds and then she saw him thrash out with his arms. As if trying to regain his balance, or to chase something away, banish it from all existence.

"What's Wrong?" Peg cried.

And her brother came bolting backward out of the backseat, badly frightening Peg. Eric was rolling on the dirty floor of the garage, to put as much distance between the automobile and him as humanly possible.

"Stop it, Eric," Peg told him in angry terror.

And he was somersaulting to his feet, eyes round with horror as he panted into her face, "Don't look inside!" He'd taken a step forward as if to move between the car and Peg but stopped at once and was edging away, motioning for her to follow him. "Don't look inside!"

Little sister looked.

For one long moment, Peg believed that she was looking down at a creature carved from black stone, with a mammoth head and four dead and gaping eyes.

But it was the bodies of Bernard and Sue, her cousins, and they were fused by fire until their heads had become a single, charred skull.

"Come away, come away," Eric called from behind Peg, but he hadn't moved near enough to snatch at her and drag her away. "Come on, come on!"

Part of Bernard's face was unburned and

affably expressionless beneath a patch of similarly unharmed dark hair.

But most of the flesh of Sue's sweet face was gone so that splotches of off-white bone emphasized the general charcoal motif. The one, unblemished dead eye stared at Peg, or seemed to. It made Peg think of a black olive sitting on colorless lettuce. Of a horsefly grossly dead on a white sheet of paper.

"Let's go!" Eric. She knew it was Eric, knew he didn't matter, she didn't matter, these things *in the backseat of her daddy's car hadn't mattered, nothing mattered so long as ol' Lynn lived. But the cousins were interesting, in a way, just fascinating to look at and go on looking at 'cause—'cause—*

Three sticklike fingers were raised to Peg, she saw just as she was on the verge of turning back to her brother, groping afresh for sanity. One of the cousins was bidding her a sad adieu, but it was impossible to detect which one's ghastly digits were lifted in macabre farewell. The fourth finger had apparently burned off somewhere enroute to the garage and the thumb was a teensy white nub, as if only the first joint had cooked and fallen off. Peg shuddered.

And the motion of her frail body against the backseat made one of the blackened arms snap off and fall to the floorboard of the car, the fingers caressing the calf of her leg as the arm thunked, pointy bone aimed at Peg like some Australian native's supernatural weapon.

Then other fingers broke away from the big fused body. One of them rolled out of the Chevy as if in pursuit of Peg.

And she'd run with frantic, panicky terror with her big brother Eric toward the place all children go when hopelessly scared out of their wits, their screams of mind-teetering horror carving the night as they rushed toward their confrontation with the Offspring.

Their first confrontation with It.

Jennie Spandorff looked like something mechanical; a robot, or an android.

They were almost up with her when, to Eric's renewed fear and horror, she stepped dreamily into the deserted garage.

8

Eric, with Danny behind him, stopped just inside the door of the old frame garage and spoke Jennie's name once more, in little more than a whisper. She should have heard him but she did not seem to, nor did she appear to have been harmed. She was walking directly but slowly toward the dilapidated, discarded car that once had been Eric's father's, as if drawn to it, invisibly. The old Chevy did not, at a glance, look appreciably different to Eric than it had when he and Peg, as children, found the burnt bodies of cousins Bernard and Sue. By the same token, however, it looked older and more rusted out, enough so that there was nothing weird or supernatural about it.

At first. Because, while Eric and Danny stood

watching, uncertain whether to dart forward and awaken Jennie from her apparent trance, the interior of the garage, scantly illuminated by light that pierced the driving rain outside and periodic flashes of distant lightning, grew lighter. For a moment, neither young man was able to determine the source of illumination. It simply widened, and deepened, until most of the deteriorating building was bright enough to identify human features, if not to read by.

Then, the youths realized simultaneously, they understood the origin of the light and Eric, who had spent minutes of hell inside this garage, gasped and steeled himself to dash after Jennie and draw her to safety: *The luminosity was provided by the interior lights of the car itself.* From one standpoint, there was nothing unusual about it. Automotive lights in good working order could conceivably have pushed back darkness to the same degree, if the doors of the vehicle had been open. But they were not, and, staring at the filth-fleshed windshield of the Chevy, Eric and Danny perceived that the lights were no brighter, no harsher, inside the car. They weren't harsh at all. Indeed, they glowed, modestly, beckoningly, as if someone they could not see, in the interior of the automobile, controlled the lighting.

And there was no living thing inside of it, unless he, she, or *it* was crouched on bended knee behind the vehicle's dashboard.

"If it starts, if that motor turns over," Stanwall said under his breath, "I'm out of here!"

"Movies," Eric murmured, deciding at last to sidle toward his girl. "That's movie stuff." And he took one, firm step toward Jennie.

The unmistakable sound of a car door being opened, from inside, froze him in place.

Burnt-twig fingers; heads and bodies fused together; fingers falling away and rolling—all that and more went off in terrible images in Eric Porter's memory. Heart racing dangerously, he waited for the charred *thing* that cousins Sue and Bernard had become to come lurching out of the car, toward them. But Kasem had found their *skeletons*, Eric recalled. They were good people, decent folks. Surely they'd gone to their reward over ten years ago. *Ghosts are ghosts*, those three words rocketed into his frightened thoughts. The car door creaked all the way open.

And the hypnotized Jennie Spandorff and the terrified young men saw a towering, gelatinous mass come floating out of the old Chevy, a yard and a half from the young woman. It began materializing at once but seemed inept at it, unpracticed. Portions of a face, a torso, legs and arms flickered like the film in old silent movies, on and off and, in different anotomical locations. And it carried something, where the hand should have been, and would be when the apparition got its act and its parts together—

something that looked somehow more substantial, more real, than the rest of the segments coming haltingly together . . .

Grandfather! Eric realized, shocked and awed and unsure of his emotions . . .

"Lynn didn't live through any *of our times," Eric said, trying to take advantage of this rare moment when Senator Adam Baldwin was conversant, when he appeared willing to begin explaining his and Lynn's intentions for the world. "So you figured there was no one better to judge what happens to us?"*

Grandfather had been overjoyed. "Precisely!" he declared. "You follow me admirably, Eric. Who else could be as objective about modern man as a being created before *our time?"*

There'd been an answer to that, or objections. Something about the Offspring also not having experienced any of the times when modern man did worthwhile things, and a spirit of communion and community made humankind one for a short, meaningful moment. But it hadn't mattered, Eric knew, that he couldn't quite express himself to the old man. Grandfather had lost all the belief he'd ever had when the world refused to let him take it, as scientist or president; but he'd rebuilt his own belief system and invested all his faith in the Offspring.

"With Lynn's freshness of approach and viewpoint," the old man went on, "all that indescribable latent ability to devise new realities beyond our wildest dreams, there was also an insatiable hunger for knowledge which I can describe only as God-granted. Lynn began consuming facts, data, theories, of every variety, devouring books and disciplines, each and every aspect concerning the entire body of man's organized information—and always, I furnished the guidance and pointed the direction, while Lynn saw with dazzling clarity where civilizations failed! Perceiving perfectly what must be done to establish a genuine order based upon logic and peace in this contemporaneous world which is simultaneously Lynn's prison, and toy!"

And when Grandfather had grown angry at both Peg and Eric, then at Mildred, their housekeeper and governness, he'd amplified his views about those "secrets in the emotional hearts of those who control the destiny of this planet." "Lynn finds it laughable." The old man had promised those who cooperated with Lynn and with him "a chance to be lieutenants in our scientific army of the future—or we can give them fear." That was the choice everyone would be making.

It was Mildred who understood before Adam Baldwin admitted it that what he and Lynn planned was making it "unnecessary" for anyone but geniuses to be born—or permitted to live. "Only for a while," Grandfather had temporized, "until the population decreases and all people know how to limit the number of their progeny." He'd told them all, that astounding but awful night when Eric and Peg met Lynn, that people would come around, would learn to love the Offspring. "The average citizen despises computers, doesn't trust the government. But Lynn is human, yet reasons the way a computer reasons! Lynn is honest—immovable by lobby, beyond bribe!"

And it was moments after that when Eric had seized his grandfather's cane and poked a hole in the life-sustaining oxygen tent enclosing the brilliant monstrosity in the double-sized hospital bed.

But Eric had not remembered his part in it, until now; he had not understood until now, as the shade of Senator Adam Baldwin gradually assumed shape at the side of the aged Chevrolet, that it was he who had in effect, killed the Offspring and wrecked all of his grandfather's cherished plans!

He shrunk back in mortal fear, away from the apparition, from Jennie too, and saw, grasped solidly in the old specter's filmy hand, the cane he himself had used to deprive the Offspring of its life-sustaining oxygen. The degree of hatred Grandfather surely felt for him now, the extent of his malice and desire to get even, seemed incalculable to Eric Porter, almost more frightening than the Offspring's constant threat, because Eric had never accepted the androgynous Lynn as an authority figure.

It didn't occur to him at all that the dark spirit of a man such as Senator Baldwin would surely know there were better ways to bring torment and misery upon a young man like Eric Porter than personally and directly inflicting pain upon him.

But was this, this gaunt horror of a ghost, what remained of distinguished Adam Baldwin? For Grandfather, while balding, had retained an enormous masculine dignity that, combined with his considerable height and powerful torso, added up to the kind of handsomeness and charisma that had enabled him to run for the highest office in the United States.

Hovering above the dazed, disoriented and vulnerable Jeniffer Spandorff, quiet as the grave yet with haunted and haunting eyes that still blazed his detestation for the whole human race, Grandfather's horrific shade was a caricature of what he'd been in life. From the dully gleaming, pasty skull to the kind of shoes morticians foisted upon grieving loved ones, the apparition was maggoty, a worm-eaten remnant of mortal corruption, the best argument for the

Golden Rule and against self-serving sin Eric had ever seen. Holes were scattered all over the craggy countenance, as if Grandfather's pores had opened and spread like cancers, but from most of them small insects squirmed in hiding or extruded pearly, blanched little heads alive with miniature rows of glittering teeth. Scraps of parchmentlike skin were rubbed or rotted away from bone, at the corner of the wide shark's mouth, over one sallow cheek, and under an ear that was nearly chewed away and seemed to flop whenever the ghost moved its immense head. Instead of looking broad-shouldered, erect, Grandfather Baldwin's phantom seemed stooped in malign threat, and the undeniable strength it projected so clearly came not from human muscles that had waged a winning war against the inroads of time but from the old man's ultimate capitulation to the power of evil. Redolent about the apparition was the stark and covert kind of obvious menace that sometimes showed in the living human face but only when such a man no longer concealed his clear and murderous intent—because he had already experienced and fractionally survived the punishments of the damned and was one, now, with those who had meted it out.

Eric had seen Lynn. When once exposed to absolute, repellent monstrosity, anything less than that was, in terms of sheer capacity to terrify or revulse, a grotesque fascination of the moment. What gripped Eric that moment wasn't his dead grandfather's Grand Guignol guise as a shade but the way Grandfather first twisted his cane lovingly between his milky hands, then brandished it, and now began to lift it above his head, all in such stony silence that Eric was able to hear Danny Stanwall's incoherent mumbling and the frantic throbbing of both their hearts. For one second more, Eric was too horrified by the sight and threat of the cane his grandparent had leaned upon in life to realize that the old hoodoo was no less purposive or self-serving than he had been in life.

Then the cane, clutched by both of the specter's hands, was poised directly over Jennie's unflinching head and both Eric and Danny Stanwall realized for the first time that he fully intended to *use* it—on Jennie!

"Grandfather," Eric whispered, trying to raise the volume of his voice. "No. Don't hurt her. Please—*don't*."

Adam Baldwin's ghost, for the first time, looked toward his grandson and recognition was merely the most readily accepted expression in eyes that were more vacant sockets with reddish orbs shining from the brain itself than the eyes of any human being. The word *Demon* wriggled and then shot through Eric's mind and he knew then that this was truly his grandfather's spirit, but that Adam Baldwin's soul was no longer even remotely human. When Eric began to blink, as if disbelieving the evidence of his own sight, the shade of his grandfather nodded its head in curt acknowledgement and then, as if it had no other option or choice left to it, returned his forbidding gaze to the dreaming and mesmerized woman standing passively beneath his uplifted stick.

That was when Eric understood that the vengeance to be served upon him would be bestowed indirectly through Jennie. For another moment, the grandson strove to gather his wits and courage. At any second, it would be too late. But this was still, in the most hideous of ways, the grandparent whose word had been law in the Baldwin mansion during Eric's formative years. Trying to attack Senator Baldwin that instant was tantamount to defending Jennie against one's first grade school principal, a commanding officer in the military, even God Himself.

The brandished cane was at its farthest rise above the dead and living heads of Grandfather and Jennie Spandorff, trembling tensely there, ready to descend with all the real and otherworldly might the old phantom possessed.

When, shouting that there was no such thing as a ghost, Danny Stanwall was rushing past Eric and the dark-haired woman to dive, pellmell, at the haunting titan.

Grandfather's cane came down with the power and authority of an evil divinity. At that moment, Eric acted, pulled Jennie out of harm's way.

And the great, sturdy cane crushed Danny's neck, behind the head, the driving force so cruel and so mighty that the cane itself seemed to split, and the young athlete was knocked face-first to the garage floor. "No!" Eric yelled, too late.

And Grandfather's glittering black eyes stared mercilessly into the youth's bespectacled eyes . . . and Grandfather smiled, broadly, the rotted stumps of his ectoplasmic teeth exposed in an expression that was the most sinister Eric had ever seen. Grandfather was reversing his grip on the cane so that he was able to pummel Danny's exposed head with the blunt, unbending grip of the stick. "Stop it," Eric shouted, running toward the heavy-breathing specter; "Leave him alone!"

But something unseen rose before Eric, halting him, obliging him to see . . . the *rest* . . . of what Adam Baldwin's ghost did to the motionless head of Danny Stanwall.

There's nothing to fear. Grandfather spoke, with a mad strain that tore the corners of his spirit mouth until the things existing in his ruined face squirmed and crawled upon his cheeks and over his bloodless lips, words he had uttered to the Porter children long years before. For the first time, Eric saw that the ghost was quite mad, and saw the cruel justice that what

Senator Baldwin had prized most, his own soaring intellect, had been taken from him for eternity. *This is a time for celebration, children*! Incredibly, revoltingly, the mad phantom was laughing and viscuous tears of yellow, like pus, were rolling down his nightmare face. *It's over—and it's just beginning*! With chortling sounds like railroad cars backing up, Grandfather reached out with taloned hands for Jennie, but Eric drew her away. *Allow me to introduce—Lynn*!

Then, with no warning, parts of the apparition began to wink-out like black stars being swallowed up by universal night skies. The entire, stooped body shimmered in streams of twinking black light and most of it was gone in a second.

The last to go was the cane, soaked with Stanwall's blood. Grandfather had dropped it beside the corpse and Eric and Jennie, glancing down at Danny, saw that the back of the head had been completely hammered away and what remained was a pulpy gray mass with veins of pretty pinks and crimsons. The cane shot into the air, dripping; it was suspended there for a moment and it, too, had vanished as if it had never existed.

"Are you all r-right?" Eric tilted Jennie's chin so that he could peer, with infinite concern, into her wide eyes. "*Jennie*?"

"I am." She pressed her nose and cheek

against his face, fleetingly, then pulled back to stretch her neck and spine. Color was starting to return and she was able to stand without support. "I *think* I'm all right."

"Do you know what happened here?"

She nodded. "I remember everything from the moment that"—she hesitated, groping for words and frowning. "Was that your grandfather?"

"It was. What's left of him." A cold spasm ran down Eric's neck and back.

"It was so horrible." Jennie wrapped her arms round herself, starting to shake now. "I saw what he meant to do. To kill me, just the way he murdered my father in Iraq. I saw you and Danny try to help, to save me." She indicated the athlete's body with a nod of her head, but her eyes were averted. "The poor son of a bitch."

Eric nodded. He thought, *Danny was like most of us. Made up of so much, most of it decent enough at heart and all of it shaped or warped by the way we have to grow up*. But distrusting himself to say anything without overpowering emotion, he turned Jennie and himself away from Danny and the dilapidated old car and started toward the garage door.

"I'm sorry I deceived you," Jennie said, shakily. "It wasn't like that after we . . . moved in together. I—really liked you a lot, by then."

"And I'm sorry I started to blow," Eric

replied. "Do we have a chance?"

She gave him her lopsided smile. "I don't see why not. Once we're out of here, we've already managed to make it through more than most people—" She stopped, surprised by Eric's expression. "What is it? What's wrong now?"

"My grandfather never said anything without a purpose," Eric answered grimly, "and I don't think he'd begin now, even when he's mad as a hatter."

"What do you mean?"

He faced her squarely at the garage door. "What he . . . said, in that eerie, crackling voice—he was quoting things he'd said to me before. Why, I don't know. But he was introducing us to Lynn, all over again!"

Jennie shook her head. "I don't follow, York."

"Jen, I think that's exactly what Grandfather was doing: Introducing us—to the way Lynn is now!"

Jennie groaned, turned toward the door. "Of course," she said, her low voice filled with anxiety and understanding. "Of course!" Her eyes were simultaneously furious and filled with concern as she glanced at Eric. "It wanted me out here! IT lured me out here, Eric, so it could get at your sister without any of us in the way!"

Cursing, Eric threw the door open.

But behind the two of them, the old Chevy

door slammed shut with a report like that of an antiaircraft burst and the lights in the car went out, plunging them into darkness.

9

By the time Eric and her lover had been gone four minutes into the miserably rainy night, Peggy Porter was virtually convinced she would never see either of them again. Being a modern young woman who had trained her conscious mind to be glib and accept anything she stored in it, she'd told herself that both young men would return any minute and imagined that she believed it. Any other consideration was simply intolerable, and Peggy's recovery of her old aplomb or poise was too fresh, fragile and tenuous, to think of being alone. In the Baldwin place, or life itself.

Besides, Jennie What's-her-face had lied to Eric and very probably intended still to kill him, if she got a chance. She was the most independent female Peggy had ever met and she was quite capable, Peg also believed, of looking out for herself.

Until Jennifer's sudden confession, Peg had rather looked up to her for those same qualities for which she now condemned her. While Verblin Spandorff's daughter was much older, practically thirty, an age that seemed little different to Peggy than forty-nine, or sixty-three, she was marvelously well-preserved and really appeared scarcely older (in Peg's view) then Peg herself. Besides, Bro had liked her, and that had been enough.

But *using* Eric, making him fall for her—even if she had the best reasons in all the world—and causing his beloved, goofy face to seem so shocked and unhappy was one of the cardinal sins in which Peggy Porter still believed. Nobody hurt her Bro if she could do anything about it! And when you really took a close look at the Spandorff bitch, a person saw a lot that didn't immediately catch one's eye: Kasem Chamanan, for example—by what right had the bitch asked him to their house? Worse, the Thai had been killed, right in the Baldwin and Porter family home! And if the police ever asked any questions, Eric could be in a perfectly ghastly mess! All because of Jennie What's-Her-Name!

Peggy washed the few dishes and glasses they had dirtied during dinner and the period when Eric did his best to tell everyone everything he remembered about growing up, Grandfather Baldwin, and Lynn. That had been so sweet of him, and, for a second, Peggy'd sensed all her memories starting to take form, only to meet some kind of mental block, and start to shred. But she'd made progress, she was sure of that, and all because of Bro, her Bro.

Going upstairs to lie down until Eric, Danny, and the bitch got back, Peggy sighed heavily and began to feel that she was slogging along through mud—psychic mud. Before this night, she'd been reasonably content most of the time, although vague and not quite herself and, of course, increasingly anxious to tell the menfolk that she was pregnant. She hadn't meant for a minute to say what she'd said about being uncertain that the baby was entirely Danny's, and now, walking heavily up the hall to her room and Dan's, she felt vague again and confused about the truth, or accuracy, of what she had said. Pregnant women always got neurotic; Peggy had heard that all her developing years and she supposed she wasn't immune or exempt from it. For the life of her, she thought somewhat querulously as she folded back the blanket and top sheets to stretch out, she couldn't recall *why* she'd believed such an odd, probably impossible thing. Who else had she ever allowed to make love to her but Danny Stanwall, after all? She was no tramp, no hooker! What in the world did he and Bro think of her now?

Fretting, feeling bulky and uncomfortable even though she hadn't put on enough weight even for anybody else to notice, Peggy shut her eyes, opened them, forced them closed again. Even when she was a little girl, naps always fired her up, renewed her physical vigor and—until the past few months, at least—her mental sharpness. And she wanted to be cute and cunning when she attempted to tell Eric and Danny that she had simply blurted out a momentary, passing feeling, not actually meant what she had told them. *Allow a mother to be a little leeway, a little space, guys,* she practiced her approach. *Next thing, it'll be oatmeal and pickles in the middle of the night!* Smiling privately, satisfied with the way she had worded that, Peggy shut her eyes and relaxed.

And opened them to find the Offspring sort-of rolling at the foot of her bed.

For one hideous instant, Peggy thought Lynn was still alive. There was no easily grasped, significant change from the last time she'd seen the creature—before Eric poked a hole in Lynn's oxygen tent with Grandfather's cane, right after Grandfather was made to disappear by Lynn—and no visible improvement. It was just as obscenely, monstrously fat, it's baby-blue eyes were still psychically androgynous, it was still repulsively naked and trapped between the two worlds of the sexes. If Lynn had had a sexual lifestyle, almost anyone at all would have been physically ideal.

But then she discerned *two* important differences between this Lynn and the "cousin down the hall" whom she had witnessed only one time in her whole life.

First of all, this Offspring was not lying down, but erect.

Secondly, Peggy saw with a rise of scalpel-sharp terror, *this* Offspring wasn't standing on the floor, it was *hovering* above it, some four to six inches, as if all the unsavory bulk she saw waiting silently for her to acknowledge it had become weightless.

"Hullo, Lynn," she said simply, aloud, and with her open verification of the being's presence in her room, all the old apprehension and shock and fear for both her life and her soul flooded back into her conscious thoughts, and, with it, most of the nightmarish recollections of what Lynn was able to do.

"Thanks for not giving me any more nightmares after . . . after our visit, back in June."

"DEAD." Lynn floated, effortlessly. The expression didn't alter. "YOUR PERSON NAMED STANWALL"—now, a smile, broad as a watermelon sliced in two—"NO MORE. GRANDFATHER BROKE HIS NECK. BEAT HEAD UNTIL IT WAS NO MORE EITHER." Incredibly, the smile widened, It was a look of real pleasure the Offspring wore.

"That isn't true." Peggy sat up in bed. "You *lie*—don't you? I won't believe that! You can't make me accept that lie."

"YES." the titanic pumpkin of a head bobbed, as if emphasizing the truth of what it said. "YOU WILL ACCEPT IT."

And the creature with the pale, juvenile demeanor allowed its fluttering, feminine eyelashes to close over the squinty eyes, then raised one flesh-dripping arm to point:

From nowhere at all—to the best of Peggy's sight and knowledge, materializing from nothingness—Danny Stanwall appeared in midair. Arriving there, he fell, hard, to the bedroom floor, arms and legs flying.

Peggy screamed but promptly went to him, dropped to her knees. "Oh, Danny," she groaned, and rested his battered head on her arm while she caressed his face gently. The head lolled and Danny moaned as if he might be regaining consciousness following a painful, coma-like sleep. "You're like ice, lover," she said anxiously. It seemed a wonder he was still alive. "Honey, can you speak? Say something! What's gone and happened to you?"

For answer, Danny opened his already hardening and decaying eyes to peer up at her. Mostly, Peg saw whites, like egg yolks; they rolled grittily in the sockets. When he parted his colorless lips to speak, his tongue was crusted with dried blood, and pink fluid trailed out the side of his mouth. Peggy gasped.

"Give me a big kiss, gorgeous," Danny croaked—and other things rushed out from under his black tongue like rats leaving a sinking ship. Spidery, miniature things with innumerable quick-crawling legs followed by inch-long, wormy creatures which had a carapace; small bits of Danny's gums and the roof of his mouth were pinched in their tiny pincers. His breath must have come up from some recently emptied region of the bowels.

Staggered, revulsed, Peggy dropped his head from her arm. It became detached at once and rolled lazily, nauseatingly, across the floor toward the levitating Lynn. Beneath his fat bare feet, the head—and the headless body still squirming before Peggy—disappeared.

"PLAY TIME," the Offspring's high-pitched wailing clip of a voice intoned, "IS OVER. LEARNING TIME BEGINS."

And the dead monster's single student was a rapt pupil. Pressed as far back as she could get against her bed, Peggy nodded brightly, attentively, gaping at the gross and nude shade who called the shots now and had always called the shots in the Baldwin house. For Peg, nothing else existed then but the apparitional Offspring with the boyish skin and the beautiful breasts.

Not even when the levitating creature began to *grow*.

Not in height, at first, but in bulk, in volume and sheer repugnance. She tried terribly hard not to cry out in disgust that was obvious, but what emerged from her mouth was just a whimper so it was all right, acceptable to the burgeoning monstrosity, who liked misery and psychic agony.

But what Lynn was doing to itself wasn't in the least acceptable to Peggy.

Effortlessly, it seemed, the obese thing was slowly but surely starting to fill the entire room. In moments, the hairless head seemed as wide as the bed and was bobbling close to the ceiling; the largely-feminine torso had expanded until it dwarfed all the busts of beauties in men's magazines and X-rated movies since modern smut began; and the utterly gargantuan midsection of the Offspring was ballooning in depth and width until the overflowing doughboy segments of the belly brushed against the walls and bobbed above the mortal Peggy's brow and nose as if filled with helium.

She gazed up, up, trying to peer over the Brobdingnagian stomach to make certain that Lynn was not displeased. And when It's porcine eyes met hers, she heard the next command as much in her disbelieving, disoriented brain as she did with her ears.

"NOW—*YOU,*" said the Offspring.

* * *

At the sound of the old Chevrolet door slamming shut, Jennie had spurted out of the garage and began to run, heading simply wherever she was headed after she knew that she was safely on open ground.

She was running straight for the woods, and Eric, following her, didn't realize where Jennie had gone until he'd already raced halfway down the driveway toward the house.

When he did not see her ahead of him, however, he whirled and dashed toward the woods, in time to see Jennie just before the trees swallowed her up.

"*Jen-nie . . .*" She hesitated, half turning at the sound of her name—but Eric's voice seemed to come from everywhere and nowhere. "*Jjjenn-nnnieee . . .*"

"I'm here!" she called, turning round and round until she was entirely lost.

And that was when she heard *thrashing* noises, not far away, and froze where she stood in abject, new terror.

How could she possibly have vanished in here so fast? Eric wondered, anger and frustration momentarily eclipsing his fear for Jennie.

Behind him, just out of the woods, it was still

pouring rain and only the faintest illumination was provided by moonlight.

Ahead of him, however, deeper into the woods, it didn't seem to be raining at all and he could not remember ever being able to see so clearly among the trees, not even during the afternoon. *It's another trick,* he thought, madder than ever, almost insulted because the Offspring considered him so stupid that he could be deceived by such an obvious deception.

On the other hand, he reflected, *anytime it's raining one place and not raining somewhere else, there must be a line of demarcation, an interface or cusp. If there is such as thing as the 'Twilight Zone,' it must be directly on that border . . .*

"Er-ricccc . . ." He spun to see, expecting to find Jennie, reaching for him. But he saw nothing. "*Er-rriicccc . . .*"

Ahead of him, only fractionally deeper into the woods, his mother, his *Mama*, looking as sweetly beautiful as she had in life, was calling to him, motioning to him to follow her! "Mama!" he exclaimed.

Her large, deepset, mournfully intelligent eyes were like floodlights. She stood between two enormous weeping willows, frail but in command of herself, in command of her only son, her worshipping son. Unlike the time when Lynn had used his childish fear of death to show her to him as something corrupted and foul, that was the Mama he and Peg had adored in childhood, vibrant, youthful, loving.

"It is I, my foolish little one!" She laughed her marvelous, musical laugh and again waved to him, called Eric to join her. "Here, it is Heaven if you know the way—here, we can all be together again, without Father or Lynn."

He was already walking slowly toward her, anxious to be nearer, to speak with and hear her speak to him. He shook his head, wonderingly; in this midnight of the spirit, on such a wild night but in this wonderland woods, when it was no longer scowling and sinister, when it was brighter than day and Mama was there to welcome him. It was not too much to believe that his dark and lonely journey was ended.

"*Come*, my Eric." she encouraged him, spreading her maternal arms wide. "Come with me, and soon we shall collect your sister as well!"

He stopped, frozen by duty that he had willingly, gladly performed, for as long as he could remember.

"Mama, I can't," he called to her. She was still ten yards away from him and he saw her face cloud with sadness. "Peg is back there, alone. And Jennie—have you seen my Jènnie? She's in here, somewhere . . . lost!"

"My Eric," Mama said, and straightened. For the first time he realized that her feet were not touching the moist, nocturnal earth. "You must come with me—*now*!" For the first time, he saw that her face looked . . . different . . . as if it had been washed with a wet sponge, and the beautiful features were running. "I command you, Eric! Come to me at once!"

You're not my mother, he thought, but could not say it. Shaking his head, he edged back from the night vision, began to turn away. *Mama would understand. Mama wouldn't want me to leave Peg to that thing.*

And he whirled, began to run, even as the voice of the image changed, became that of cousin Sue, then cousin Bernard, of Kasem Chamanan, of Danny Stanwall, hurling vile epithets at him as he ran.

And realized that he did not know how to get out of the woods. Because the unnatural light had fled, and he had never been in a place so dark in all his life.

At first, Jennie did not even recognize the man who passed her, farther down the matted trail in the woods upon which she had stumbled—although she'd hoped against hope that it was Eric and he simply had not noticed her.

Then, however, she realized that the man—he

walked as if he were burdened, as if he were carrying something in his arms—was shorter than Eric and moved more nimbly, as if he knew the old woods well.

At the instant that the light went out behind her, Jennie did not even notice, because the little man had turned his head to glance back at her, was chuckling warmly and yet kindly at her expression of amazement, and, with a nod of his head, was indicating that she should follow him.

"Father!" Jennie exclaimed, astounded but overjoyed. "Father—*you're alive*!"

"Of *course*, I'm alive!" he shot back, over his shoulder. "You didn't seriously believe that mountainous ogre of a politician could get the best of Verblin Spandorff?" His always giddy laugh trailed after him like a hero's banner.

Jennie, hurrying to keep pace with him, stumbled and almost fell. But she didn't mind. She could not recall when she had felt such happiness. "I don't understand, Father. Where have you been? Why haven't you contacted me?"

"Oh, here and there," he laughed, "hither and yon with a bit of thither thrown in for good measure!" His bronzed-monkey face flashed another brazen grin at her but Spandorff kept hurrying along. "Adam Baldwin left me for dead, you were correct about *that*, my daughter! Which is why, once I recovered from my head wound, the archeologists on my team bore me away to Lhasa, where I posed as a Norwegian explorer named Sigerson. I had to remain hidden. You see, I had no proof, no witnesses, to support me in any legal claim against the wily old son of a bitch. As a matter of fact, I didn't even know what Baldwin was up to with my discovery until a few years ago, when I finally dared return home."

"You still could have contacted me," Jennie called after him, reproachfully. But he did not reply and, in a moment, she let it drop. Verblin Spandorff had always possessed the reputation of a total independent; reliability and sentiment weren't among his more famous qualities. It was wonderful enough that she had a father again and that this nightmare would be ending! "What do you have in your arms, Father? And where are we going?"

He spun to face her, with such speed that she was again astonished and halted in her tracks. But he was only showing her what it was he had in his arms, and she stared across the distance between them with another expression of surprise. "Lynn's late lamented mother wasn't the only one I found in Iraq!" he exclaimed.

Spandorff, grinning from ear to ear, was clutching a motionless figure wrapped in ancient folds of treated cloth—a *mummy*.

"But Father," she began, starting to run to him, disappointed in the innovative archeologist and afraid for them all, "you know what happened the last time! Lynn, that's what!" Once more, the little man was trotting quickly and unerringly among the trees. But now, some of the bandages swathing the mummified creature appeared to be coming undone. "Are you sure it's wise to—to bring another of those horrors back to the United States?"

"One question at a time, Jennifer my girl!" he shouted back, slowing his pace slightly. Now an entire trail of ancient cloth was fluttering over his shoulder. "You asked what I had in my arms, and I answered that. Your next query, if memory serves me well, went something like this: Where am I going?"

Nodding, Jennie rushed to catch up. Apparently her father was almost at his destination and was slowing down, ready to explain. Although all that she really wanted of Verblin Spandorff was to go back to Dayton with him, to sit with him and listen to all he had to say while she caught him up on all the details of her life, she meant to be patient with Father, to hear him out now. Who knows what wondrous discovery he might have made about the Baldwin mystery, or what he had found here in the woods? "Well, Father," she called, "where *are* you going so quickly?"

"HERE!" his voice boomed back at her, and he was trotting out over empty space, walking on air—because she saw nothing whatever beneath his booted feet, and Jennie realized that instant that she was following him, with only the wafted cloth of the unraveling mummy to clutch for support!

Arms locked around her waist, heaved. Suddenly she was falling, but backward, landing hard upon the person who had grabbed her and upon concrete.

Beneath her, Jennie saw the figure of her father plummeting toward a busy city street. Her own feet dangled over the edge of the overpass, and she realized, with sickening horror, that she had almost been lured into empty air, high above rainswept 38th Street. A glance told her it was Eric who had found her, saved her. He was struggling to get his breath and to drag him back from the edge.

"All—a delay," he gasped. "To keep us from getting to Peg in time."

But Jennie was gazing first at the illusory image of her long-dead father, vanishing in a distant puff of swarthy smoke.

And at what she saw on the other end of the unreeling mummy tape, far below the two living mortals:

A vividly yellow cat, screeching and pawing at the air, then vaulting somehow toward the hill beneath Jennie and Eric. And she knew it had succeeded in landing there.

Because despite her terror, despite the cruel trick played upon her, she heard it's maddened yowling and mewling as it clambered up the hill toward them.

10

Eric, following Jennie Spandorff, and Jennie, following nothing but a mental projection of the Offspring's ranting and sadistic spirit, had gone completely through the woods and out onto an overpass, nearly a mile from the Baldwin house. The choice, when Eric urged Jennie to her feet and they saw the urgency of getting home as swiftly as possible, if they were to save Peggy, was returning through that appalling and intimidating woods, or skirting it and going the long way.

But the shortest distance between two points wasn't a straight line if, in getting there, their minds or their lives were lost.

Besides, the Offspring and the other spectral terrors of the Baldwin place had shown no ability to extend their living nightmares beyond the front and back yards of the estate or the woods. Hoping that they would be permitted to run the long way back, staying at the sidewalk and circling back through the neighborhood, they began at a dead run and gradually slowed to a jog. While each of them was young and had been in reasonably trim shape before going to Indianapolis, the nerve-jangling events of the past three months had taken a severe toll and rain, a steady, dark drizzle now, made their progress hazardous.

Strange, how much we take for granted, Eric thought as they scurried along the rainswept sidewalks. He'd begun glancing toward the neighboring houses, gripping his girl's hand tightly and trying to match his pace to hers, and he was surprised by how many of the houses they passed were well-lit, at an hour well beyond midnight. *By day, we see people who look like us, entering or leaving these houses, and never give them another thought.* But statistics compiled by dozens of well-meaning organizations clearly indicated that terror, violence, and evil by whatever name were not limited to the Baldwin place but epidemic, city-wide, state-wide, and national.

Wife-beaters. Child batterers. Eric saw one two-story house with all the lights burning on the second floor and shuddered, urged Jennie on by. Old people left by the city to freeze in winter, suffer malnutrition in spring. Teenagers convinced by the clothing they had to wear that they were boys when they were actually girls, and vice versa; other children crammed, unwanted or for reasons of malign punishment, into cellars and closets. Incest, apparently, was common, or more so than anybody suspected. Men would leave houses just like these they were passing, get drunk or stoned out of their minds, and run down other human beings without pausing to drive on, for fear of losing their driving privileges. Housewives in buildings like these would have sex tomorrow with maintenance men, delivery boys, hubby's best friend, brothers and sisters, or sell their favors without a second thought. Latchkey kids, left to their own devices, would invite pushers into their homes, ransack their parents' things to find valuables to pawn, discover handguns with which they'd commit holdups, or kill their playmates in a passion of role-playing and gaming.

Maybe there's nowhere for Jennie and I to go, Eric thought, *nowhere it's safe—safe from easy vice and worse influence. And maybe I should be happy that such a horror as the Offspring exists, dead or alive, because it's a reminder that evil exists, and thrives.* Breathing hard, aware that Jennie was exhausted, cold with rain blowing in their faces and leaving their clothes sticking to them, Eric saw the Baldwin house as they rounded a corner and drew in his breath for a fast finish. *Because in the "real" world, dark horror hides behind new clothes, good jobs, and houses just like these. And when night comes, they close their doors, and lock them, and only the victims even suspect how close the Offspring has come to winning.*

What if the door doesn't open? Jennie wondered, gasping for air as she ran up the front walkway with Eric at her side. *Couldn't we just shrug and turn away—turn and run, or get back into the car and drive . . . anywhere?*

That moment before Eric reached out to turn the knob and open the door so they could enter Hell again, the two of them hesitated. With the only illumination on the doorstep provided by a streetlamp diagonally across the street, the Baldwin house loomed above and around them like a black cave in which there might not be any ending, or any other exit. Although each of them knew what was in every room by now, could have identified every piece of garish and cheap or incongruous furnishings, and how to get from one room or one part of the place to the other, the old Baldwin house seemed that instant like an alien building they'd never visited before, and had never wished to.

Even as they entered it and passed through the foyer, feeling microsopically small and insignificant, and hesitated to whisper Peggy Porter's name, the big house seemed . . . uncomfortable; queer, and grotesque; pest-ridden and malevolent. There was, particularly for the psychic Jennie, a sense of *foreshadowing*. No, she realized, a sense that longbuilding, covert, and anomalous planning was coming to a fruition, to a head. *Whatever happens tonight,* she thought, *before dawn, will finish it. Either the living or the dead must go.*

Across the great living room, as they virtually tiptoed through it, toward the staircase, the organ that was no longer there began playing. A sad, sobbing strain, melodic, but performed in groaning minors that one felt behind the tongue and teeth, in the very root of the brain, until one's own internal system resonated and moaned with the sounds and experienced them almost as vision, and at every point of flesh and bone where nerve centers knotted like fists.

She plays for herself, Jennie mused, almost out of the room now and being half dragged by the man who loved her. Still, she hung back, turned her own dark-colored face to make out the shimmering essence of Elizabeth Baldwin and her beloved instrument. *Not to alert, or alarm.* And, as she found herself in the hall on the other side of the front room: *She's only minimally part of this world, at all. Eric's Mama survives more in the past, the way we all come to do, than in the present.* And she had no existence, could have none, in the future.

Eric was glancing toward the dining room. A couple of yards from the stairs leading to the second floor upon which so much had happened to him, the bespectacled young man was staring at light with no apparent source pooled on the dining room table. It enveloped, in part, condiments his sister Peg had left there, and as he and Jennie watched, a bottle of Heinz catsup along with a salt-and-pepper set crawled across the dining room table, balanced precariously on the edge, and seemed to jump over the side. The catsup struck the floor at once with a sickening sound of heavy shattering and left a puddle like thick blood. But the pepper shaker, and then the salt, fell s-l-o-w-l-y, as if filmed at a slower rate, and only the pepper shaker smashed when it hit the floor.

The salt shaker stopped an inch above the dining room floor, as if somebody, or something, had caught it.

Anxious then to get upstairs and finish it all, bring everything to a climax and leave the Baldwin place, Eric spun toward the stairs, groping in the dark for the bannister.

"*Ow*!" he cried, tugging his hand away and putting two fingers in his mouth. "It's boiling *hot*!" He gazed at Jennie in new amazement.

"Look," Jennie said. He did, and each of them saw steam rising from every step of the long stairway.

"It doesn't want us to go," Eric whispered, "up there."

"Fine!" Jennie snapped, frightened. She would have headed for the front door if his hand hadn't reached for and restrained her. "For once, I agree with Lynn. I don't want to go up there either!"

Dim lighting from the bulb on the second floor landing revealed Eric's look of surprise and disappointment. Then his expression changed and he touched Jennie's cheek. "I don't blame you, but Peg's up there, in danger. Go on; get out of this place. We'll join you in the car . . . if we're able."

"Don't turn macho on me, York!" she said, turning to face the stairs. "I only meant that we're going to have to run, if we want to avoid getting our feet blistered!"

And with that, she suited action to words. Astonished, Eric saw her go, climbing the steps two at a time and avoiding the bannister completely.

"I knew you'd do it," he told her when he had followed her to the second floor. His feet felt lightly scorched, singed, to the extent of first degree burns or close to it. He glanced down at her smouldering shoes. "It's probably only illusion, anyway."

"At least, it dried me up from the rain a little," she murmured bravely.

Together, they started the long walk up the hall toward Peggy's room. Without discussing it in the slightest, each of them knew that was where they'd find the teenage blonde. From beneath them, the organist had resumed playing but she was getting careless, or fumblefingered, making mistakes. *She senses her children are in danger,* Jennie thought, arm locked in Eric's as they walked. *I don't believe she even knows Lynn survived. And she never meant to terrify us, the way the materializing Verblin Spandorff killer intended it.*

The rooms on either side of the hallway were silent, *too* silent, Eric noticed. Each of them gave him the impression of containing at least one nightmarish force, but if they were present, they were holding it down—keeping their "peace." Presumably because Lynn had commanded it.

Then, from within the room which he and Jennie had shared—the Offspring's old bedroom—he heard odd gurgling sounds, and identified stentorian breathing. Jennie looked at him, mirroring his own startlement and rising fear. Listening attentively, they heard the noises stop, for a moment—as if the occupants of the dark room had heard them in the hallway and instantly sought silence. The door was open, was ajar, and Eric took two steps toward it, pushed the door open the rest of the way.

One baleful, bizarrely amused eye screened by lustrous lashes glowed in the center of that room, near the ceiling. It wasn't as if the creature was trying to hide or expressing any faint fear, Eric realized. It had simply not wished to waste the expenditure of a total materialization.

"TOO *LATE*!" a voice intoned. It came from all around them, where they stood motionless inside the room, and it sounded more satisfied and amused than ominous. "TOO LATE,

DELAYED, TOO TARDY." There was a small *creaking* noise at their backs and Eric whirled, caught the bedroom door with his fingers before it could close.

"Hurry!" his hissed at Jennie—"Get out in the hallway!" Because there was a powerful force that continually gained strength, and it was all Eric could do to keep the door ajar. "This was a trap!"

Jennie didn't have to be told twice. And Eric was right behind her in the long corridor just before the Offspring's door slammed shut with a noise that was violent and terrifying.

Again, at a light switch, as he'd done twice downstairs, Eric tried to provide them with better light but nothing happened when he hit and then wiggled the switch.

Unless there was a bulb burning in Peg's room—poor Danny hadn't been able to make his skepticism act as a shield against this house's murderous forces—they'd have to learn what Lynn had done to her in near darkness, Eric realized. And that, of course, was the point of it: the Offspring *preferred* that they saw little, clearly; right up to the last, Lynn had controlled everything and acquired what gamblers called an "edge," at each and every crucial turn of their odyssey.

From outside the room, with the door closed, there seemed to be no light of any kind burning in there. "Peg?" Eric called. And louder, "Peg!"

No reply.

"Stay behind me," Eric told Jennie, and tried the doorknob.

The door opened at his slight touch, and it needed oiling. The damned thing creaked and wailed like a banshee until it was thrown back entirely.

And Peggy Porter's bedlamp was burning. Quite enough to enable them to see what had happened. *It really wanted us to see for ourselves,* Jennie thought from behind Eric, trying to peer over his shoulder. *The rest of it was another one of Lynn's kid games.* She locked her curved hands to Eric's shoulders.

And felt him tense, turn into knots, beneath her fingers. "Oh-h, Sis, *no*," he groaned with enormous sadness and shock.

Peggy was fully conscious, sitting up in bed the best she was able. She'd drawn a blanket up over her feet and legs, partly for reasons of modesty. Because most of her flannel shirt had torn free from the buttons and Peggy's stomach protruded like a ripe, burgeoning melon.

She was, Eric and Jennifer saw, no longer three months pregnant.

She was nine months pregnant if she was a day and it would not have astonished either her brother or Jennie if childbirth began immediately. Neither of them had seen a woman that pregnant before; Peg looked as if her due date was at least a month earlier.

Then all Eric was able to see was his little sister's eyes, the feverishly bright, forcibly self-adjusted, infinitely frightened expression in them. Approaching her where she lay, propped up against the headboard of what had always appeared to be Mama's bed, Eric saw that Peg was sweating profusely and, when he touched her forehead and one cheek with gentle fingers, she felt clammy, cold with terror.

"I guess it . . . didn't want to wait," she said so softly he could scarcely hear her.

Jennie met Eric's shocked, weary gaze when he looked back at her with as encouraging and nurturing a smile as possible, but her own thoughts raced with the implied horror of young Peggy's plight. Maybe the child on its way was actually Danny's and hers, but expecting mothers did not develop grossly distended bellies in a matter of one hour. Perhaps it was an hysterical pregnancy, always had been. But again, how could Peggy Porter have passed from seeming her ordinary, slender self to a condition like this during the time that Eric and she were out of the house?

Jennie walked slowly, sympathetically, toward Peggy knowing that the complete horror of what was happening to the girl was undeniable now, and could not be entirely, hysterically realized until they all saw what the Offspring looked like when it entered the body of a newborn infant.

"Who's that?"

Peggy had cried out in fresh alarm. Now she was raising an arm that quaked to point toward the bedroom door, and what lay beyond it. The others had not heard a noise, but they listened, now.

Slow, trudging, heavy footsteps sounded from the hallway. While the three of them held their breaths, none of them capable of rushing to the door to see who was approaching, panic welled up and each of them knew that they were too used up, too exhausted and drained of emotional resources, to wage any kind of defense or attack against the interloper. For Eric, knowing that the nightmare had already taken a grim and harrowing new turn because of what his sister's ballooning pregnancy meant, and faced now with yet another agonizing disclosure right outside the door, it was the end of his youth and vitality. Because it was the end of his own egotistical attitude, his own soaring but unreal aspirations. How could he possibly be as important as he'd believed himself when he had repeatedly fallen for every devious trick the Offspring threw his way?

And if Lynn had been menacingly perfect—invulnerable, or close to it—in the original form it had taken, and immeasurably more awesome as an astral body, what chance would anyone in heaven or hell have against it when Lynn was reborn in the healthy flesh of his sister Peg and the athletic Danny Stanwall? Before it had reached kindergarten, the reincarnated Offspring would undoubtedly be able to protect itself in every way that was necessary—because now it would be able to get up and move. Travel. Do what it wished directly, not with Grandfather Baldwin's assistance nor with its mind projections alone.

The bedroom door, which Jennie had closed behind her, started to open. Which was when Eric Porter confronted his worst fear for his little sister: the unnatural fetus she carried in her womb. Even now, her stomach was visibly swelling, getting larger by the second, was not going to be delivered in the usual way. That was not Lynn's style; never had been. For a self-creating, one-hundred-percent self-serving monstrosity such as the Offspring.

Bursting through its new mother would seem the only way. And no longer androgynous, either, Eric thought with enervated anxiety. If the Offspring had its way, and it almost always had, *he* would be *he*, this time . . . physically normal, tall, strong, and charming.

A pale white hand clutched the door.

And Mildred Manning Moag—Mildred, their beloved Mildred!—was slipping into the bedroom with her customary expression of concealed caring and unspoken disapproval, even as her glance barely took in the presence of her Eric and Jennie Spandorff and went maternally in search of her Margaret.

The moment was such that, while neither of her former charges had seen the aged housekeeper for months, no words were necessary. They were in the house of Senator Adam

Baldwin and Lynn, whom Mildred had served faithfully, and that meant that her charges were in peril. Awful peril. Questions did not need to be put, in addition, because of the businesslike way of the once-powerfully built housekeeper. After locating Peggy, she headed unveeringly toward the pregnant girl and, without the first sign of surprise or dismay, began helping her out of bed.

"Mildred—" said Peggy, startled and abruptly filled with questions.

But throughout all the time they had been together, it was the loyal, almost tireless housekeeper who had taken upon herself not only the complete responsibility for the well-being of her "little ones," but the dogmatic right to direct them since Peg and Eric grew up. When no explanation was forthcoming from the crone except for a characteristic compression of the corrugated lips and a curt nod of the head, Peggy was standing, balanced awkwardly, her abdomen surging before her almost as if its fetal passenger already possessed a mind of its own.

My Lord, Eric thought, *she almost looks like Lynn that way*! And why not, he wondered, *because it's obvious that Peg is going to give birth any minute and that must mean that Lynn's brain or spirit is already inside her!* Eric shook his head, became frantic. *That part-human thing she's carrying is going to pop right through her stomach unless ol' Mildred really knows what she's doing.*

With Peg partly supported on the old woman's sturdy shoulders, the two of them began trudging quietly toward the bedroom door. Eric saw then what Mildred meant to do: to flee the Baldwin house, once and for all—to leave the place forever, as Mildred had wanted them to do.

Jennie, who had finally figured out the identity of the reliable old woman, started following the others toward the door. Her heart sang with the realization that they *were* going to get safely away at last!

Then Jennie paused, badly shaken by what had occurred—or been transmitted—to her. For one instant she could not quite believe the higher evidence of her specialized senses and had to lean wobblingly against a wall of the bedroom for support. Hanging back, she shook her head even when Eric glanced around and held out an affectionate, encouraging hand. The organ music began again from downstairs and she mustered an artificial smile and her courage, shook off a mood of positively disenfranchising terror that had overcome her momentarily, and joined the rest of the little escape party in the corridor. It was preternaturally quiet, Jennie thought; it was so quiet it might have been any house in the neighborhood then, but it was not. Elsewhere, any evil that flourished was disguised under other names.

Eric was marveling at the bravery and boldness, the audacity, of their aged friend who was hustling his sister down the hallway to safety as swiftly as she dared—although Peg was desperately pale and unsteady, and Eric could not imagine what Mildred might do about his sister's imminent delivery. He remembered, though, the way she had brought them to safety that first time, when he and Peg were small children—the way he had almost been driven to insanity or dead nothingness by the igniting Offspring, and then found himself in the drifts of snow outside the house, Mildred gripping his small hand. With her face bathed by intermittent shadows and light, she had whispered a prayer that might have been for all humankind, and they watched red flames burst like rockets from every window. " 'And the beast was taken,' " Mildred intoned, then, " 'and with him the false prophet that wrought miracles before him.' "

But the house had not truly burned down, and Lynn had not truly perished. *It* had survived—marginally, miraculously, more menacingly than even before. Wasn't that, in a perverse way, an affirmation of the belief that there *was* no death, really?

And how could she have known we needed her tonight? Eric wondered. He saw that his sister and the aged housekeeper had reached the head of the stairs and were ready to descend, to make the escape complete. But how could Mildred have known or swiftly understood that Lynn was using Peg even as it had used the mouldering, mummified carcass of its original mother, thousands of years ago—and how in the world could Mildred have come to them, this way, and just in the nick of time? Was it possible that she wasn't as she seemed, that she was yet another demoralizing ploy of Lynn, an illusion?

He peered curiously around at Mildred's dogged, patient, compassionate old profile, and then past her.

And discovered, climbing the stairs toward them in the most feral crouch he'd ever seen, the furry, yellow thing that was the clone—or the ghost of the clone—of Peg's long-dead cat, Krazy! He saw then with horror that it was only three steps, then two, beneath his unsteady pregnant sister—saw that Peg's gaze was centered directly on the very next step she'd have to take—saw that Mildred, between him and Peg, was devotedly, carefully, watching her "Margaret."

"Look out, Sis!" he shouted.

"Peggy, you're about to trip!" cried Jennie. She tried to squeeze past Eric and the crone, to catch Peggy's arm.

Then the yellow fluff of death and fury was somehow caught between Peggy's feet and ankles, yowling and scratching at Peg with claws like rusty nails.

And, to the sickening dismay of Eric and Jennie, she was falling heavily upon the steps and then beginning to roll, end for end, all the rest of the way down the stairs.

Nobody else moved.

Motionless, Peggy Porter lay crumpled with her blond hair in a small pool of blood, and the yellow feline was vanishing in an acrid puff of black smoke.

11

Peggy was sitting up, very slowly, laboriously. Her manner and the slightly dazed look on her vivacious face resembled those of a young woman awakening from a long and busy, maddening sleep—from dreaming so deep and pervasive that she appeared distantly surprised to find herself awakened at all, and simultaneously uncertain of her moment's reality.

By the time all the others had rushed down the steps to cluster around Peg like so many mourners amazed to discover the deceased erect in her casket, she appeared ready to talk to them, able to reassure them that she was quite unharmed. Nothing about her registered pain or psychic anguish.

But Peggy Porter, rather than speaking or

reacting to the anxious expressions on their faces, was merely peering down at herself, at her own youthful body. One by one, the others silently looked where she was looking, and gasped. What they saw was surely an impossibility—but they saw it.

As if a slow motion camera of the sort utilized to capture in time lapse photography the image of an emerging flower had been forced to run in reverse, Peggy was shedding the pounds she had accumulated so swiftly—was losing all the natural and the unnatural bulk of her pregnancy, and steadily shrinking back into the childless Peggy Porter who's been the reason they went to Indianapolis and the haunted Baldwin house.

She wasn't bleeding. She didn't seem to be experiencing terrible pain. The fall had apparently hurt the strange, partly otherworld infant she had been carrying but, because it had not truly existed, it had simply disappeared, leaving young Peggy with its psychic memory, but with no physical remnant of its existence as a part of her.

"Oh, God—what's that!" Eric exclaimed, leaping a foot away and rubbing at his cheek with his fingertips. Glancing down, he saw the redness adhering to them.

"*L-look.*" Jennie said, pointing up.

From rents in the room's ceiling, droplets of blood had begun raining and some of them had splattered against Eric's cheek. They carried with them a foul stink that reminded Jennie of dead flesh left too long in the sun. Now the rents were spreading, enlarging.

"It's going to come through like a shower of gore!" Eric said, gasping in digust.

But it didn't. Instead, he and the others heard sounds at their feet and, peering anxiously down, they saw a series of seven gelatinous, tubular masses take form on the living-room floor, and crawl. They were identical monstrosities, neither quite as much insect as worm, or some cursed kind of diabolical slug. Their backs were rigid, and humped while they crawled; they had blind eyes and feelers sprouting from their paperwad heads which quivered in the air as if seeking their destination and, finding it, they made for the foyer as if to block the nearest exit.

But the winged things, tiny and ferocious as flying piranha, had beaten them to it. While Jennie and the increasingly alert Peg shuddered, these ebony birds plummeted and rose again, challengingly, studying the humans with deepset, black, knowing eyes that contained cunning, animal madness, and a bald vindictiveness that made Eric blanche and look away. That moment, first one and then two of the winged demons darted out of the foyer and flew in his face, batting their wings crazily and viciously pecking at his bespectacled eyes. Scratches instantly appeared on the lenses. When Eric swung frantically at them with his fist, the lot of them flew on a straight line back into the foyer, their sound like that of crackling paper set freshly afire. All the hummingbird-sized, flapping creatures then hovered all but soundlessly in the air, defiantly gazing at Eric and the other people.

Toilets, all the toilets in the old house, began flushing. But this time, the supernatural was fully evoked in the guise of unlikelihood or impossibility. As fast as one rushing noise of flushing finished, water was somehow shot immediately into the bowl again as if unseen hands, or claws, were repeatedly coaxing the lavatories into unnatural action. The rising bedlam of the noise was less like a Niagara of ordinary rushing water, to Jennie, and more like that of dozens of people vomiting wrenchingly. Then Verblin Spandorff's daughter felt herself begin to gag and choke in empathy and put her palms over her ears in a desperate effort to block the sounds out.

Throughout all of it, Mildred stood resolutely and unmoved beside her Margaret, her Eric. Her chin was thrust our grimly and her hands were firmly locked with those of her young charges. Eric glanced at Mildred, saw that she appeared entirely unfazed, unimpressed, even frigidly aloof. He sensed, however, how much she feared the danger to the youths she had raised through times of trial and her own hazardous exposure to the Offspring.

"I guess they're just Lynn's illusions," he

shouted above the tumult to the old woman, trying to make Mildred hear him distinctly. Although it was impossible for him not to feel fear, he was attempting to remain down-to-earth and also allay any unneeded anxiety on the old woman's part.

"*No . . .*" The old housekeeper turned just slightly toward him and her voice, to Eric Porter, seemed to emerge directly inside his head instead of through the normal means of hearing. He saw her shudder; he realized for the first time how old and frail she had become. "You haven't got it figured out even now, Eric," she said sharply. "Which means you're no genius like your grandfather. And without his brilliance, you're not like Adam Baldwin at all." She must have known how much her outwardly analytical comment uplifted Eric, but when she squeezed his hand, her touch was chill, oddly distant. Then her eyes bore into his. "The creatures who try, now, to keep you here in this hellish place forever aren't Lynn's doing. You should see that, boy. These things are the result of the dreadful alliance which Lynn made with them, years ago."

"I . . . don't understand," Eric said. For a second he wondered if she could have heard him above the manic racket in the front room.

"Yes, you do." Her rough but fond tones again sounded in his brain. "You want to believe that these are further manifestations of the Offspring's imagination, and will." At that instant, the noises desisted and Mildred's voice was louder than it needed to be. "You forget that Lynn is helpless, now that Margaret's fall has ruined its physical manifestation. Again, the Offspring is neither fish nor fowl. And for that reason, there is no way Lynn can get to you or your sister."

Then *who*, and *what*, wondered Eric. Before he could speak, Jennie answered his question and pressed against his shoulder for safety.

"These are the devil forces—the evil spirits—that existed in this house even before Lynn's partial demise," she said. "Lynn gained their cooperation through the dominance of its great intellect, convinced them to do what Lynn desired." Jennie swallowed, hard. "I sense all that now, Eric, and sense that it's corroborated by this woman who reared Peggy and you. What we're confronted with right this moment is a large number of terrible lieutenants, York—demonic allies of Lynn." She clutched his bicep, shivered. "I sense that they're mustering their own attack now, and that they don't like the way we've interfered with Lynn's plans."

"I think," Eric began, his face boyishly eager, "I know how we can get through them and the foyer. Maybe if—"

He felt that moment as if lightning had struck and left him deaf. With no warning, every frightening noise in the Baldwin house was sucked away, like water running down an open drain.

While Jennie could see the others, perceive that Eric's lips were moving, she heard . . . nothing.

Which was when still more beings of the soul's dark night began to materialize.

Floating and crawling, darting and skittering things were manifested and moved boldly, terrifyingly, among them. Worse, not all of them retained the shape they revealed at first glimpse; one moment they seemed tiny, roach-sized but incredibly fast, and the next they appeared enormous and weighty and bunched against Peggy or Jennifer, leaving shiny and viscuous trails on their clothes like mucus. Others were principally possessed of enormous claws, which they sheathed only at the last instant before creeping by; one such thing scratched Peggy's calf, producing a noiseless outcry of pain, then showed a toothy grin of mad promise: *we'll get you when we're ready.* That was its message; *if you try to escape this house, we'll tear you to bits.*

It had dawned on Eric, who had also found the world soundless, that he could not even hear his heart beat or sense the steady throb of his pulse. And it had occurred to him that they might change direction, might bolt for the back of the house and try to beat the demons outside. But that meant facing the garage, and the heart-stopping terrors of the woods beyond, and he was unable anyway to convey his idea to the others because they could not hear him. Urgently craving something, anything, that was normal, real, he lifted his hands to one ear and clapped them together with all his strength. Nothing. He tried again.

This time, distantly and tenuously, he could hear the faint sound of flesh as if it had touched other flesh in some furtive caress. In a way, it had been worse than the total silence. The experience left him feeling ghostlike, apparitional, and he wondered then if that was the common way for discarnate spirits—if the mischief they wrought mightn't be the product of finding the afterlife insane, or bereft of human commonplace.

Around them, spurts of lightning flashed like darting, illuminated sperm; other shapes whizzed or trudged doggedly by, one thing mounting his foot and momentarily hammering at his ankle as if trying to penetrate it sexually. Horrified, Eric shook his foot, reached down to brush at the shadowy demon and, raising his hand, saw upon his fingertips a cold slime that writhed and made swirling motions as if seeking an imitation of new life. Shrieking soundlessly, he half-brushed, half-shook the stuff away and glanced up with wild eyes.

To see the image of Grandfather Baldwin, leaning like a cruel cavalier upon his murderer's stick—and Danny Stanwall, levitated at the foyer entrance in a stark, malign pose of savage Satanic belligerance.

You don't exist; you're not real! Eric believed that he shouted his words at them, unable to judge whether he meant what he'd said or not.

And a smoke-gray gauze like a gossamer curtain fell before and around Mildred as Eric screamed *No*!, then descended to hide his sister, next his lover Jennie.

Until, for the first time in his life, Eric Porter learned the meaning of claustrophobia and understood the menace and alienation of it.

The draping phenomenon was his, now; and as it concealed him completely from the other living human beings craving escape from the Baldwin place, Eric discovered that it was quite impossible to see anything except the gray, gossamer curtain. Formed on all sides of him, shimmering so that it gave the appearance of transparency, the stuff could not be seen through at all and it was, for Eric, as if he had been marooned somewhere in outer space—kept alive, marginally, for dark purposes which were beyond his ken. Utterly isolated, he found himself almost instantly assailed by neurotic notions of helplessness, of sheer worthlessness, that made him moan in shame and terror simultaneously. Because the draping effect prevented him even from seeing his own legs and feet or the carpeted floor, he knew then that there was no reason to hope that the curtain would ever open, or rise, understood that the evil entities of the Baldwin house could do with him as they wished.

It did not even occur to him to reach out to the gauzy drapery and try to brush it away, or tear it. Because it was not meant for him to think coolly, logically.

A moment later, Eric realized that he was sinking to his knees, starting to bury his shame and lonely face in his hands, and felt incapable of doing anything else. *All I am is a chunk of meat, and without food, water, companionship,* he thought, *I'll be dead meat in a matter of hours.* He began sobbing, lost tears of self-pity welling up from his eyes, his soul.

"Eric . . ." For another second he did not even raise his head. "Help me, Bro—please?" His sister Peg. "Eric? Where *are* you . . . ?"

A radiance back-lit the nearly colorless curtain to his left. Straining his eyes, willing it, he made out—or believed that he saw—the slender shape of the young woman he had tried so often before to spare from the ultimate harm. "I'm here, Peg!" he exclaimed, and launched his whole body in the direction of her luminosity.

"You did it!" she exulted, beginning to cry. Eric stood next to her again, reaching out to hug her. "You did it!"

"I think I had to," Eric said softly, peering around him and reaching out to take the hands of both Jennie and a gently smiling Mildred, "if we were to get out of here." Then it dawned on him that he had not only destroyed his own gossamer prison but that of the others.

And that their voices had become audible again!

When the four of them turned once more toward the foyer beyond which lay freedom, Eric saw that the bizarre creatures which had filled it were gone. He urged the others forward.

But he stopped in his tracks when a new figure, another threat, materalized in the entranceway to the foyer.

Kasem Chamanan—at least, it looked like him, precisely; the little Thai did not appear to have changed at all—blocked the entrance, and their exit. Kasem, who had known ancient magic, who had known fighting techniques few Westerners ever learned.

Their friend Kasem—but now he held both palms up, imperiously, and it was immediately obvious that he did not intend to let them pass.

Although his regular yet somewhat Oriental features had not altered—that was part of the horror, for Jennie Spandorff, as she realized the clear intent of the ghost; because one expects disgusting and ugly spirits to pose a threat, but not one's well-loved companion—and Kasem seemed entirely real, there was about the purposive curve of his down-plunging and heavy brows and the contorted twist of his smiling mouth a controlled or husbanded fury, a vindictive malice that might have been created by resentment for his own untimely demise.

Fleetingly, Jennie tried, valiantly, to touch the intellect of the Thai shade, to reach him with her own compassion and the feminine charm to which Kasem had responded. But even partly connecting with that functioning mouldering mind caused her to recoil, physically as well as psychically. She had to clutch at Eric's arm for support. Jennie trembled, glanced away from Kasem. Even in contact with the Offspring, she had not become attuned to a more murderous, mad, and ruthless intellect. Whether it was actually Kasem Chamanan—and his specter, or something of an imp cast in the little Thai's image—it was an intelligence for a sensitive with far greater preparation and experience. Proximity to that rabid personality could take a normal, living mind and chase it down the corridors of careening lunacy.

Eric, Jennie saw, was edging cautiously toward the Chamanan shade once more, trying hard to smile and putting out a hand in friendship. Her gaze met Peggy's and what each woman thought leapt between them as if crossing a telegraph wire: *He mustn't touch that creature's hand*, thought Jennie; *but what else can any of us do*? And, *You must stop him*, thought the little sister; *he's doing this for me, and our past—for you, and his future. But he isn't* psychic! He doesn't know *what he's doing, what Kasem's ghost may do*!

So, because it seemed that Peggy Porter was right and only she might have a chance to reason with the phantom, Jennie drew in a long, quavering breath and started walking toward Chamanan, who was moving his hands swiftly in unnecessary preparation for defense—or in remembered preparation for nightmarish attack.

Let me. The old woman, Mildred, herself little more than a shade in the protectionless clustering of her numerous years, froze Jennie Spandorff in her tracks and was gently calling Eric's name. *Er-ic*, she wailed, in a voice like high winds toying with human words at a distance far above the mundane earth, *Eerr-rrric . . . it's I who will deal with your poor, driven friend.*

Immediately, the haunted eyes of the small, nimble spirit turned toward Mildred and Kasem Chamanan made a noise midway between apprehension and bloodlust. When the old woman was abreast of Eric Porter, a nod of her unbowed authoritative head caused him to stop and, after a moment, retreat.

"Plato said, 'Fear old age,' " Eric quoted, tense between the two women he adored, " 'for it does not come alone.' "

"I remember," Jennie whispered, her own eyes focussed upon the woman and the ghost of the Thai journalist, "reading that psychic energy increases as the years pass. Some tribes say that the curse of an old person works better than one from a young person." She glanced at Eric with hope, with absorption in what she was saying. "That the aged acquire a repository of archetypal knowledge, because like an infant, they're closer to the . . . other side."

Without looking away, Peggy told them both, "Maybe the barrier between the world of the living and the world of the dead sort-of pulls apart, with old age, if the person is at all preparing for the afterlife."

"But that's a misnomer," Eric whispered; "that word 'afterlife.' Because where we must go, actually is the after-death!"

Now Mildred Manning Moag was three feet, then two, from the Thai who had been so athletic in life, but Peggy wondered if either of them was actually walking, or moving, in the same time frame that other people knew. Kasem had ceased to waggle his hands ominously, slowly, and was abruptly raising the palms to Mildred; but it was difficult to say whether he was reemphasizing his intention to let them advance no farther toward escape, or if he was subtly asking Mildred to stop. What was clear to see was the marble-bright bewilderment in Kasem's smoky eyes—the way he could not seem to judge whether he should strive to intimidate the slight female form approaching him, or to deal with her violently, at once.

"You've no business taking the face or form

of the good man you and the Offspring killed here," Mildred declaimed. Apparently, she had made up her mind about the being. She was speaking in her own voice, aloud, for the first time since her arrival at the old Indianapolis house. But Eric, who knew her well, imagined that it cost her greatly. "You are not what you seem. None of you ever are!"

Snarling like a cornered animal, Kasem backed quickly into the foyer. Eric, Peg, and Jennie, rushing to follow, stopped at the entranceway and stared in surprise and shock at the aged woman who had raised the Porters.

Encompassing Mildred's body from head to toe was a thin, bluish flame.

At first glance, then a second, the old housekeeper and substitute mother appeared to be bathed in light similar to that which was given-off by a gas-burning range. Although it wasn't harsh and didn't make any of them feel like turning their heads from the glare, that light-blue fire which outlined the old woman's body sizzled and seemed to feed angrily upon itself. None of the other three real people staring at her understood, for a moment, what was happening.

Then, Eric *did* remember what he'd read about the meaning of the blue flame: well-known psychics for at least two-hundred years—primarily, Hindus—had consistently claimed that the elderly possessed, at their finest, an aura exactly like bluish fire, and that they were often granted permission to live quite long lives because their presence, alone, could revivify or revitalize the imperiled young! Surely, oh, *surely* that was appropriate for Mildred now, the youth pondered, half-praying. He felt filled with guilt for the way he and his sister had rebelled against her authority, sought to banish her from their lives, and remembered reading about the primitive Germans who had routinely slaughtered their aged relatives, and the *Buriats* of Siberia, who gave banquets for the old, then strangled them while they were drinking and laughing.

"And something more," Jennie said, as if she'd read Eric's mind. Her gaze, too, remained fixed on the aged, courageous woman and the image of their friend. "The Offspring was androgynous. After the reproductive years, ancients taught that the very old were also sexless, and magically gifted."

Jennie, Eric, and Peggy saw Mildred raise her arms, as if concentrating the azure flame in them and in her hands and her fingers. Now they knew the other was not Kasem, or that he had forgotten all the supernatural tricks he had known in the face of his own rising cowardice.

"The old woman was the sage-femme, or perhaps she still is," Jennie whispered. Her heart, like Eric's and Peggy's, was beating violently; only Mildred could win their way to the outside, to freedom. "She was keeper of the tribe's lore, its medium, prophetess, priestess.

The natural healer, the—"

Mildred simply touched the temples of the demon barring the front door.

And any wild possibility that the creature had within it the soul of their murdered friend was, that instant, dismissed.

For the smallest part of a second, the Baldwin house's possessing demon stood nakedly in its own petrifying guise. Gone were Kasem Chamanan's face, and form; present was the emaciated face, neck, limbs and body of what only grotesquely represented or mocked that which was human. Peggy had a glimpse of mammoth eyesockets lit at their tunneled roots by fiery, othernatural orbs like coals of fire that had burned since time began. Eric saw the seemingly plasticized muscles of the skinned arms and legs, the Hell-transplanted organs rotting behind the ribcage. Jennie perceived—mercifully for the instant that it lived, or remained—the unreasoning, bitchy bigotry and self-serving graspingness of its hateful mind.

Then it did not exist there any longer and the bluish flame haloing Mildred Manning Moag was also gone; but the old woman was throwing the front door wide, seeming merely to touch it; and she was gesturing for them to follow, cajoling and mentally dragging the three young people to midnight liberty, just as she had rescued her pair of charges when they were little.

Eric, turning from the front lane to look back

into the house of his childhood, saw that a uremic blaze of something that moved like a miasma just above the floor was trying to follow them. He heard—no, *sensed*—a gathering of coercive forces from the bowels of the place, then definitely overheard a sequence of rasping whispers that plotted, that fomented new plans, and felt his senses begin to teeter.

Never go into that house again! Mildred's authoritative alto seemed to singe the interior of Eric's brain and he jumped back just in time. The front door slammed shut with definitive, frightening force for which he would not have given the old woman credit, and without daring to check, he felt sure the door would not open. *Stay away, Eric Porter. Never return to this terrible place*!

Not wanting to look at her, he nodded, a badly shaken young man, and saw that his sister and Jennie were staring at the Baldwin house. Even though the door was shut and, if they did not return to it, they were probably safe, they were all aware that the whole building was atremble, like a furious, frustrated fat man who could scarcely contain his anger. Light that gleamed like coal issued from every opening of the place with laserlike vividness. And without saying another word about it, Eric, Peg and Jennie turned and rushed down the lane to the waiting automobiles.

"Mildred?" called Eric, finding her nowhere near his car. He glanced back, toward the house, and then at his sister. "Where did she go?"

Peg's lips formed the words, "I don't know."

But Jennifer Spandorff slipped her arms around both brother and sister and whispered softly, gently, in their ears. "She was never here tonight, Porters." She hesitated before adding, "I've known that for some time now." Seeing the look of astonishment in their eyes, she looked away, smiled sadly, and opened the car door. "I mean that your Mildred wasn't here . . . physically."

Peg saw her brother begin a dubious remark, touched his lips with her fingers. When Eric stared wonderingly into her eyes, she found that all three of them were quietly weeping. "I believe we'll find that Mildred died tonight, Eric," she said chokingly. "That her . . . her good soul came to help us. One last time."

Jennie kissed her on the cheek and they climbed into Eric's car. They needed company now, needed to be together; they could make arrangements for Danny Stanwall's "wheels." Sighing heavily, aware of how badly his head ached and how urgently he wanted them all to be back in Dayton, Eric started the car and found himself shuddering. For a second, he had unconsciously doubted that the engine would turn over.

Eyes. He was—he knew it, then, he felt certain of it—being watched.

With great deliberation, wishing it might take

him hours to do it, Eric turned his head until he could stare back at the Baldwin house for a final time. The rain had let up, he saw; tomorrow might even be a nice day.

The lights were on in the house. On the second floor. Inevitably, Eric, and then his sister, looked up until they were able to see the window of that room in which the Offspring had lived twice.

In a flash, no more, brother and sister identified the shape of an incredibly enormous, obscenely ugly, naked body . . . just the height of a newborn child. Its knowing eyes smirked coyly at them.

Then the lights went off.

AFTERTHOUGHTS

My first thought was to tell you about the origin of the two OFFSPRING novels upfront, as a foreword. Then I realized that I could scarcely speak freely about Lynn since those of you who had not read the first book would have the present one ruined by what I want to say.

Stick around for another few moments, if you wish, there's no additional charge, or, if personal remarks embarrass you, simply reach out for the next book on your stack. You do have another one there, don't you; a whole stack of novels? Whether they bear my byline or not, I hope so. The only thing arguably better to do with your time is to write your own book!

"Where d'you get your ideas?" is a question many writers shrink from, not because we mind letting you know but because, in part, our answers are often greeted with blank stares. Or stares of disbelief. But I've been asked about the origin of the Offspring, and maybe you've wondered, too.

It had a suitably strange genesis.

You see, the not-identified-as-the-first Offspring was the first novel I ever wrote, but it was the twenty-first J.N. Williamson novel to be published. For anybody who has written but not placed a book, there's something encouraging about that fact, I think. But that's just the first bizarre fact involving what might be termed "Offspring origins."

The first Offspring was the product of a nightmare. It was such an uncannily complete nightmare that Lynn "itself" and the children who were to be plagued by Lynn were present, and many of the horrors visited upon them. I awakened in the cold sweat of dread cliche and, for two days, I could not stop thinking from time to time about my androgynous creation.

Ultimately, I perceived that I had literally been given the concept and knew what I had to do with it.

One of the sources of my ideas, for over a decade, then, has been my own unconscious mind and my memory. Or maybe there are two sources there; hard to say. While my wife Mary and I were bringing up six children—including a quartet by her first marriage—there wasn't much time for writing. Or so it seemed then.

Before our romance was rekindled—we had dated in our teens; I'd never forgotten her—some short stories of mine had been published in *Ellery Queen's* and elsewhere and I'd always longed to become a full-time, much-published wordsmith. While we were raising the kids, and vice versa, I managed only a few more new tales. Candidly, it appeared probable that my bookish dreams were doomed to disaster. Because of many pressures linked to the cost of bringing up a half-dozen children and other reasons, I was down to writing only when sheer inspiration was upon me—and that is quite possibly the least-acceptable excuse ever invented by a writer.

But our progeny were wandering off—springing away, one by one—that night when obese Lynn winked at me from the cover of nightmare. It was as if God, my creative mindright, or relentless stubbornness noticed and shouted: *now.*

Kirby McCauley nearly represented me, as literary agent, when I'd finished *The Offspring,* but it was the man behind *Ellery Queen,* Frederic Dannay, who pointed the way to Milwaukee agent Ray Puechner, who loved the book and promptly sent it away to a major hard-cover house. Ray sent me back to the typewriter with the startling, sterling counsel, "Forget about it now; it's out of your hands. So write another novel. Then another!"

His advice paid off. I did it—well, no author

really forgets his first book—and right before Christmas in 1978, Leisure's editor Jane Thornton went wonderfully gaga over book two: *The Ritual*. And by then, I'd become the prolific weirdworder I'm presently considered to be.

A few thoughts about being prolific: whether the term is compliment or condemnation depends entirely upon the reader, or critic. But it has always amused me when anyone is amazed that I am a producer, because I was merely following the guidance of my agent! You see, I was unemployed at the time and the one way I could look my family in the collective eye was by seeing myself, instead, as "a full-time writer." People who held full-time jobs arose in the morning and put in eight-hour days. It didn't seem unreasonable that *I* should do so, as a novelist. Besides, I hate doing nothing. As a consequence, I began putting in my eight hours, six days a week with five hours work on Sundays—in the writing of more novels. Remember, I was in my forties when The Career began; I was fully accustomed to spending the day at work!

Before Ms. Thornton of Leisure came to like *The Ritual*, and bought it, I'd already written, either as finished manuscripts or partials, *The Houngan* (later reprinted as *Profits*), *The Tulpa, Death-Coach* (which I'd named *PI*) and portions of three *other* novels, two of them since abandoned. But a year passed before *The Ritual* came out and, by then, I'd written early-draft portions of *Horror House, the Banished,* and *Playmates!*

It came to this: twelve novels of mine were published in a period of fewer than twenty-four months. Which leads to the next strange surprise in the saga of *The Offspring*.

Nobody thought to submit *Offspring* to Ms. Thornton or Milburn D. Smith, Jr., of Leisure Books, until almost *eight years* after I'd begun to write it!

Perhaps it involves the metamorphoses of *Offspring I,* an unusual number of rewrites for most modern novels: as originally conceived, Senator Baldwin's blueprint for Lynn involved what was called Legionnaire's Disease. In the seventies, the nature of the terrible "plague" that struck down so many people at an eastern hotel was utterly mysterious, and I was as agog over it as anybody. My intention was to "solve" the mystery fictionally—while introducing the most genuinely unusual "monster" to appear in horror novels for years. *How,* I thought while I was writing the first version of *Offspring, can this book miss*? Additionally, I'd anticipated the public fascination with androgyny by several years.

Well, the major league hardcover house never did accept or reject my first novel. As far as I know, they still have it and may make a bid for it anytime! When the cause of Legionnaire's Disease was found, the enigmatic heart of *The*

Offspring was carved out and away and, with new book projects in my works, poor Lynn appeared doomed.

But Ray Puechner and Mary, who became my literary agent (and that of others), insisted that book one was salvageable. Goaded, prodded, and encouraged, I hauled out the yellowing manuscript one inactive day and tried—by now it was the fourth time I'd striven, like Dr. Frankenstein, to breathe new life into it—once more. The result: rejection by a house I had come to rely upon. Now, truly, the all-but-infallible Lynn looked moribund. I believed it needed to be buried forever.

But in 1982, again faced with one of those rare days when I was "between contracts," I began to think about my first novel; just that. Lynn was in a box somewhere, continuing its claustrophobic existence, and only I knew its whereabouts. Suddenly, I perceived what should have been apparent to me all along: Lynn was quite a terrifying enough antagonist or villain without a great need for the subplots I'd given most of my more-recent novels. With Grandfather Baldwin's egomaniacal aspirations thrust another notch up the ladder, there was quite enough of a storyline to sustain reader interest! At once, I saw that what was needed was a different kind of introduction to Lynn, a new prologue that would provide the origin of the brilliant monster itself—a few more scenes of foreshadowing and overt horror—and the strengthening of the secondary characters. It sold. And people wanted a sequel.

An instant problem presented itself, however: Lynn had been *burned to death.* I wasn't about to pretend that Lynn had been miraculously saved; I wouldn't do that to my readers, some of whom know the names and bios of my least significant characters, and twists of plotting I've quite forgotten. Indeed, my description at the close of *Offspring I* was graphic; indisputable.

Happily, I am often engaged in the mulling-around of pseudo-philosophical speculation on the questions of life and death. My first idea, then, involved the enthusiastic notion of Lynn as a ghost. My second thought was that I'd published other novel-length ghost stories recently—*The Longest Night* and *Ghost*—and I knew that this one would have to be different, if I was to keep and please Williamson readers.

What if, I wondered—as all fantasists and many other writers so often do—Lynn could be experienced in Part One as a menacing, versatile spirit who, we discover, wants to be reborn? That, I perceived, would set up part two as primarily a tale of horror, and readers would get two kinds of novel for the cost of one! Ghost story and horror novel!

From there, it was a quick skip to the typer to devise an outline in which Lynn would require a female body in order to assume new, fleshly substance—and big bro Eric, of course, would once more be Peg's protector.

From what deep-seated, personal, mental supply department do ideas of this kind come? All writers in my genre are frequently asked this question, and none too politely unless the interviewer also adores horror and supernatural fiction. In the case of Lynn, the question needs to be reframed: what was a thing like the Offspring doing in your unconscious mind?

What I can furnish is a series of guesses; clues, at best. I'd turned forty a couple of years before writing novel one and perhaps, with the addition of surplus pounds and the gradual departure of our *own* offspring, I was dreaming of what I feared I might become. Or possibly it involves the way that the word "unisex" was just beginning to wend its way into print; because the truth is, I *do* think we should attempt to be men, or women, just as soon as we can figure out precisely what that entails! Maybe it was an unconscious reaction to the business people in power, the authority figures, whom I tended to see as bloated with self-righteousness, ever inclined to dominate anyone with a different viewpoint.

Or perhaps I was recalling a moment in my boyhood when, growing up in an alcoholic-stained family, I was unwilling to arise one morning and heard, quite distinctly, *music* playing outside my window. There was no reasonable source for it but it was the most beautiful sound I'd heard, midway between harps and bells. And possibly I didn't remain in bed but went outside in quest of the source, and that evocative, tranquil-but-tantalizing, uncanny music was the work of a creature as strange, obese, and awe-inspiring as the Offspring.

I can tell you that the characters in *Offspring* were based on real people, to one extent or another (because I didn't know better, then, than to do so): my stepson Eric, as Eric Porter; my stepdaughter Mary, as Peg; actor Andrew Duggan as Adam Baldwin; Mildred as a mental blending of Bette Davis and my high school freshman music teacher.

Only Lynn and Mama were wholly created from my creative mind-right.

I think.

We know so little of ourselves, really, the origins of our most essential beliefs or fantasies, dreams and nightmares. Our aspirations are surely a compound of those factors which motivate us, and others we will never even guess at. Which is why—if there's any single theme or foundation beneath the storylines of my fiction, long and short—it is a wondering, delving, probing, awe-filled affirmation of the belief I hold that the Creator has revealed merely a fraction of fact, and loves to watch us grope and stumble toward Truth. And while He knows everything, He therefore knows that we only believe we do. While He tells us very little, He sometimes likes for us to try to learn and does not resent it in the slightest when we succeed.

And although He doesn't mind or interfere unless He is asked, He knows that our quests and our questioning will never, quite, locate all the answers. It is, I feel, a head game we can't win—but we can't lose it, either, when we *try*. As openmindedly, creatively, and unharmfully as we are able.

J.N. Williamson
Indianapolis
April, 1986

EVIL STALKS THE NIGHT

Kathryn Meyer Griffith

THE WOODS—where twenty years ago, only Sarah and her brother Jim escaped the slaughter that claimed the lives of their brothers and sisters.

THE WOODS—where now it begins again. Sarah is drawn back to her childhood home with her young son Jeremy. Once more, she and Jim confront the terrifying power of an evil that will not die, an evil that kills.

THE WOODS—where something inhuman continues to stalk its victims, fulfilling its age-old quest for blood . . .

2329-6 $3.50 US, $3.95 Can